MM9

BY HIROSHI YAMAMOTO

MM9
MONSTER MAGNITUDE

HIROSHI YAMAMOTO

TRANSLATED BY NATHAN COLLINS

SAN FRANCISCO

MM9
© 2007 by Hiroshi Yamamoto
English translation rights arranged with TOKYO SOGENSHA CO., LTD.
through Japan UNI Agency, Inc., Tokyo

English translation © 2012 VIZ Media, LLC
Cover photo and design by Izumi Evers
All rights reserved.

HAIKASORU
Published by VIZ Media, LLC
295 Bay Street
San Francisco, CA 94133

www.haikasoru.com

Library of Congress Cataloging-in-Publication Data

Yamamoto, Hiroshi, 1956-
 [MM9. English]
 MM9 / by Hiroshi Yamamoto ; translation by Nathan Collins.
    p.   cm.
 ISBN 978-1-4215-4089-4
 1. Yamamoto, Hiroshi, 1956—Translations into English. I. Collins, Nathan. II. Title.
 PL877.5.A46M6113   2011
 895.6'36--dc23

                                    2011042037

The rights of the author of the work in this publication to be so identified have been
asserted in accordance with the Copyright, Designs and Patents Act 1988. A CIP
catalogue record for this book is available from the British Library.

Printed in the U.S.A.
First printing, January 2012

Japan Meteorological Agency
Monsterological Measures Department (MMD)

Ryo Haida · Mobile Unit

Sakura Fujisawa · · · · · · · Mobile Unit, Vehicles and Transportation

Asaya Koide · · · · · · Mobile Unit, Photography and Communications

Kiichi Awashima · Mobile Unit

Yojiro Muromachi · · · · · · · · · · · · · · Mobile Unit, Director

Toshio Yamagiwa · Operator

Kensuke Sogabe · · · · · · · · · · · · · · Operator, Military Geek

Koichiro Morihashi · · · · · · · · · · · · · · Operator, New Hire

Yuri Anno · Astrophysicist

Shoichi Kurihama · · · · · · · · · · · · · · · Department Chief

Other

Ikki Anno · · · · · · · · · · · · · · · · · Yuri's Son, Third Grade

Mikio Izuno · Astrophysicist

Eiko Hamaguchi · · · · · · · · · · · · · · · · · · · Ryo's Girlfriend

TABLE OF CONTENTS

PART ONE

CRISIS! KAIJU ALERT!

May, 2005. Yokohama, Ishikawa Train Station—

At 6:53 PM, Ryo Haida's cell phone rang. The ringtone—Mussorgsky's *Night on Bald Mountain*—identified the caller: Yojiro Muromachi, head of the Mobile Unit.

Ryo scowled, said, "Oh, come on," and took the cell from his pocket. He had just stepped through the station exit, headed for the coffee shop where his date awaited. It was just past sunset, but the sky was overcast, the city painted with the vivid colors of neon lights.

"This is Ryo," he said. Early in his childhood, he learned never to give his full name over the phone. With part of his name meaning "yes" in Japanese, *"This is Haida Ryo,"* could also mean, *"Yes, this is Daryo,"* and often elicited the same confused—and tiresome—response, *"Your name is Daryo?"*

"It's me," Yojiro said, his words coming like rapid fire. As usual, he didn't waste any time getting to the point. "Thirty minutes ago, a JMSDF submarine near the Ogasa Islands collided with an unknown. Our estimates—"

"No, wait, hang on there. I'm meeting up with a date."

"You'll have to cancel."

"You're killing me here. This is that college girl. The future starlet? You don't know how hard I've worked just to get this far. Can't you ask Kiichi or somebody—*anybody* else?"

"He's in Kumamoto on business. And I'm not asking just you. We're all hands on deck for this one."

That gave Ryo pause. Now that Yojiro mentioned it, Ryo could hear Chief Kurihama in the background hurriedly shouting out orders.

"Is this a big one?"

"Our estimates put it at MM8. Maybe even nine."

Ryo gasped. "Off Ogasa, you said?"

"And heading north at forty klicks. The SDF is already on alert."

"Understood. I'll head back to the office."

"Where are you now?"

"Yokohama."

"Then go straight to Atsugi. The JMSDF is readying an S-1 helicopter to take you to the site. Asaya and Sakura have already left here with the equipment. You can rendezvous with them at the Atsugi air base."

"What about you?"

"I'll be gathering data here for the time being. We're still pulling everyone back in from the holiday, and it's chaos here. I'll leave the site to you guys for now. I might join you by helicopter if I can get away."

"Understood. Can I grab a taxi?"

"Hold on."

Ryo could hear Yojiro say, "Ryo is asking if he can take a taxi," and Chief Kurihama reply, "I don't give a damn! Just make sure he gets a receipt!"

"Did you hear that?" Yojiro asked.

"Got it." Ryo raised his hand to catch the attention of a passing taxi. "By the way, what type of kaiju is it?"

"Unknown. We don't know anything beyond its size and speed. I'll send you everything we have on it when I have a moment."

"Got it."

Ryo hung up his phone, climbed in the taxi, and said, "Ayase. And step on it."

As soon as they were moving, Ryo called his date to apologize.

The storm broke, and raindrops dotted the car windows.

A few minutes later, Ryo received an email with the full report.

First contact was made by the Japan Maritime Self-Defense Force SS571 *Amashio* (2,450 tons standard surface displacement) with the 2nd Submarine Squadron. At 6:21 PM, the *Amashio*'s passive sonar system picked up an unknown entity swimming northward in the seas near the Osaga Island Group, south of Japan's main island. In order to better determine its shape, crewmen sent out a number of active sonar pings, when the unknown suddenly changed course to head straight for the submarine. Evasive countermeasures were attempted but ultimately failed, and the unknown collided with the ship's stern. The *Amashio* was spun around and received critical damage to its forward trim tank. The submarine was forced to make an emergency surfacing. There were no casualties. The unknown returned to its northerly heading. From the sonar's echoes, the creature was estimated to be between eighty and one hundred meters in length. Because it swam at a steady depth, without bobbing up or sinking down, it likely possessed a density similar to that of the ocean water. A reptilian kaiju that size would displace anywhere from 1,400 to 4,200 tons of water.

Seated inside the taxi as it sped through the rain down Highway 16 toward Atsugi, Ryo murmured, "MM8 . . ."

"MM" was short for "Monster Magnitude," a scale established in the late nineteenth century by an American kaiju researcher named Guthrie. He conceived it as a measure, based on size, for the potential destructive power of a particular monster—the number of people affected, the number of casualties and destroyed houses, the economic damages, etc.—with six distinct levels on a scale of zero to five. When he devised the scale, the greatest kaiju disaster in America to date had been in Minnesota in 1894, when a reptilian monster estimated to weigh one hundred tons destroyed over ten small towns and left six hundred dead. Guthrie accordingly set that at the top of the scale, with the lower end reserved for small-scale disasters with no more than one or two victims.

According to Guthrie, "With an increase in volume of a kaiju by a factor of 2.5, the amount of damage inflicted on a populated region will increase by a factor of up to 4."

The thickness of kaiju skin was proportional to the cubic root of their total mass, and the thicker their skin, the less effect medium-caliber ammunition had. The number of injuries needed to put down the beasts was proportional to their volume. The amount of strength per unit of cross-sectional area of muscle and bone was proportional to the cubic root of their volume squared, and their land speed was proportional to their volume to the one-sixth power. Their destructive capabilities toward buildings was proportional to the cubic root of their volume to the fourth power. All those calculations combined to give the maximum amount of destruction that could spread within a populated region before the military—at least as it was then constituted in the United States—could destroy the kaiju.

The scale was expanded to MM8 in 1923, when 140,000 Japanese lost their lives in a single kaiju disaster, and in the time since, there had been several more revisions. At the present time, the monster magnitude was calculated by the water displacement equal to the kaiju's volume. Kaiju of one ton or less rated at MM0, and each increase of a point on the scale was equivalent to a 2.5 times increase in volume.

Due to advances in military power and the prevalence of sturdy, high-rise buildings, Guthrie's Law no longer held true. But his scale of monster magnitude continued to be used to estimate the destructive power of kaiju.

MM8 was the equivalent of 1,600 to 4,000 tons of water. In the case of the most common type of kaiju, bipedal reptilians, their height could range anywhere between forty and fifty meters. Even Japan, often called the "kaiju nation," saw only a few such creatures over the course of a century.

And this one might be a 4,200-ton MM9.

"Is this happening?"

Ryo was on edge. The biggest kaiju on record was 3,600 tons—an MM8.9. Only ancient legends told of any kaiju on par with an MM9. All reports of modern-day appearances had boiled down to unreliable and unverifiable eyewitness accounts. Yet believers of the existence of MM9 kaiju remained—if only because no proof had surfaced to indicate otherwise.

If this one is an MM9—no, even an MM8—this is serious.

If their countermeasures failed, and the kaiju was permitted to reach land, there could be a repeat of the 1923 catastrophe that claimed 140,000 lives.

An announcement over the taxi radio snapped Ryo back from his thoughts.

"At 7:10 PM local Japan time, a kaiju warning was issued. Kaiju Three has been confirmed in the sea off the Ogasa Island Group, 26 degrees latitude and 139 degrees longitude, moving northward at a speed of forty kilometers per hour. Projections indicate a strong possibility of landfall tomorrow evening on the Pacific shore between central and eastern Japan. The monster magnitude has been estimated at eight. The Japan Meteorological Agency urges all seacraft in the area to exercise extreme caution, and—"

"Not again," the driver said wearily. "Last time they said there'd be a huge one to hit Tanzawa, and they were wrong about that, weren't they?"

"Huh? Oh, yeah, I guess so." Inside, Ryo was chills and sweat.

"The Daisan Keihin was completely backed up with evacuees' cars. It was horrible. Then the kaiju turned out to be a frickin' *three*? The SDF just took it out with their rifles."

"Yeah . . ."

Ryo felt ashamed. It was his unit that had estimated the underground kaiju at MM6 and advised the alert for western Kanagawa. It happened during the holidays and had cost the hot springs and amusement parks a lot of business. The Odawara Board of Tourism nearly sued the Monsterological Measures Department over it.

"The MMD'd better get *something* right," the driver went on, "or nobody'll believe them anymore. Like the boy who cried wolf in Grimm's tales."

That was Aesop, Ryo thought. But he didn't feel like arguing. The man was right. The predictions of the Japan Meteorological Agency Monsterological Measures Department *were* wrong from time to time. Of course, they were right most of the time, but all people seemed to remember were the times their advisories and warnings struck out and the times of catastrophe when they failed to predict a kaiju.

A wrong prediction could put thousands, even tens of thousands of lives in danger or cause tens of millions of yen in economic damages. The men and women of the MMD shared a heavy responsibility. Despite that—or rather, because of it—their critics were severe. Although they saved many lives, few gave them recognition.

Theirs was a thankless job.

The radio announcer continued to read off the warning, "This warning covers the areas of Chiba, Tokyo, Kanagawa, Shizuoka, Aichi . . ."

Takebashi, Chiyoda Ward, Tokyo—

The head office of the Japan Meteorological Agency stood across from the Imperial Palace's East Garden and its surrounding Ote Moat.

"Sorry I'm late!"

By the time Yuri Anno came dashing into the office, the Department of MMD was at battle stations. All around her, phones were ringing off the hook, and the staff were yelling at each other, "Have you reached them yet?" "I've got a call from the Ministry of Transportation!" "Where's that data?" People rushed back and forth with armfuls of folders. A giant display of Japan occupied one wall, and on it the areas affected by the warning were lit orange.

"Hey," said veteran operator Toshio Yamagiwa. He looked up at her from his computer screen with affable little eyes. "Is Ikki all right?"

"I left him with my mother-in-law." Yuri removed her coat. "We had plans to go to the amusement park tomorrow, so he's pretty mad at me."

"It's gonna rain anyway."

His answer wasn't much of a comfort, and she responded with a noncommittal smile. *It's a lousy mom who can't be with her son on the weekend*, she thought. But what could she do? The MMD had plenty of specialists in biology, environmental science, folklore, and so on, but she was the only astrophysicist. In the event of a major kaiju event, she had to rush to the office no matter what her circumstances.

There were few astrophysicists involved in the field in any nation. Until quite recently, quantum physics and cosmology were not thought to be useful in dealing with kaiju. Biology provided understanding of their ecology; geology, environmental science, oceanography, and the like detected kaiju wherever they dwelled; chemistry analyzed flames, poisons, and other chemicals emitted by the giant monsters; biomechanics estimated the effectiveness of bullets and missiles against them. Astrophysics held no similar purpose.

Many still doubted its place, and some even protested Yuri's employment. But she had faith. She believed, even if the world at large didn't, that astrophysics—the anthropic principle in particular—held the key to solving the mystery of kaiju. If she felt any other way, she wouldn't have given up her associate professorship at the Meteorological College when she was scouted by the MMD.

Yuri turned to Chief Kurihama. "What's the situation?"

"A JMSDF ship is keeping pace with the unknown, holding its distance beside it. Its heading and speed remain unchanged."

Shoichi Kurihama fidgeted with his glasses, his countenance bitter. He headed the MMD but was never prideful about it. In the event of a kaiju-inflicted disaster, his was the unpleasant task of facing public criticism. He fervently hoped for a transfer to another department.

And this time, his responsibility was heavier than ever. The pressure had already caused his stomach to ache. He took his trusty medicine bottle from his desk drawer and shook out a pill into his palm.

"We still don't have any clues about the nature of this kaiju," the chief said. "Our best estimates from the sonar reading put it at just shy of one hundred meters long. Ryo and Asaya have already left to investigate."

Suddenly, there was a loud noise. Chief Kurihama choked on the pill in his throat and coughed violently. The noise—like a strong rush of water mixed with popping bubbles—was similar to what a microphone might pick up when thrust out into a downpour on a rainy day.

"What the hell is that?"

"Sorry, Chief." Koichiro Morihashi, a newly hired operator, scrambled to turn down the volume of his computer. "It's a file just sent to us by the JMSDF ship—the sound of the kaiju's swimming picked up by their passive sonar."

Yuri listened. The rest of the staff stopped their work and gave their full attention to the recording.

Any creature as large as a kaiju would create sound just by passing through the water. Just as the propellers of different ships created different cavitation noise, each kaiju's aquatic motion carried a distinct audio signature. Unlike the echo of an active sonar, this sound couldn't give them a clear outline of the creature's shape, but it was at least a clue toward the nature of the monster.

Yojiro Muromachi frowned. "There's a lot of background noise."

Yojiro had been with the Meteorological Agency for over twenty years. With a well-rounded knowledge including expertise in biology, folklore, and archaeology, he was a veritable specialist in kaiju prediction. He was forty-eight, the same age as Chief Kurihama, but in stark contrast with the chief's narrow, bookish face, Yojiro's build was akin to that of a mountain climber or a professional soccer player. He loathed keeping inside the office and preferred fieldwork—which is why he had been chosen to lead the Mobile Unit.

"The ship's at quite a distance," Koichiro explained, "and the current is strong, so they're picking up a lot of interference. But I'll see what I can do with it."

Chief Kurihama grumbled, "This is just noise. Can't they get any closer?"

"No, that would be dangerous," Yojiro said. "We're dealing with a big one here. It's already taken out one submarine. That ship is out there alone, and one strike could incapacitate it."

Yuri asked, "Is this all we've got on it?"

Yojiro shook his head. "Another report came in just before you got here. Two hours before the submarine incident and seventy kilometers south, a worker on a Mexican freighter claims he saw a sea serpent."

"A sea serpent?"

"That's what he says. He only saw part of its back sticking out from the water, but he puts that at about thirty meters long, so we're talking about something of substantial size. Judging from the time and location of the observation, I think it's safe to assume it's the same monster that collided with the submarine."

"Did he get any photos?"

"No. But they have a fax machine on board, and we're getting him to draw us a picture."

"That's an eyewitness account—why did it take two whole hours to get to us?"

"I don't know," Chief Kurihama said, clearly annoyed. "And right now, we don't have the leisure of digging into it."

"Right." Yuri thought for moment. "If it's a sea serpent, there's little probability of a landfall. And with a thin body, it could be as small as an MM7."

Sea serpents, a variety of marine reptile kaiju, had been spotted in waters across the globe since times of old. Although some were discovered to have four short limbs, few ever climbed onto land.

"MM7 or snake," the chief said, "we have to take it seriously."

Veteran operator Toshio pointed to his computer screen. He had been searching for similar creatures in the central kaiju database. On his display was a photograph of a kaiju with four short legs and a long body like a Chinese dragon's, slumped against the side of a building. It was from 1952, found in the Baltic Sea, and an MM6. It was named after the person who first sighted it, Eve. It had a dopey face one might even call cute.

It had killed one hundred and fifty before it was taken out.

Yuri sighed and slowly scanned the room, which was once again filled with the disarray of ringing phones, heated shouts, pleas, and inquiries. A NHK breaking news report ran on one of the wall-mounted flatscreens, but the newscaster's voice was mostly lost in the chaos. A crawl on the bottom of the screen read, *Mysteries of the Wild will be broadcast at eight thirty.*

"What?" Yuri said.

Yojiro asked what was wrong.

"Oh, nothing, excuse me."

Yuri moved to the corner of the room, took out her cell phone, and called home.

"Mom? It's me. I set the ten o'clock *No Sleep Tonight*—yeah, you know, the one with Kazuaki Godai? I set the DVR for it, but it might get pushed back by the news. Would you mind changing it to record an hour longer? No, don't worry, I can walk you through it. Do you have the remote? First, press the timer button . . ."

The streets were emptier than usual, and Ryo arrived at the Atsugi JMSDF Air Base just after eight. A patrol helicopter with Fleet Squadron 51 had already been pulled from the hangar; it waited for Ryo under the rain and the lights of the helipad.

But Sakura Fujisawa and Asaya Koide, who had left from Tokyo before him, hadn't shown up yet. Twenty minutes later, the Meteorological Agency van finally pulled in through the base gate.

Sakura stepped out from the driver's side, her eyes brimming with tears. "I-I'm sorry!"

She wasn't exactly gorgeous, but she had a cute round face like a baby raccoon. Her looks often caused her to be mistaken for a young teenager. After graduating from high school, Sakura took the public service exam and made it into the Meteorological Agency as a third-class recruit. Although Sakura had only been with the agency for two years, she was placed on the front lines in the Mobile Unit as part of her training. With the least experience of anyone on the team, she was almost exclusively put in charge of driving and transportation.

"This is my first time in Atsugi," she said, "and I thought the base would be in the city, and I went all the way to the Atsugi interchange."

"Don't sweat it. It's just the kind of mistake any rookie's bound to make." Ryo flashed a wry smile. Until he joined the Mobile Unit, he himself hadn't known that Atsugi Air Base was not, in fact, located in Atsugi, but rather in the neighboring Ayase.

Asaya Koide was cheerfully unloading equipment from the rear of the van. "I'm sorry too. I should have been paying better attention. By the time I noticed, we were already past the Machida exit."

Asaya was twenty-seven, one year younger than Ryo. He primarily handled the cameras and communications equipment.

"Well," Ryo said, "it was just a little detour. Don't worry about it. Let's just get going."

Ryo and Asaya started walking the large cases of equipment to the helicopter. Sakura hustled behind them, pushing a cart with a trunk-sized metal case, the pole of her clear plastic umbrella wedged between her cheek and her shoulder. If nothing else, she had spunk.

The three bowed deeply to greet the helicopter crew.

"Thanks for coming out in this tonight," Ryo said.

He turned to the side. "So this is the S-1."

A white cylinder hung from a pylon on the right rear of the rain-soaked SH-60J Seahawk. Except for its clear reinforced-plastic nose and the cable running inside the helicopter, it looked exactly like a torpedo.

"Isn't that your guys' equipment?" said one of the Navy men with a laugh. "I thought we were just keeping an eye on it for you."

"This is my first time seeing one," Ryo explained.

"Mine too," Sakura said. "I've run lots of simulations on it though."

"That's right. I guess this'll be its first time out. I just hope it'll be useful," Ryo said.

Sakura folded her umbrella and climbed inside the helicopter. "It had better be. It cost us four hundred million yen."

As he ran through the preflight checklist, the middle-aged pilot said, "Doesn't the MMD have their own helicopter?"

Again Ryo felt ashamed. "We just don't have the kind of budget for that."

After the kaiju disaster at Kobe ten years ago, a major debate arose in the media about the MMD's lack of even a single helicopter and the reliance of their predictions on observations made from Self Defense Force and the Fire and Disaster Management Agency helicopters. The MMD was restructured from the ground up, which led to the formation of the Mobile Unit, but now a decade had passed with still not even a plan to procure their own helicopter.

Kaiju disasters occurred all across Japan. The MMD would either require one large helicopter capable of long-distance flight or many smaller helicopters stationed in air bases around the country. Where would they get the budget for that? Most citizens were of the opinion that it would be a waste of tax revenue—when the MMD could just get free use of the SDF fleet, what need did they have for their own? Sometimes Ryo could understand the sentiment—except when he saw the same members of the Diet who slashed their budget every year, on TV, with their free bullet train passes and extravagant taxpayer-funded housing.

A soldier asked, "But your salary's good, right?"

"Huh? Well, not *that* good."

"What about those nice clothes?"

"Oh, these?" Ryo looked down at his rain-slick brand-name suit and chuckled. "No, I was just called in when I was on a date."

"That's rough."

"Yeah. Yeah, it is."

The pilot cut in. "The heavy stuff's really coming down now." Countless streaks of rain ran down the canopy. "Hey, miss, do you get airsick?"

"No," Sakura said, "I do fine."

"I'm sure, but the sea is going to be pretty choppy. Landing's going to be interesting."

"Ah."

The rotors spun up. The roaring wind slapped against the helipad and sent up a white cloud of spray. The helicopter lifted off and flew toward the south.

"We've got an incoming fax!"

The MMD staff crowded around, watching with bated breath as the machine stuttered out the crudely drawn picture.

"It has scales," one of them whispered.

The drawing was of the creature's back, thrust out of the water like an island. Its surface was covered with scales, reminiscent of the *Shachihoko*, the statues of mythical dragon-headed carp atop Nagoya Castle.

"That's it?" said another. "Where's its head?"

"He never saw it," a third explained. "But its back was out of the water for about half a minute, and he got a good look at that, at least."

Yojiro groaned. "It doesn't have any fins."

If the kaiju was a piscene type, it would have had fins. Even most sea serpents had bumps, or a mane or horns—*something*.

The circle of people talked back and forth.

"So it's not a sea serpent, but some other type of reptile?"

"Almost certainly."

"Don't those scales look like Eve's?"

"Doesn't that mean it's likely to make it onto land?"

All across the office, the tension rose. Yojiro turned to Chief Kurihama. "We should issue an alert."

"An alert . . ."

Kurihama glanced at the large monitor at his side and shrank back. The kaiju's projected course was indicated on the display along with its predicted location in twenty-four hours—a large circle that covered all of Eastern and part of Central Japan.

Unlike the simple warning already issued, an alert would trigger an evacuation from the affected areas. All commerce would come to a halt, and the effect on daily life would be immense.

"But with a radius like this," the chief protested, "that's a huge move."

"It's a vacation day. The economic impact will be the least possible."

"Even still, if there's a repeat of Tanzawa, and nothing happens—"

"If nothing happens, we'll be lucky! This is an MM8 or an MM9. If it gets to shore, it'll be 1923 all over again," Yojiro said.

"We don't even know if it *will* go on land."

"That's nothing more than an optimistic conjecture!"

"It might even change course," Kurihama said. "And the SDF will likely destroy it. The modern military is nothing like it was back in the Taisho Era. Don't you agree, Kensuke?"

Kensuke Sogabe, an operator and military geek, scrambled to his feet and straightened his glasses. "Y-yes, sir. Mathematically speaking, even with an MM8 with skin fifty centimeters thick, an anti-ship missile like the Harpoon with the Munroe effect—"

"This is a *kaiju*!" Yojiro barked. "When did they ever give a damn about adhering to science!"

Kensuke didn't have a counterargument. It was true. No creature weighing a hundred tons could possibly stand up straight and walk itself across the surface of the earth. Not while following the laws of science anyway. No matter how the numbers were crunched, bones and muscles of that size just wouldn't be capable of supporting their own weight. And yet kaiju over MM5 appeared all over the world, and on a regular basis. Even dissection and anatomical analysis had never been able to solve that mystery.

Moreover, in previous encounters with MM6 to MM8-class kaiju, tank and battlecruiser cannon fire were less effective than projections would have suggested—an indication that the laws of physics were broken by not only the strength of kaiju bones and muscles, but likely their skin as well. Yuri's field of study, cosmology, received so much attention partly out of the hope that it could explain the phenomenon.

Yojiro took a deep breath and collected himself. "A Harpoon has never been used against an MM8. And if there's a low-density layer of tissue beneath its shell, it could have the same effect as spaced armor. We can't know if the missile will be effective or not when we don't even know what we're dealing with."

"It might be!" the chief said.

"And it might not. We have to assume the worst."

"And if we're wrong, we'll be humiliated."

"Are you willing to put people's lives in danger to avoid looking bad?" Yojiro asked.

"No! I'm just saying we need to observe a little *prudence* with respect to our situation here!"

The two glared at each other, their faces barely a foot apart. Yojiro had the physical advantage, but Chief Kurihama didn't back down. The rest of the staff stood around them and watched uneasily. The bustling, noisy room quieted, and the ringing telephones and the TV news report suddenly seemed to blare.

"Ummm . . ." One of the female operators timidly raised her hand. "Can I ask something?"

The chief, his glare still aimed at Yojiro, snapped, "What?"

"Calls keep coming in from the media. They want us to hurry up and name the kaiju."

"A name . . ." Kurihama spun and pursed his lips in thought. With this being the third kaiju of the year, it was temporarily designated Kaiju Three, but the creatures were always named. Western countries tended to bestow their monsters with common names. Japan, however, out of concern for the feelings of people who might otherwise share a monster's name, coined unique names for them— a task that fell to the MMD.

"But how can I name it when I don't even know what it really looks like?"

"What if we named it after a place?" Kensuke offered. "Like Ogasawara?"

"We have to take this seriously or we'll hear about it later. Let's think about it. Carefully. We don't even know if it's reptilian or not. Until we know what it is, it'll remain Kaiju Three."

He turned back to Yojiro. "We don't have enough information to put out an alert. We wait until we've identified what kind of creature it is and determined whether it's capable of going on land. Or until it gets within two hundred kilometers of the coastline, whichever happens first. All right?"

Yojiro opened his mouth to argue, but then realized that the chief was right. Besides, it wasn't wise for two of the managers to be seen arguing in the middle of a crisis.

"At least issue an alert for the southern islands like Aogajima, Hachijojima, and Miyakejima."

"When the kaiju is within two hundred kilometers, I will. That should give them five hours to evacuate. Is that all right?"

Grudgingly, Yojiro said, "I don't object."

The destroyer escort ship **Suzuka,** *standard displacement five thousand tons—*

The *Suzuka* sailed through the stormy seas. Viewed from the sky, its outer lights blurred behind the falling rain. On its front were two five-inch rapid-fire cannons and an ASROC launcher. Two 20mm Vulcan Phalanx systems, resembling enormous drug capsules, stood one on each side of the bridge.

Like the helicopter pilot had said, the landing was interesting. Not only was the storm wind strong, but the ship rocked on the waves. Sakura shrieked when, moments before they touched down, the deck rose up and struck the Seahawk's front wheel with a mighty clang.

The Mobile Unit team was led to the Combat Information Center, or CIC, where Captain Toshiya Kawamura awaited them. After a short greeting, Kawamura abruptly said, "I have bad news. Fifteen minutes ago, we lost the kaiju. There's a lot of noise from the ocean surface, and not only that, the monster entered a thermocline in the rip current."

Ryo wasn't about to blame them. Thermoclines, ocean layers where the water temperature changes more rapidly with depth, often formed along the edges of the Kuroshio Current and interfered with noise picked up by passive sonar. Even most veterans would have been unable to sort through the pattern.

Ryo asked, "What about active sonar?"

"We're not using it. The report from the *Amashio* suggests a possibility the kaiju was provoked by the sonar pulse."

"That's smart. Do you think you can find it again?"

"Take a look at this."

Captain Kawamura pointed to a table. Under the glass top was a large monitor with a nautical chart of the area from the Ogasawara Islands to Hachijojima. The *Suzuka* was marked by a red triangle, and other vessels with black ones.

"This," the captain said, pointing to an orange oval, "is the possible location of the kaiju. Of course, as more time passes, the radius will only grow larger. Seven more destroyer escort ships and two submarines are en route. By tomorrow morning, we'll have ten vessels surrounding it. And if the weather clears, we'll send out patrol boats and helicopters. The sea is projected to calm by morning, so the search should be easier."

"Sounds good."

"There's something else I want to show you," Kawamura said.

Ryo looked up from the screen. "What is it?"

The captain gave an order, and a man brought in a large Styrofoam case, one of the ones used to store fish in the ship's mess cooler. It smelled like the ocean.

Captain Kawamura said, "This was brought to us from the *Amashio*. It was caught in their propeller."

He opened the lid. Ryo, Sakura, and Asaya gasped in unison.

Inside was a meter-long lobster with a dark, wide shell.

Yojiro looked at the image transmitted from the *Suzuka* and said, "It looks like it's related to the fan lobster, a species of slipper lobsters. I think I saw something like it in pictures taken by *Shinkai 7500*, the research sub. Koichiro!"

"Yes, sir!" The rookie operator pulled up the archive search and typed in the query. "Here it is. 1992. It was found in the Mariana Trench 3,700 meters below sea level."

The large wall display filled with a video of a crustacean crawling backward along the seafloor. Its body was flat, like a crab, and its tail widened out in a fan shape. It did look similar to the one caught in the *Amashio*'s propeller.

Biology not being one of her strengths, Yuri asked, "Why is it walking backward?"

Koichiro read the archive report. "No one knows. It was only filmed the one time, and its behavioral patterns remain unknown. It hasn't even been given a scientific name."

Yojiro said, "The deep sea is an undiscovered country. Some say that humans have yet to encounter even one percent of the creatures inhabiting the depths of the oceans. No one can say what lives down there."

Ryo spoke over the video feed. "Sorry to cut in, but Captain Kawamura wants to speak with you."

"Go ahead, put him on."

The captain appeared on-screen. "This is Captain Toshiya Kawamura with the JDS *Suzuka*."

"I'm Yojiro Muromachi with the MMD Mobile Unit."

"These are just my own personal thoughts, but isn't there a possibility that the kaiju is a giant version of this lobster? If so, it will have an incredibly strong shell, and we should proceed with a strategy based that premise."

Yojiro thought it over. "No, I don't think that's likely. First of all, crustaceans crawl along the seafloor and can't swim quickly. Secondly, a sailor on a Mexican freighter claims he saw a sea serpent. We have our doubts as to whether or not it's actually a sea serpent, but I find it hard to believe anyone would mistake a lobster for one.

"I can think of at least one example that might help explain what happened," Yojiro continued. "In the 1923 disaster, a *leanchoilia*, a species from the Cambrian Period, was found in a footprint left behind by the kaiju. It's speculated that the monster lived on the ocean floor, and when it rose up, it brought the arthropod with it."

"I see. We'll proceed with the assumption that we're dealing with a reptile."

Yojiro bowed his head. "Thank you, sir."

The MMD never directly engaged a kaiju. Attacking the creatures was solely the job of the SDF. The MMD's task was to analyze the monsters and to provide the SDF with effective tactical and operational advice. Because bad advice could hinder combat operations, they had to gather information as carefully as possible and provide proper judgment.

After they gave their advice, all they could do was leave the rest to the SDF—and pray.

Two cans from the mess hall vending machine in hand, Ryo joined Sakura, who was standing in a corridor looking out of place.

"Juice or sports drink, your pick."

"Thanks." She took the sports drink. She pulled the tab and laughed. "I messed up."

"How?"

"I forgot to bring a change of underwear. And now I'm all sweaty and gross."

"If you ask, I'm sure they'll let you use a shower. You might even be able to borrow some clothes from one of the women officers."

"Yeah, but I'm not sure how to ask." Sakura looked up at a pipe running the length of the passageway. "I've never done anything like this before."

"You don't need to feel nervous about it. Military officers are people too. They'll understand," Ryo said.

"I guess."

"Also, you need to get some sleep tonight. It looks like tomorrow's going to be the big day. You don't want to be caught underslept when it counts. That's the worst."

"Okay, I will. And . . ."

"Yes?"

"I've been thinking. This kaiju chases after sonar pulses, right?"

"Seems like it. Many deep-sea organisms are sensitive to sound. Low-pitched noises from factories and ports might even be what's causing it to head straight for Japan."

"Then instead of killing it, why can't we use sonar to lead it out to the ocean? To somewhere safe?"

"Hmmm . . ." Ryo scratched his head. "That might be risky. What if it came back to Japan? We only found it this early because of two ships that happened to cross its path. We might not be so lucky if there's a next time. It could make it to the shore undetected and cause a huge disaster. And if it went to Russia or China or some other country, Japan could be held responsible."

"Either way, wouldn't it be better to lead it away from Japan? What if we attack here in the nearby sea and we just make it angry, and it really does go after Japan?"

"You're still thinking too soft," Ryo said. "We'd have trouble amassing enough firepower."

"What do you mean?"

"With this massive a kaiju, the naval forces won't be enough. They'll need the help of the air and ground forces. The Ministry of Defense is setting up a defensive line on the sea 120 kilometers south of Izu in the waters between Miyakejima and Hachijojima. The JGSDF Type 88 Surface-to-Ship Missiles have a range of 150 kilometers. Factoring in the flight range of the attack helicopters, an assault at that location will allow for the greatest concentration of firepower. Of course, if the kaiju makes for land on one of the islands, like Hachijojima, the naval forces will attempt an attack on their own.

"Part of the danger with a half-cocked assault is that it could cause the kaiju to alter course. If the predicted location of its landfall were to change, the land forces would be in chaos. We have to keep its course as straight as possible and ambush it just before it reaches shore. That's the only way."

"Wow, thanks." Sakura seemed impressed, although Ryo knew he'd just covered basic cryptomilitary theory.

Ryo grinned. "And we have to worry about appearances."

"Appearances?"

"The Ministry of Defense would rather stop the giant monster right at the water's edge. It projects a better image. Attacking a kaiju in the far-off sea just doesn't have much of a punch, right? If Japan sees itself saved at only a hair's breadth away from disaster, the people's stock in the SDF will go up all the more."

Sakura was speechless.

"Don't look at me like that." Ryo laughed and slapped her shoulder. "Who cares if we help their public image, as long as we prevent the kaiju from causing destruction? Just think of it as a bouquet for the JSDF, an extra bonus for them. They're the stars. We're just the stagehands."

Sakura seemed deep in thought. Thinking the conversation over, Ryo turned to walk away.

"Ryo?"

He stopped. "Yes?"

"Why did you pick this job?"

"That's a good question." He chuckled, then thought about it. "It wasn't a dream of mine or anything. I came in as a third-class recruit, just like you. I started in another department but was shuffled to the MMD. And then I guess I just found myself here. But it's not a boring job, by any means. And the pay's not bad either."

"I see . . ."

"What about you, Sakura? Why did you choose to work here?"

She cast her eyes down. She spoke in a whisper, as if embarrassed, her words nearly drowned out by the ship's hum. "I wanted to . . ."

"Go on."

"I wanted to protect people's happiness."

Ryo gaped at her.

She explained. "I was a girl when the Kobe disaster happened. On TV, I saw refugees, their homes burnt down, and children who had lost their parents. It hurt to watch. And I asked myself if I could do anything for them—and what I could do to keep it from happening again."

Suddenly she noticed Ryo's expression. She waved her hands and tried to laugh it off. "Oh my God! What a dork! I'm not that passionate about it anymore. I mean, come on, how naive can I be, right?"

Ryo's face was serious. "No, I think it's good."

"What is?"

"What you said. I think the MMD probably needs people who think like that too."

Sakura hurriedly raised the can of sports drink to her mouth with both hands to hide her blushing face.

3:35 AM—

On her way from the nap room to the restroom, Yuri decided to check on the MMD office. The department was quiet now, vastly different from how it had been only a few hours earlier. After the *Suzuka* lost the kaiju, almost no new information had come from the ship. Even the media were stuck waiting for new releases from the Meteorological Agency and the Ministry of Defense. The picture on the TV screen was of the Tokyo skyline with a crawl at the bottom that read, *Kaiju report airing at 4:00 AM.* The department staff were taking turns napping, with everyone to be woken only when new information came in.

Yuri noticed Yojiro and Toshio staring at their computer monitors. "Are you two *still* up?"

Yojiro usually took command on-site, but the weather hadn't yet cleared and he hadn't been able to find a helicopter to take him to the scene. Faced with nothing else to do, he sat in the main office and helped gather information.

A quiet buzzing noise came from his speakers.

"Yeah, there's something that's been bugging me. Here, take a listen." Yojiro pointed his finger straight up as if piercing it straight through the noise. "This is the swimming sound of an MM8 reptilian kaiju found off the coast of Ireland back in '52."

"Eugene, right?"

Eugene had attacked London, destroyed Big Ben and the Tower Bridge, and killed four thousand people. It was the largest kaiju disaster in Europe in the twentieth century.

"Yeah. Can you hear how there are waves in the sound?"

"Yes," Yuri said.

"Now compare it to this."

He clicked his mouse, and the sound changed. It was similar to the previous one, but the modulations were much shorter.

"This is Ray, the MM5 that attacked the eastern coast of America. In both cases, the alligator and the marine iguana, they move their bodies left and right as they swim, so there is a rhythmic wave to their sound signature. But this . . ."

Yojiro pointed to three spiky waveforms on his screen. The top two were Eugene and Ray, which both clearly shared a similar up-and-down wavelike pattern, although with differing periods. But the bottommost one was nearly flat.

"This is from our kaiju. It has no apparent periodicity."

Yuri was taken aback. "So it's not reptilian?"

"And it's not a fish. I can't say what it is, but it isn't swimming by alternating flexion actions."

"Then how is it moving? Does it have some propeller-like organ?"

"The sound doesn't match that either. No matter how many ways I run it through the analysis software, it just comes out noise. I don't know how it's moving a hundred-meter-long body at forty klicks." The exasperated Yojiro pulled at his hair. "There's something off about this kaiju."

A bucket-sized glass of chocolate parfait sat before Sakura, who shrieked in delight. "If I eat all this I'll get fat! Well, just a taste!"

There was a rapping at the door, and Ryo spoke.

She woke up.

"Sakura, time for work!"

She sat up in bed, a bunk in the women's sleeping quarters. "Couldn't I just have had one little bite first?" She rubbed her eyes. "What time is it?"

"Nine forty-five!"

She snapped awake.

"I-I'm sorry! I overslept!" Sakura pushed her legs into her pants. "What about the kaiju?"

"One of the other ships just spotted it on their sonar. One hundred twenty klicks west-northwest of Torijima. On almost exactly the same course. The alert was just issued for Aogajima and Hajijojima."

"And the weather?"

"Clearing. Hurry, we're going to fly in," Ryo said.

"Coming!"

The Seahawk departed with Ryo, Sakura, and Asaya inside. The sea was deep blue and the sky cloudless, as if yesterday's storm had never been.

After some time, the pilot said, "We're approaching the *Hakuba,*" the pilot said.

The *Hakuba*, an Aegis-equipped destroyer (7,250 tons), appeared on the horizon. Several P-3C patrol aircraft circled over it.

"Where's the kaiju?" Ryo asked.

"Three klicks south of the *Hakuba.*" The pilot pointed. "About there, I'd reckon."

Asaya read from the screen of his netbook. "Its depth is holding steady at thirty meters." He frowned. "We can't use the S-1 that far down."

"They're going to see if a sonobuoy can lure it to the surface," Ryo said. "Either way, the sonar pings will give us its silhouette."

Attacking an unknown kaiju would be reckless. Sonar was a good first step, but actual visual contact with the monster was preferred.

Ryo asked, "Are you connected with the meteorological agency right now?"

"Yes. I'll be able to stream the active sonar data to the MMD in real time." Just as Asaya finished the sentence, a small black object dropped from one of the P-3C patrol planes and landed in the ocean.

Ryo said, "All right," and unknowingly clenched his fists.

The sonobuoy's sonar pulses rang through the sea.

"I have the silhouette!" Toshio shouted.

The MMD office filled with energy. The audio analysis program made short work of the data, and Toshio sent the image to the main wall-mounted display.

"What the—"

Chief Kurihama's mouth dropped. The silhouette was a single pencil-shaped rod. The outline was unusually blurry, and there were no apparent limbs or even fins.

Yuri tilted her head. "Is that . . . a submarine?" *Did we mistake some foreign nation's submarine for a living creature?*

"No, it can't be," Toshio said. "The sound waves are being scattered by its surface. It's bumpy. Submarines are smooth."

Kensuke offered, "Maybe those are spikes then, of some sort?"

"I don't think so," Yuri said. "With that shape, there'd be an awful lot of water resistance."

Then someone shouted, "It's changing course!"

The front tip of the silhouette bent slightly to the right, then, like a freight train on a curve, it painted a slow arc as it turned. As had been expected, it was drawn toward the sonobuoy.

"Just like we thought!" Muromachi said. "Its body isn't winding at all! So how in the hell is it moving?"

The kaiju thumbed its nose at the conventions of biology and physics, its hundred-meter-long cylindrical body gliding through the ocean at forty kilometers an hour.

"It's surfacing!" Asaya shouted. "Forty meters, thirty-five, thirty . . ."

"Bring us in!" Ryo said.

The Seahawk reduced altitude until it nearly touched the ocean's surface. It hovered directly above the kaiju's coordinates sent back from the sonobuoy.

Sakura pressed her face to the glass. "Below! Below!" Excitement filled her voice. "There it is!"

Ryo looked out his window. The shadow of the giant creature, maybe ten meters wide, appeared in the water like spilled ink. The pilot passed over it and positioned the helicopter just to the front left of the shadow.

"Come on S-1, show us what you've got!" Ryo pressed the launch button. The S-1 disengaged from its pylon, the transmission cord trailing behind it like a bungee cord, and splashed into the water.

"You're up, Sakura!"

"Yes, sir!"

Sakura gripped the controls. She had been chosen to operate the S-1 because she had proven the best in the unit at handling the controls—her love of video games had made her a natural. But although she had logged many hours simulating the machine, this was her first time attempting the real thing. Field training would have required a helicopter, and helicopters cost money.

A camera inside the front of the device sent back an underwater picture. Rays of sunlight made a waving curtain in the pale blue sea. The S-1 had been dropped a little distance away from the kaiju, and there was no picture of the creature yet.

"It's swimming at forty kilometers per hour," Ryo said. "We have to keep pace."

"I know!" Sakura's finger was already on the acceleration button. The numbers of the speedometer on the top left of the screen increased to forty-four kph. A compass sat in the top center of the display. Sakura turned the S-1 slightly to the right.

Ayase was keeping track of the sonobuoy's data feed. "It's five meters below you now. Maintain your heading . . . No, just a little more to the left. Drop your speed just a hair. Yes, perfect. You should see it soon."

Through the blurry blue veil emerged a black wall. The S-1 rocked violently in the current made by the passing creature, but somehow Sakura kept it on course, parallel with the kaiju. She panned the camera to the right.

"I'm turning on the light," she said, and did. The wall lit up on the rumbling picture. All across it, insect-like creatures packed together, jostling and crawling among each other.

"Wha—!" The *things* reminded Sakura of cockroaches, and she felt goose bumps rise on her skin.

"Get closer!" Ryo shouted.

Sakura pushed back her disgust and steered the S-1 to the right. The shaking in the screen intensified. The camera rapidly closed in on the wriggling wall, and in a second, the creatures became clearly discernible on the screen.

"Lobsters?"

The video feed streamed live to the MMD office.

"Lobsters!"

"Lobsters?"

"What, lobsters?"

All voices traded the same words across the room, *Lobsters, lobsters!* On the screen were hundreds of fan lobsters packed layers deep. The crustaceans on the outermost layer slid backward at a tremendous speed, their tails sticking straight out. If they were packed down that way all the way to the center, there would have to have been hundreds of thousands of them, all swimming together as one.

After ten seconds, the image suddenly jolted, and static came over the line.

Sakura shrieked. "They've swallowed it up!"

The swarm of lobsters didn't retain a perfectly straight cylindrical shape and slightly snaked through the water. The S-1 had been caught inside the rush.

The image on the screen was utter chaos. The innumerable lobsters' appendages and feelers and carapaces flew past the camera in an endless blur. The S-1 was knocked about inside the throng, and its compass spun wildly.

"I can't control it!" Sakura was on the verge of tears. "The cable's pulling! It's getting sucked in!"

Asaya yelled, "It's too late! Cut the connection!"

Ryo went pale. "No, wait!"

But it was too late. The cable was severed.

Ryo watched helplessly as the cable slumped to the sea. "Oh . . . four hundred million yen . . ."

Then the ocean split into two, and the kaiju's giant back revealed itself. The hundreds of lobsters, layered together, wriggled in the sunlight. From a distance, they might have looked like scales.

"It's a colonial organism!" Yoshiro said. "Like polyps, or corals. A mass of organisms functioning as one being."

"*That* was in the deep sea?" Yuri asked.

"Not necessarily. Maybe they formed that shape when their food ran out. Or maybe they behave like locusts and lemmings and move as a group when they overbreed. Moving together like that, they could find a new feeding ground much quicker."

For a moment, Yoshiro was still, struck with wonderment at the mysteries of life. Then, suddenly, he spun to face Chief Kurihama.

"Chief! Tell the SDF to stand down their attack!"

The chief too had been staring at the screen, captivated, but he came back to reality. "What?"

"A missile strike would only scatter the swarm—tens of thousands of lobsters on the continental shelf off of Japan. We don't know the impact on the local ecosystem."

"You're right!"

Kurihama recognized the implications immediately. If a large population of a foreign species of lobster made their home off the coast of Japan, there would be a massive impact on the fishing industry.

"Get the Ministry of Defense! Tell them to lead the lobsters out to the deep ocean before attacking. And let's get word to the media!"

The staff answered, "Yes, sir!" in unison.

Once again the room was filled with the activity of those contacting the Ministry of Defense, others hurriedly working to set up a press conference, and some uploading the S-1's video feed to the Meteorological Agency website.

Suddenly, one of them spoke up. "So, is this a kaiju? It's not really a monster, is it?"

"No, we need to think of it as one single creature," the chief said. "And with that size, it can't be anything but a kaiju. Don't you agree, Yojiro?"

Yojiro was still looking up information on colonial organisms, but he gave a noncommittal "Sure."

Then someone else spoke. "What will we call it? It's a lobster, so how about Lobstergon?"

Kurihama rolled his eyes. "Come on, at least try!"

Suggestions came from all over the room. "How about Lobsterlon!" "Lobsterah!" "Too awkward!" "Too flippant!" "A 'Dah' or a 'Gah' in the name helps make it sound giant!" "What are different ways of saying 'group'?" "Cluster, pride, herd, swarm, shoal . . ." "A large group of locusts can be called a cloud."

Kurihama pointed his ballpoint pen at the last man and exclaimed, "I'll take it! A cloud in the sea . . . Seacloud! I think that'll work. What do you think? Ehh?" Kurihama beamed with pride. Naming the kaiju was the chief's perogative. Nobody seemed to find a reason to object to this one, and the room gave their silent consent.

"It's decided!" he said. "Kaiju Three will be known as Seacloud. Inform the press!"

That evening—

Colonial kaiju Seacloud was led east by sonar until it was directly above the Japan Trench. Eight destroyer escorts fired a focused attack of VL-ASROC antisubmarine rockets and confirmed Seacloud's destruction. The warnings and alerts were lifted. Any surviving lobsters either sank deep into the trench or were scattered in the waters of the northern Pacific by the Kuroshio Current.

In the end, it was determined to have a displacement of three thousand tons and was designated an MM8.7.

Ryo and Sakura stood on the deck of the *Hakuba* as the sun set into the sea.

"Basically, it was like a bunch of conveyor belts one on top of the other," he explained. "One lobster atop another, atop another, atop another, and as a whole, they formed a cylinder. Each of them walked backward atop the one below. The farther out the layer, the faster it moved. The ones at the very edge were backing up at ten kilometers an hour. They had their tails stuck straight out, pushing against the water, tens of thousands of little oars all rowing at once—that's how the cloud moved so fast. Once they got to the back of the line, they were swallowed back inside until they came out the front again in an endless loop."

"How do you think they learned how to do it?"

"If you think about the algorithm, it's pretty simple. I'm sure you've seen a flock of birds turn at the same time, as if they were one creature. It's just like that. I've even seen video of spiny lobsters walking along the ocean floor in a straight line. Many crustaceans share some form of group movement or another. Seacloud's behavior likely evolved from that."

"Truly a wonder of nature," Sakura said. "But it's a little sad, don't you think?"

"What is?"

"If you think about it, all the lobsters did was repeat what they'd done for millions of years. We humans didn't come along until long after they did, and we just got rid of them because they were inconvenient."

"It's the same with all kaiju. They just follow the workings of nature. But we've found the power to defy nature. It's part of who we are. And all we've done is exercise that power—in order to protect people's happiness, like you said," Ryo said.

"I guess . . ."

"We protect people from nature's menace. It's our job. When it comes down to it, nature is our enemy. You can't let too much of your feelings get into it."

"Yeah . . ."

Ryo stretched his arms high. "Well, at least we got through this without a single death. That's something to be happy about, right?"

"Chocolate parfait."

"What?"

"I read a magazine article about this restaurant in Ginza that has the most delicious chocolate parfait. I've been wanting to go for a while, but things kept coming up . . ." Sakura laughed nervously. "I was just thinking, I'm happy that nothing happened to Ginza."

Ryo nodded. "And I'm glad nothing happened to Yokohama."

As he watched the last golden sliver of sun slip past the horizon, he thought, *As soon as I get back, I'll have to reschedule that date.*

"Damn, I have to write up my formal apology first."

"What?"

"We lost the S-1."

"Oh." Sakura was downcast. "There's no way I'm going to have to pay back four hundred million yen, right?"

"You never know!"

"What?"

"Kidding, kidding. Don't worry. It was an act of God. They'll forgive you." Then he added, "Please, just make the apology a good one!"

Night fell, the ocean at peace.

PART TWO

DANGER! GIRL AT LARGE!

"Your eggs are done!"

At his mother's cheerful call, Ikki Anno trundled down the stairs in his pajamas, stretching his little body with a big yawn. Yuri hummed as she set the living room table. It was six thirty in the morning—quite some time before her son would have to leave for school, but she enforced an early wake-up out of the belief that they should at least have some time for leisurely conversation in the mornings.

After he was done in the bathroom, sleepy-eyed Ikki sat at the table and took a bite of his fried eggs, which, along with a single slice of toast, were enough to tide over the third-grader's stomach until lunchtime.

Yuri moved on to folding the laundry. "Have you finished your homework?"

"Not my read-alouds." Ikki threw his mother a resentful look. "You didn't get back till late last night."

"Oh." She pressed her palms together in an apologetic gesture. "Mom's sorry, dear. My meeting went longer than I thought."

To complete his read-aloud homework, he needed to read selections from his Japanese textbook and have a family member sign off on the worksheet. Because his mother often got home late—or sometimes not at all—he was frequently unable to finish his work. His teacher was understanding, but Ikki always felt ashamed.

He sighed. "It's okay, it happens all the time. I guess I'll just have to turn into one of those delinquent youths."

"What?"

Ikki laughed. "Just kidding."

His smile was genuine. Despite the boy's many lonely microwave dinners and Yuri's absence from his school's parent visitation days, Ikki knew it was beyond her control. His mother's job was very important. Even though he was a young child, he understood what she did, and he was proud of her.

"I'm sorry," she said. "As soon as you finish your breakfast, I'll listen to you read." Then her cell phone rang—the ringtone the theme from an anime program.

She had a bad feeling. A call this early meant an emergency.

Her hunch was right. On the line was her coworker and MMD operator, Toshio Yamagiwa.

"It's Toshio," he said. "Sorry to call this early."

"Is it a kaiju?"

"I guess we'd have to call it that." His voice was troubled. "It was first sighted in Gifu City. I've just heard about it from Chief Kurihama myself, so I don't know the whole story."

All members of the MMD were on an emergency phone chain, and Yuri was toward the bottom of the tree. By the time her phone rang, the rest of the department would have already been informed.

"Gifu, you said? Is there any connection with that sighting of the bird—"

"No, this isn't quite like anything we've seen before. The MM is probably four or five. TBS already has a news crew on location. See for yourself."

She scrambled for the remote. "How'd they get there ahead of us?"

"One of the morning shows was on hand to record some event live, and it happened to show up where they were."

She turned on the TV. On the top right of the screen were the words *Breaking News: Kaiju in Gifu City!* Over the audio, a studio anchor and on-site reporter were describing the current state of the evacuation.

At first, Yuri couldn't tell where in the picture the kaiju was. The camera held on a tight close-up of a young girl's face, maybe between fourth and sixth grade. She looked Japanese, only with darker skin, as if she was deeply tanned, and had long disheveled hair. She was slowly looking all around her wearing an innocent, untroubled smile, like she wasn't quite aware of what was happening around her. The handheld camera was visibly shaking—it must have been zoomed in at quite a distance. Yuri wondered, *Why are they filming this girl? Why don't they just show me the monster already?*

The camera zoomed out to reveal the background. Yuri gasped.

The girl's head was sticking out over the top of a five-story apartment building. Her head was larger than the water tank on the roof.

Meanwhile, somewhere in Tokyo—

"Yeah, I'm seeing it."

The man, seated on a sofa in his pajamas, a cordless phone to his ear, watched the girl on his plasma TV. He was near fifty, and in his youth he might have been handsome. He had narrow, sleepy eyes and a thick goatee.

The person on the other end of the line was shrieking in panic.

But the bearded man remained calm. "This has to be Umemiya's doing, right? Could it be anyone else? Maybe he slipped up trying to move her, or he's getting the SDF to dispose of her because he couldn't work up the nerve to do it himself. Maybe he just wasn't thinking."

He lazily scratched his head, listening. "What should we do?" he repeated. "I don't think there's anything we *can* do, at this point. You're the one who failed to stop him. Now we just have to see how it plays out. Well, except for closing up shop here, with the Intelligence Agency and the police bound to come snooping around—yeah, I'm ditching the CCI. They were just a cover, anyway. I've already moved most of the under-the-table cash somewhere else. We'll be able to start over."

His partner was still shouting something, but he cut in. "Your time would be better spent getting out of there. Leave everything behind. It looks like there won't be time to hire movers—yeah, of course, you need to hide any evidence. Not just the documents, but be sure to wipe the hard drives. Use the program I put on there. And do a factory reset on your phone and throw it away. Don't forget that. I'm hanging up now."

He did. The man gazed around the lavishly furnished room, a 250,000-yen apartment in one of the city's most exclusive districts.

"And I liked this place, too."

He sighed. Ceremoniously, he stood and began to dress.

The girl was excited, buoyant. She'd never seen such a wide space. Or if she had, it had already vanished from her memory. All she did remember was a dim lightbulb, four gray walls, a gray floor, and a gray ceiling.

At night, she lay down in a wooded valley and stared up at the dark sky. She was shocked by what she saw. *Is the world really this big? Was there always this much out there beyond those walls? Above that gray ceiling, and its filth and its cracks, had there always been another, gigantic and black, with these beautiful sparkling specks of light?* This new reality was more than the child's imagination had ever contained.

At first, when the sky quickly brightened and the stars faded, she was a little disappointed. But then the clouds were painted in vivid colors and an enormous, dazzling lightbulb appeared beyond the mountains. The sight of it moved her so much that she gasped. The light was so bright it hurt her eyes to look straight at it. She lowered her head. On the floor beneath her were countless boxes, almost like building blocks. Drawn by her curiosity, the girl cautiously came down from the mountainside.

The smallest of the boxes came up to her shins, and the tallest to her head. All had transparent panels inset in their sides. Many of the shorter ones had colorful lids from which sharp wirelike bits protruded. The girl had never before seen so many different colors and shapes at once. Compared with the dark, gray, flat world she knew, this was a fairyland.

In the gaps between the boxes were narrow paths paved with some blackish substance. The top layer was thin and fragile, and the material beneath was spongy. With each step, the weight of the girl's body sank into it, and the black layer cracked. Fountains of water shot up through some of the cracks. Gray sticks stood along each side of the paths with black threads strung along at the height of her shins. When her leg tugged at one of them, it snapped with a tiny spark and a light sting—nothing serious, but enough to startle her. After that, she was careful to step over the strings when she crossed them.

Below she saw throngs of small creatures, shining and white, squeaking as they scattered down the roads. They were about the size of mice, but they bustled about on two legs. Although the girl found something comical about their flurried movements, the boxes—for the time being—drew her interest, and she didn't think to chase after the scurrying creatures.

She crouched to look inside one of the boxes. Behind the window something shone—a smaller box, one she could fit in her hand. The front of it twinkled and she could hear a faint sound come from within. *A magic box!* She wanted it. Slowly, she reached for it. With a gentle press of her finger, the thin, clear windowpane shattered. Her hand easily passed inside and she grabbed the box.

But when she pulled it out from the larger container, the front of the magic box turned gray, and its sound ceased.

"Oouh," she groaned and threw the box aside. But her disappointment was only fleeting. What did it matter if she broke one? There would be plenty more toys in this big big room.

With so many things around, what would it matter if she broke some of them?

Takebashi, Chiyoda Ward, Tokyo: Japan Meteorological Agency HQ—

A jittery reporter on the flatscreen TV was saying, "The child—no, the kaiju with the *appearance* of a child—just sat down in the Nagara riverside road and is holding a car, pushing it back and forth, playing with it like a toy. Oh! She's lifted it up now. Oh, that's really high. There doesn't appear to be anyone inside, but . . ."

Kurihama fumed. "Enough of her face! Show us below her neck! Below her neck!"

"Chief," Toshio said soothingly, "you know they can't. It's broadcast TV."

Yuri grumbled, "Really, this doesn't give us anything."

Five hours had passed since the kaiju was first sighted, and all the networks had teams of reporters on-site—but all of them broadcast images with a digital mosaic obscuring the girl's body below her neck. It was self-censorship, each network independently coming to the same conclusion—an uncensored image might have run afoul of child pornography laws. But even so, it was frustrating for the MMD not to have full knowledge of the kaiju they were dealing with.

Chief Kurihama asked one of the younger operators, "Do you have the Gifu office on the line?"

"We still can't reach them. They seem to have run into a bit of trouble."

"What about Yojiro's team?"

"They got to Nagoya thirty minutes ago. They're probably nearing the site now."

"What the hell are they doing?" Kurihama threw his elbows on his desk and fretfully twirled his pen in his fingers. "The army's already deployed, ready and waiting for our advice, and we can't do anything because we're still not even there. The media's going to be all over us."

"Chief," said a female operator with one hand covering her phone receiver, "I'm getting several inquiries from the networks. They want to know if we have a name for Kaiju Six yet."

"How the hell can we? We haven't even seen what she looks like yet!"

One of the other operators happily reported, "Chief! I have a connection with Yojiro on-site!"

"Put him on the main screen."

Yojiro's face appeared on the flatpanel display. Visible behind him were a six-wheeled Type 82 Command and Communication Vehicle and a Type 89 Infantry Fighting Vehicle with SDF soldiers scurrying between them.

"Sorry it took us so long to get here," Yojiro said. "But we're here now."

"What's the situation?" the chief asked.

"Kaiju Six was moving westward but stopped northwest of Mt. Kinka, near the Nagara Bridge. We are located roughly two klicks downstream by the Chusetsu Bridge. Currently, the kaiju doesn't seem to be making any major movements. I'll put it on camera now."

The camera panned right to show the Nagara River upstream. The image zoomed in. All eyes were on the screen.

The room buzzed.

A bare-naked girl, sitting on the right-hand shore of the river, was playing with a car in her hand. At first glance, it was a tranquil scene. Her long hair hung down to her waist and covered her upper body like a cloak. The bridge in the foreground obscured her from the waist down. Aside from her darker skin, she looked like a normal Japanese girl—and nothing like a kaiju. This perception was heightened by the lack of a sense of scale in the long distance shot. She looked like a child of normal height playing with a miniature car.

Without thinking, Yuri said, "She's pretty."

The others in the room shared her sentiment. If the girl were a human, she would have been around ten years old. Her chest, though mostly covered by her hair, was clearly that of a child.

Yojiro continued his report. "The 10th Division and the 35th Infantry Regiment have been deployed along Highways 77, 157, and 248, forming a cordon around Kaiju Six. The evacuation of Gifu City is only about halfway complete, but the northern area of the city and everything within a three-kilometer radius of the kaiju are pretty much all clear. Security forces are checking for any stragglers. Once we've confirmed the evacuation is complete, we can commence the attack. We estimate Six to be twenty meters tall—MM5 at most. We anticipate that tank-mounted cannons or anti-tank missiles will be enough to destroy it. The only problem is—"

"Its appearance," Kurihama said.

"Exactly."

A kaiju in the form of a human—or, more simply, a giant—was not entirely unprecedented. All living things on Earth had the capability of massive increases in size, although the cause or causes remained unknown. The press often called the transformations "sudden mutations," but they were incorrect. The sudden changes weren't the result of a biological process, but rather developments contrary to the laws of physics, specifically, the law of conservation of mass. There have been many examples of giant-sized life-forms in all regions of the globe: ants, grasshoppers, praying mantises, spiders, scorpions, snails, octopuses, lizards, snakes, crocodiles, chickens, mice, moles, rabbits, monkeys, and so on. As humans were also living creatures, it shouldn't have been a wonder to find a human kaiju. Indeed, cultures all over the world had legends of giant people, and there was no doubt that a race of giants, distinct from *Homo sapiens*, were once widespread. Some of them had even been found slumbering beneath the earth in a state of cryptobiosis—an indefinite suspension of metabolic processes to survive adverse conditions—only to awaken once more.

In the twentieth century, there were ten incidents involving giant humans—two in America alone. The larger or more violent were killed, and some between MM0 and MM3 had been caught and held in captivity.

But the MMD now faced a unique problem. Those giants were all adults. There were no previous cases with human children kaiju. Even more troubling was her size. At MM5 (one hundred tons), she had surpassed the biggest humanoid kaiju on record, Glen (1952, Nevada Desert, eighteen meters tall, MM4.7).

"From what we're observing," Yojiro said, "she is of low intelligence. She hasn't spoken anything resembling language. Therefore, she seems not to be a normal girl who suddenly grew to giant size—although we can't know that for sure."

And until they knew, the SDF couldn't act. If she wasn't human, and if she had only the intelligence of an animal, she could be declared a kaiju. All kaiju MM5 and larger—even docile herbivores—were a danger by their very existence, and once near a population center, could be terminated at the discretion of the SDF. Even smaller kaiju would be put down if they proved aggressive. But there was no proof yet that this girl wasn't human. Beyond that, even if she was a kaiju, and they killed something that only *looked* like a girl, Kurihama could well imagine the public's condemnation.

The chief asked, "Is it MM5 or not?"

"If so, only barely. A visual estimate at this distance can only be so accurate. We'd have to get a better measurement of its height."

"This is giving me a headache." Kurihama sighed. "Do we have any leads on what it is? Where it came from?"

"It seems to have come from the south face of Mt. Gongen, but that would have been before daybreak, and we have no witnesses. We *have* heard there's been some damage to the mountain face. I'm thinking about going with Kiichi to check it out."

Yuri said, "I'd like a picture from closer up. And to see her walking, if possible."

"Ryo and the others are going to take a vehicle in closer," Yojiro said. "They should be ready to head out shortly."

Kurihama asked, "Are those kids going to be okay on their own?"

Yojiro grinned. "Don't shortchange Sakura's skill behind the wheel."

Ryo, Asaya, and Sakura climbed into the van prepared by the Gifu branch office. Ryo and Asaya were still in their twenties, and Sakura was nineteen, fresh out of high school. The junior MMD employees were often the ones sent to the front lines.

Their protection, two army men, got in the back. The older, Sergeant Kashihara, carried a 84mm caliber recoilless rifle commonly known as the Carl Gustav. His subordinate, Corporal Izaki, was on hand to assist with ammunition and reloading, and also carried a Howa Type 89 Assault Rifle. The 84mm shells wouldn't be enough to take out a monster with a height dozens of times taller than a human—nor would the 5.56mm rifle cartridges, of course—but they might be enough to pierce through a kaiju's skin and cause it pain—and hopefully slow it down.

As Sakura adjusted her seat and the driver's mirrors, Sergeant Kashihara asked her, "Is it really okay, us riding with you? Maybe we should've brought our own vehicle."

"Oh, no, you're fine." Sakura game him a nervous glance in the rearview mirror. "It's easier to maneuver with just one car. When it comes time to escape, things can get crazy. If you were behind us in a Jeep or something and we crashed into each other, it wouldn't be something to laugh at."

Ryo added, "It's happened before. Ten years ago, give or take. In America. The scientists were in one car, military support in another. The two escaping vehicles crashed into each other, and the kaiju squashed them both. Ever since, all attempts to get close to one of the monsters have been made in one vehicle."

"I see," said the sergeant, though he seemed to still have reservations. Maybe he felt nervous putting his life in the hands of a teenage driver.

Sakura eased on the gas. "And we're off."

The van traveled up the Nagara riverside roadway toward Kaiju Six.

Sakura stopped at the north end of Kinka Bridge, one kilometer away, and turned the car around. From that point on, she would drive in reverse. That too was standard procedure. Too slow a U-turn might make the difference between escape and a kaiju's foot smashing through a vehicle's roof. Ryo looked out the rear window and helped guide her steering. Asaya pushed his body out the sunroof and took pictures of the giant girl through his camera's telephoto lens.

Just before the Nagara Bridge, Sakura parked the van at the Nagara River Convention Center. From there, they could see all 250 meters of the bridge. The girl, sitting with her back against a hotel, was still playing with a car and hadn't noticed their approach.

Ryo whispered into his headset, "We're about four hundred meters away. We're getting out of the van to take pictures on foot."

Ryo, Asaya, and the two soldiers quietly stepped outside. Sakura remained at the wheel. They left the doors open and the engine idling to make for a quick escape.

Asaya set up his camera and tripod on the pavement. He checked the GPS for coordinates to send back to the head office, where the distance from the kaiju and her size on the screen would be analyzed to determine her height.

Sakura slid over to the passenger seat and stuck her head out the open door. "She really messes with your sense of scale, doesn't she?"

The girl made the four hundred meters separating them feel like thirty. They could hear her low rumble of a voice saying, *"Goooo goooo,"* as she played with the car, repeatedly tossing it into the air and catching it again. Each time the vehicle landed in her hand, the sound of jolting metal resounded off the riverbanks.

Ryo asked, "Is that just like a beanbag to her?"

Sakura shrugged. "But she looks fairly docile, right?"

But just then, as if she had suddenly grown bored of her game, the girl threw the car as high up into the air as she could. The vehicle arced through the air and crashed into the railing of Nagara Bridge, bursting into pieces and sending a chunk of the railing into the river below.

Then she noticed the van parked on the bank of the river—and the tiny creatures beside it.

"*Oo-oah?*"

She slowly rose, sending the wall of the hotel crumbling behind her. Debris scattered down from her back. Her dark, innocent eyes glimmered with excitement at the discovery of a newfound toy. She moved as if in slow motion and walked across the embankment and into the river. She splashed through the shin-deep water, upending moored cormorant fishing boats, and approached the van.

Ryo and the others rushed back into the car, and Sakura urged the vehicle forward without even waiting for them to shut the doors.

They drove along the riverside road. Asaya stood up and recorded video from the roof. The girl had made it out of the water and scrambled up the embankment and onto the road. She clomped after them, laughing merrily.

"She's fast!" Ryo said with a shudder.

The girl's movements were slow, but her stride was bigger than that of ten men, and so she covered distance quickly. The needle on the van's speedometer had already pushed past fifty kph, but the giant was keeping pace. Her black hair, at least ten meters long, tossed about in the air. With each of her steps came a rumble like exploding dynamite, and the asphalt visibly cracked. No one could have expected the pavement to hold up against the force of dozens of tons falling from several meters in the air.

If she stepped on them, they'd be crushed.

"Shake her!" Ryo yelled.

Sakura was already speeding up the van. They were almost to Kinka Bridge, with the line of armored vehicles on the Chusetsu Bridge visible, their cannons aimed upriver.

At the northern end of the Kinka Bridge, Sakura yanked the

wheel to the left, tires squealing as the van spun ninety degrees. Ryo cursed, smushed against the side of the van by centrifugal force, but Sakura ignored his outcries and floored it down the length of the bridge. The girl jumped down from the road to cut diagonally across the river and head them off. At the other end of the bridge, Sakura took another left, and drove upstream on the southern side of the water. The girl came at them from the side.

Near Kinka Elementary School, it looked like the girl might catch them, but the van narrowly escaped her outstretched arm. She climbed onto the road and resumed chase.

Ryo barked, "What the hell are you trying to do?" but Sakura again ignored him as she urged the van down the road. The girl was behind them, jumping over power lines as though they were hurdles. Corporal Izaki raised his assault rifle to fire out the open rear hatch, but the road was too bumpy for him to take effective aim. Kashihara's recoilless rifle was out of the question—the backblast of exhaust would severely injure the other passengers.

The van sped straight down the road and into the Mt. Kinka Tunnel. The girl dove headfirst, like a baseball player, and slid along the asphalt. Chunks of pavement sprayed into the air. She slammed thunderously into the tunnel's entrance with her arm thrust inside. But the van was out of reach. The girl moaned, *"Gaaa-oooo!"* and slapped at the earth in frustration.

Out the other side of the tunnel, Sakura stopped the van.

Ryo's breath was ragged. "What was that about?"

Sakura felt the glares of the four men on the back of her head. Softly, she said, "If . . . if I kept driving straight . . ."

She turned. "If I kept driving straight, the tanks would have fired upon her. Right?"

Seeing the tears in her eyes, Ryo shrank back. But he quickly recovered. "Next time, don't get us involved with your feelings. If you're going to die, do it alone."

Sakura, dejected, said nothing.

Chief Kurihama was leaning forward, watching the scene through his computer screen, and when he saw they were all safe, he slumped against the back of his chair. "Are they trying to *kill* me?"

The young operator Kensuke said, "But this video—this is important stuff! The American military kept all their footage of Glen secret, and Alison was killed before anyone recorded her in motion. This might be the world's first video of a giant over ten meters tall running at full tilt."

But Kurihama was too busy muttering to himself to listen. "I'll have to reprimand her when she gets back. As long as I'm chief, I won't let anyone be a martyr."

The rest of the team in the office let the chief be and began work on the analysis of the images. Toshio took a still frame of the girl just as she'd stood up, and overlaid a one-meter grid to determine her height. There was plenty of work for the others, including the construction a full 3-D computer-simulated model of the girl.

Kensuke used footage of the girl running to calculate her speed. "When she's running in a straight line, she covers a hundred meters in six seconds. In kilometers per hour, that's . . . Whoa! She's going sixty!"

"If she can move that quickly," said one of the men, "we have to rethink the evacuation radius."

Another pointed to a zoomed-in picture of the girl's face. "What's this? At her neck."

Over his shoulder, someone said, "Part of her skin looks darker. A bruise, maybe?"

Toshio finished his measurements. "She's twenty meters tall, just as we thought. Plus or minus fifty centimeters. Let's see, if a normal girl her age is a hundred and forty centimeters . . ."

Yuri did the math in her head. "She's fourteen times normal size." She punched the numbers into her calculator to find the square root, then looked to Kensuke and asked, "Could you replay the footage of her running and speed it up by 3.7 times?"

"Make it an even four, and I can."

"That's fine. Please go ahead."

At four times the speed, the girl looked like a normal-sized child moving in real time.

"Just like I thought," Yuri said. "Unlike the reptiles, with a humanoid kaiju you can really sense the difference in time scale."

"Time scale?" Kensuke asked.

"She's living in time 3.7 times slower than ours. To her, we seem like we're scurrying around at 3.7 times speed. Since this effect would extend to the frequency of electromagnetic waves, she sees in the infrared spectrum. And because humans give off heat, I imagine we shine white."

Toshio nodded. "You're talking about the parallel anthropic principle, right? She's living in a different reality."

A younger worker lamely offered, "So she's from another dimension?"

Yuri laughed. "No, she's a being from our world. But she's operating under a different set of physical laws. That includes gravity. She must feel no heavier than a normal girl does."

If she was fourteen times taller than a human, the area of her cross section would be two hundred times larger, and her weight would be 2,700 times greater. Bones and muscle weren't able to hold up that much weight. She shouldn't have been able to stand. The reason kaiju could walk the earth remained a great mystery.

The parallel anthropic principle provided one possible solution. Kaiju were the result of a so-called "paradigm shift" three thousand years ago. They came from a parallel universe with an origin different from our Big Bang, and our laws of physics didn't apply to them.

"But there's still many unknowns," Yuri said. "For example, to her scale, the earth has a radius of only 450 kilometers, and yet she feels gravity at one G. The only way the math works out is if the earth is fourteen times more dense than it is. Unless the law of universal gravitation is different for her too—"

"Yuri," a female receptionist cut in. "Someone's here for you. Something about an interview."

"Now? I don't have time to talk to a reporter now. Have them wait until after we're done here."

"No, he's with the Public Security Intelligence Agency. A Mr. Azekura. It's about this incident."

"Azekura?" Chief Kurihama swiveled his chair. "Taichi Azekura? With the PSIA?"

"Y-yes, sir."

"What's *he* doing here?"

Kurihama pinched his lips together and squeezed the ballpoint pen in his hand.

Taichi Azekura, a plain-looking middle-aged man, could have been mistaken for a homeowners insurance salesman. He was nothing like the steely-eyed secret agent the movies led Yuri to expect from a special agent with the Intelligence Agency.

He walked into the meeting room and gave the chief and Yuri an affable grin. "Hey, Kurihama, long time no see. And you must be Ms. Anno. Nice to meet you."

With a sour expression, Chief Kurihama plopped down on the sofa. "I hoped never to meet you again."

"Come now, don't be like that. I wouldn't be here if it wasn't my job. Half of why I'm here is to ask some questions. The other half, to give you some information."

"To give *us* information?"

"It's like this," Azekura said. "If we held on to what we know, kept it our secret, then you wouldn't be able to see the whole picture, which might be trouble for you."

"And I should be thankful?"

"Well, yeah. About a half a year ago, we started tracking this group calling themselves CCI."

"What, leftists?"

"No. CCI stands for the Creative Cosmology Institute—a legitimate-sounding name, but in truth, they're a cult, suckering people in with nonsense about some super-ancient civilization of gods in Japan."

"So the PSIA's finally paying attention to destructive cults?"

Azekura easily parried Kurihama's sarcasm. "We don't want a repeat of the incident ten years ago."

A cult called the Zeta Transcendents secretly raised a kaiju underground and unleashed it beneath Tokyo. It was an act that rocked Japan, the first instance of kaiju terrorism—and the Intelligence Agency had failed to see it coming. Even though some among the press and the police had held the Zetas in suspicion, the PSIA was focused entirely on left-wing extremist groups and North Korean spies, and paid little attention to cult formations. The agency, having utterly lost face, began to put efforts into watching cult activity.

"This CCI," Azekura said, "is quite dangerous. We've had unconfirmed reports indicating they are importing machine guns and antitank missiles from Russia. And that's not all. We received intelligence that they are raising a kaiju."

Kurihama's face went pale. "A kaiju?"

"Yes. We found one of their internal writings. But we weren't able to find out anything about the kaiju itself. In the document, they only called it 'X'—nothing about its real name or what it looks like."

Yuri said, "Kaiju X . . ."

"But we were able to find out, roughly, its location. Around Kagamigahara City, Gifu Prefecture, there are still several air-raid shelters left over from the Pacific War. We believe it is—or was— inside one of them. In truth, we were already in talks with the prefectural police to search the shelters when this happened."

Kurihama said, "You're saying this incident is . . ."

"There's a high chance this may be another Zeta Incident."

Yuri shuddered. One after another, the images of victims being carried out of the subways flashed vividly through her mind. *Could that innocent-looking child be carrying a terrible destructive power?* She looked at Azekura. "But what does this have to do with me?"

"Yeah, about that. Do you know a Mikio Izuno?"

Now *that* was a name she hadn't heard in a while. "Yes. He's an astrophysicist. He was a pupil of my father's. My dad took a liking to him, and back when he was a student, he often came over to our house."

Fragments of her childhood replayed in her mind.

Mikio, who always picked her up and said, "Hey, little Yuri, how are you?"

Mikio, whose interests and manner of speaking were older than his age.

Mikio, who loved sukiyaki.

Mikio, who gave her a book for Christmas.

At some point unbeknownst to her, her little heart had started to flutter every time he came over. The last time Yuri saw him, she had just entered high school. She still remembered how hot her cheeks felt when he looked at her and said, "To think little Yuri's grown into such a woman."

It was a distant memory. Even now, she didn't know if that budding feeling had been love.

Keeping her tone professional, she said, "But twenty years ago he suddenly went missing. I haven't heard from him since."

"Did he ever talk about anything . . . unorthodox?" Azekura asked.

"You mean the parallel anthropic principle? An English physicist named Asprin came up with the idea in 1983, but back then, few took him seriously. Mikio was the first in Japan to draw attention to his work."

"Do you think he could have been cast out of academia because of it?"

Yuri laughed. "Cast out of academia? That's something out of fiction. The real world doesn't work like that. And even though the parallel anthropic principle had few backers back then, it's only gained support in the field of physics."

"Then why did he disappear?"

"I don't know. He put all his affairs in order before he went, so it must have been of his own volition. Back then, I worried that he'd gotten involved with something."

"I see. Now, I have a few questions about this." Azekura pulled a small tape recorder from his pocket and placed it on the coffee table. "It's a wiretap recording of a CCI phone call from three days ago."

Kurihama broke in. "The Intelligence Agency doesn't have the right to do that."

Azekura laughed it off. "Yeah, well, it's a little more complicated than that. Anyway, Mikio's name comes up in the recording—his last name, actually. And the analysts were clear on this—the voice says 'Izuno,' which is a fairly rare name—not 'Mizuno' or some other common one. Since few share that name, we have a high degree of certainty that it's the same man. We just need you to confirm it. Of course, this recording is all off the record, so please, you didn't hear any of it from me."

He pushed the play button.

A man was talking. ". . . don't know why you keep that thing alive. You have to take care of it. Now!"

The other speaker, also male, said, "Mr. Umemiya, please, compose yourself. This project is my responsibility. Why are you interfering with the plan we decided on?"

Yuri's heart jumped. It was the same voice that twenty years earlier had said, "*Little Yuri, look how you've grown.*"

The first voice came back. "Mr. Izuno, you haven't grown fond of Princess after raising her all these years, have you? Maybe that's why you don't want to kill her."

"You're wrong." Mikio's sneer was practically audible. "She's just a valuable specimen, nothing more."

"Then there shouldn't be a problem. We have One, it should be enough. That was the purpose of the project, wasn't it? Princess's power is too dangerous. If she got free—"

"I know that better than anyone."

"So why are you being like this? Why are you endangering our plans?"

"How many times do I have to explain it? She's insurance. She's a card up our sleeve in case something happens. We need to keep her."

"But—"

"One's just as dangerous, isn't it? Come now, Mr. Umemiya, surely you don't think it will always act exactly according to our expectations? If it were that easy to control, we wouldn't have needed the project in the first place."

"But the Intelligence Agency is starting to sniff around!"

"They don't have the slightest clue of her purpose."

The recording stopped. "How about it?" Azekura asked. "Is that the voice of Mikio Izuno?"

Yuri softly nodded. "Yes. It is."

"Do you have any recordings of his voice? Maybe an old video tape with him speaking? If you did, we could run audio fingerprinting."

"No, I don't think so. But what would *Mikio* be doing in a cult?" Yuri said.

"I don't know. We don't have him on any of the membership lists. He might be using a false name. But we've been led to believe that he is in charge of the group raising Kaiju X."

Yuri couldn't believe it. The Mikio she knew was rational, intelligent—not the sort of person she could see connected with a cult.

"This Princess they were talking about," she said, "is it the girl, Kaiju Six?"

"That's a valid assumption. Maybe this Umemiya guy, or someone else, noticed our investigation, panicked, and set her free. Maybe they thought it would be better to let her rampage than to have her captured by the police."

Kurihama frowned, deep in thought. "They also used the term 'One.' Could that be the name of another kaiju?"

"Could be. There were several occurrences of the number in documents we obtained. We're still looking into it."

"Like Yuri, I'm also having trouble understanding why a physicist would raise a kaiju for a cult."

"The problem is not why, but how." Azekura raised a finger. "That kaiju—Princess—couldn't always have been that size. First of all, the air-raid shelters don't have that much space to hide her in. Moreover, she'd require over one ton of food every day. It would be too obvious. She must have become a giant in the past few days at most."

"So you're saying . . ."

"Yes. That physicist, Mikio, has developed a technique to radically increase the size of living creatures. That's the only explanation. Possibly utilizing, somehow, the parallel anthropic principle."

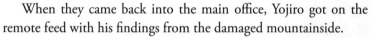

When they came back into the main office, Yojiro got on the remote feed with his findings from the damaged mountainside.

"This was an old air-raid shelter," he said. "And it wasn't just destroyed. It burst out from within. The dirt's been scattered outward, away from the site. I think it's safe to conclude this is where Kaiju Six emerged."

Chief Kurihama asked, "Are there any other signs of activity?"

"Yes. The locals say this place was off-limits, but there are empty bowls of cup ramen and plastic sacks from convenience stores all over the place. No doubt about it, this place was in use. I did find something I feel to be particularly interesting."

Yojiro lifted up his hand. Dangling at the end of a heavy, dirt-encrusted chain was a belt made of thick black leather. "It's set up to lock like a pair of handcuffs. The inside is well worn. It's clearly been in use for quite some time. The problem is its size."

He put his arm through the closed loop. It was more than twice the size of an adult wrist. "This wasn't made for a wrist or an ankle. But I couldn't fit it around my neck, either. It must be for a dog, or—"

Yuri cut in, her voice soft and her gaze distant. "A child's neck."

The bruise on the girl's neck was the same width as the belt, only fourteen times wider. She felt sick as she recalled the voice from the tape.

"*. . . raising her all these years.*"

What horrific experiments had Mikio been performing in the darkness of the old bunker?

The news from the home office struck the members of the Mobile Unit hard.

Sakura asked, "So . . . that child is *human*?"

Ryo's expression went dark. "I think we have to think of it that way. The reason she can't speak might be simply because she's been held in captivity for years, and not because she's a kaiju."

"But could it really be possible? To turn a person into a giant?"

"It's not unheard of," Ryo said. "The Nazis are said to have run experiments in an attempt to create giant super-soldiers. They used radiation or something. Supposedly the Americans used the Nazis' knowledge to run similar programs in the fifties."

Asaya added, "Some say that's why they've kept the data on Glen a secret, even half a century later. He was a failed experiment."

"I've heard that," Ryo said. "They certainly seem to have run tests on animals, at least. That giant tarantula—what was its name, Arnold? Apparently that was an escaped test subject. Whether that's true or not, the US and the Soviets both tried to weaponize kaiju during the Cold War. We can be sure of that much. Of course, none of it panned out."

"Why not?" Sakura asked.

Asaya answered. "'Cause they couldn't control 'em. Sure, you hear all the time how radiation turned one animal or another into a kaiju, but most of the time, when you throw a ton of radiation at something, it just dies. Nobody knows what conditions will make them grow. And even if you managed to come up with a process, the giant creatures just destroy whatever's around them. You can't predict where they'll go. They might attack your allies. That wouldn't make for a very good weapon, would it?"

"So nobody's doing that kind of research anymore?"

"Pretty much. There are too many humanitarian concerns over doing those kinds of tests on human subjects."

Ryo thought about it. "Humanitarian problems . . . Maybe that's their aim."

"What do you mean?" Sakura asked.

"I mean Kaiju Six. If she were a typical kaiju, the SDF would handily take her out. But because she looks like a girl, they can't attack her so easily. If they kill her, the government and the armed forces will face a great deal of criticism. So while they're struggling to decide how to deal with her, she goes about destroying things. What if they turned that child into a kaiju for precisely that reason?"

"That's—" Sakura was astonished. "You're saying they'd use a *child* for that kind of terrorism? That's too cruel! Too low! Too wicked!"

"You're telling me. I'm just as disgusted as you." He paced in a circle. "Even so, I don't see how we can let her be, with her that size. It's a pity, but we might not have any choice but to kill her."

"I won't accept it! Isn't she the victim here? Why does she have to die?" Sakura grabbed Ryo by the shoulder. "We should protect her. We can't allow her to be killed."

"Yeah, but *how*? It's not like she's a lost puppy. Do you know how much it would cost just to feed her?"

Asaya pulled a calculator out of his pocket. "Let's see, if she eats 2,700 times more than a typical child . . . Even if we only fed her once a day, that's food for nine hundred people."

"See?" Sakura objected. "That's just as much as one grade school spends."

"How do you figure that?" Ryo asked. "Do you know how many millions that costs in a year? And who will deal with her waste? And where is there space to keep her?"

"How about Minamidaito Island?"

Minamidaito was a solitary island to the east of Okinawa where several kaiju were kept for study.

"The biggest kaiju there is an MM3.5. She's four times that size. How would we make a cage big enough? How would we capture her? How much anesthesia would we need to make her sleep? And even if we got her to sleep, how would we transport her? She's too big for a semitrailer."

"We could make her walk," Sakura said.

"To Nagoya Port? Do you think she'll behave the entire way? She doesn't know language. You saw how fast she moves. Children are fickle. If she ignored our instructions and ran off, what would we do? If she ran through a crowd of onlookers, it would be a disaster."

Sakura had nothing to say.

"Not only that, it would take time. We'd need a budget of billions—the Meteorological Agency wouldn't be able to allocate that kind of money on their own. The Diet would have to debate it. How many weeks would that take? Even if we decided to protect her, it would be an enormous undertaking. Minamidaito Island would have to prepare for her, we'd have to requisition a cargo ship, we'd have to evacuate people all along the highway from here to Nagoya . . . How long will that all take?" Ryo released a helpless sigh. "Will the girl wait for us until then? She seems not to be hungry yet, but it's only a matter of time before she goes off in search of food."

"Do you really want her dead that badly?"

"I don't want her dead! But I can't think of an alternative," Ryo said.

Sergeant Kashihara had been listening to the whole conversation.

Softly, sadly, he said, "I have a daughter her age." He looked down at the Carl Gustav in his hands. "I don't want to shoot her if I don't have to."

What else could Sakura say?

At that same time, Kurihama was talking with Yojiro.

"I've decided on a name for Kaiju Six," the chief said. "Princess. From this point, Kaiju Six will be called Princess. We've also just calculated her size. Ninety-six tons. MM4.9."

"Not a five?"

"No. Until there's a possibility of her endangering lives, the use of deadly force is not authorized."

"Is that a good thing?"

"Can't say for sure."

Kurihama's feelings were mixed. Yojiro, Yuri, and the rest of the MMD all shared the same sentiment. For the moment, Princess's life had been extended. But they could see a bitter end awaiting in the not too distant future—a thought that weighed heavily upon them.

Do we really have to kill this completely innocent child?

The chief spoke. "There's one other piece of information that's bothering me. It seems some civilians have snuck back into the evacuation zone."

"Civilians?"

"Yeah. The police spotted three suspicious men prowling the streets near the Takashimaya department store. The officers gave chase but lost them."

"Rubberneckers."

"Maybe. Maybe not. Either way, they're trouble. As long as there are civilians around, the military has to watch their fire."

An operator shouted, "Kaiju Six has started to move!"

"What?" Kurihama barked.

"She's moving west from Gifu Park toward Honmachi."

The room had been as quiet as a vigil, but now it roared back to life. The main wall display showed a map of Gifu with a red arrow indicating Princess's current location as reported by the SDF helicopters.

The operator continued reporting. "Oh, she's turning south. Toward Gifu Station. She's moving at two hundred twenty meters per minute."

Kurihama asked, "Where's the SDF unit in her path?"

"Deployed at the intersection in front of a shopping center. At her current heading, she'll reach them in seven minutes."

"Isn't that where those civilians were spotted? Tell the SDF to stand down! They don't have permission to engage. Don't let them fire!"

Ryo stood outside the van to take a call from the main office.

"She's near Yajimacho? Understood. We'll follow her."

He turned in surprise as the van's engine started. While Ryo was occupied with the call, Sakura had climbed in the driver's seat of the empty vehicle. Her face, which Ryo glanced only in profile, held a determined expression.

"Hey, Sakura?"

She sped away.

"That woman!"

Ryo clicked his tongue as he watched her drive off. Then, he turned to Sergeant Kashihara.

"Get me a Jeep!"

Princess ambled south along Gifu's main road. As she walked, she looked with wonder at the buildings along the street. Occasionally, the girl ripped a sign off the side of a building or kicked over a street sign or traffic signal, but she hadn't yet wrought any serious destruction.

The SDF couldn't attack her for that. Moreover, there was the possibility that civilians were nearby. The Tetsumeicho intersection was not to be their battlefield. The tanks and soldiers were forced to pull back six hundred meters to the road just in front of Gifu Station.

But they wouldn't be able to keep backing off forever. The southern areas of the city still had many people left to evacuate. If Princess arrived there, there was a great danger of some tragedy.

At some point, inevitably, they would have to attack.

Sakura chased after her in the van. To draw the giant's attention, she got as close as two hundred meters behind the girl and honked her horn again and again. Princess kept on walking—the noise might have been too small for the girl to hear.

"Stop," Sakura pleaded. "Please stop."

Then, in front of the shopping center, Princess stopped, turned her inquisitive gaze around, and noticed the van behind her.

"All right!"

Sakura mustered her courage and stepped from the van. The girl tilted her head to the side and slowly walked toward the car.

Sakura's cell phone rang. She stood still beside the van, and with her neck craned up to watch the girl, she took out her phone with her right hand.

She opened it to be immediately assaulted by Ryo's shouts.

"You fool! What the hell are you doing?"

The Jeep with Ryo and Sergeant Kashihara stopped two hundred yards behind the van. The two saw Princess approaching Sakura and climbed out of their vehicle. Kashihara got on one knee and readied the Carl Gustav. But if he fired now, Sakura would also be in danger. The sergeant looked down the scope and kept his finger at the trigger, but he didn't move.

"Come back, Sakura!" Ryo screamed into his phone. "What are you thinking? Do you want to die?"

Sakura's voice wavered, but she spoke with a firm conviction. "I'm going to see if she can understand me."

"What?"

"If she's human, she'll be able to understand me. If she can comprehend what I'm saying, she might behave."

Princess was almost upon her now.

"Run! What if she eats you?"

"Well, then you'll be able to attack."

"Huh?"

"If she can't understand me . . . if she's a violent, man-eating kaiju, then you'll have your excuse to kill her!" Now Sakura's voice wavered not with fear but emotion. "If she's done something wrong, there won't be any other choice, but I can't allow her to be killed innocent. I won't accept it!"

"That doesn't mean you alone should—"

"There's no need for anyone else to die. I don't want to get you involved with my feelings."

Ryo was speechless.

He could understand her thinking. When it came down to it, he felt the same. He too found it impossible to accept killing an innocent girl just because of her size. The only thing separating him from Sakura was that he lacked her passion—the naive passion to put his life on the line in some futile stand against the cruel wall of reality.

A person who could do that would not enjoy a long life. But as foolish as Ryo might regard Sakura's naiveté, he couldn't deny her it.

As he stood there, paralyzed with indecision, Princess walked up to Sakura and lowered herself to one knee.

As Princess crouched down and brought her face to Sakura's, the young woman trembled and grew faint.

Sakura heard herself say, "She's huge."

That close up, Princess's size was terrifying. The giant dropped on all fours, the space beneath her as wide as a side street, the sun blocked out by her frame. The girl's face alone was bigger than Sakura's entire body. Princess opened her mouth in excitement and revealed teeth the size of paperback books and a wet wriggling tongue—plenty big enough to swallow a person whole.

Somehow, Sakura found enough of her voice to squeak out, "Oh, I, uh, I am your friend."

Princess simply tilted her head and said, *"Goooooo?"*

Then Sakura remembered the girl lived in slower time. She raised her voice and spoke slowly.

"I. Am. Your. Friend. Do. You. Un. Der. Stand?"

The girl still didn't show any sign of comprehension. But her dark eyes glittered with curiosity, and Sakura felt some presence of intelligence. Princess seemed to realize that the young woman wasn't just some small animal.

The girl's voice became calm. *"Oo-oah,"* she intoned. Slowly, she reached out her hand.

Through waves of terror, Sakura battled to keep hold of her consciousness. She stood motionless, letting the giant hand—as big as a bulldozer's blade—come to her. The girl's hand softly wrapped around her. Within those massive fingers, Sakura was only the size of a toy from a gumball machine. She felt her eyes close.

Ryo let out a wordless cry. He clenched his fist around his cell phone. All he could do now was pray, to hold on to the hope that the girl wasn't an unintelligent, bestial kaiju.

If his hopes were wrong, all Princess had to do was gently squeeze, and Sakura would be crushed.

Sakura felt a floating sensation, like an elevator arriving at a penthouse. Fearfully, she opened her eyes. Panic washed over her as she realized she was four stories above the ground.

She grabbed on to one of the girl's fingers and pleaded, "D-don't drop me! If I fall, I'll die!"

The girl smiled, perhaps entertained by Sakura's frantic display. Although the young woman was on the verge of tears, she somehow found a smile to give in return. Although the giant seemed not to be violent, the immense wall of a face before Sakura was a far more terrifying experience than she'd ever thought possible. It took all of her focus to remain conscious.

"I-I should have brought some food." In an attempt to push the fear aside, she started saying whatever thoughts came to her mind. "In the movies, th-there's always some kind of food. French bread, maybe?"

She rubbed her stomach. "Are. You. Hun. Gry?"

Another quizzical tilt of the head. The motion was cute, even when a giant was doing it. "*Guuuu?*" She still didn't seem to understand.

Sakura pointed at her mouth. "Do. You. Want. To. Eat?"

The girl opened her mouth wide. "*Ahhhhhh.*" Then the corners of her lips turned up in a grin, and she brought her mouth to the tiny woman and started to bite down.

Sakura screamed and covered her head with her arms.

Then she heard a slow, low-pitched, *"Guo, guo, guo."* Sakura fearfully lowered her arms. That sound was Princess *giggling*. When she realized it was a joke, she found herself laughing too. *She understands jokes! Does that mean she's intelligent?*

Just as she began to see hope, Sakura saw something else. People on the roof of the shopping center. People pointing weapons in her direction.

She yelled, "Watch out, Princess!" and the giant reflexively turned. In that instant, a small object trailing smoke flew just over the girl's bare shoulder.

It struck the building behind her.

And exploded.

Sergeant Kashihara looked up from the scope. "Who fired?"

Surely not the military. They hadn't received permission to engage, and besides, they'd withdrawn to the south.

Ryo pointed to the shopping center. "On the roof! It came from over there!"

Kashihara scrambled for his binoculars and pressed them to his eyes. There were three men on the roof of the building. One had a metal tube on his shoulder, and another was reloading it. The third, holding an assault rifle, began to fire on Princess. The tiny rounds stung her skin, and she raised her left arm over her face and howled in pain.

Kashihara gaped. "Who are they?"

They finished loading the second missile. This time, as not to miss again, the man with the launcher took steady aim at her head. Princess's face contorted with fury, and holding her right hand with Sakura protectively behind her back, she thrust her left hand straight in the direction of the men.

Ryo gasped. "What's that?"

Pale blue particles of light blossomed like a flame from her open palm. The light spread out into the air, then whirled into a spiral like a tiny Milky Way. It spun faster and faster until the particles blurred into a solid disc of light.

The second missile fired. It exploded at the palm of her hand. There was no damage. The man with the assault rifle fired desperately, but the bullets hit the disc of light and burst into sparks.

The men were clearly dismayed, but they didn't try to flee.

Princess gently lowered Sakura to the street and started walking toward the shopping center. The attackers tried a third missile, but the girl blocked it with the shield of light.

Finally, they started to run. But it was too late. Princess dispelled the disc of light and put her hand through one of the windows on the top floor of the six-story building. The mall was a little taller than her, and with a feral roar, she climbed up it like a ladder.

"Princess, don't!" Sakura screamed, but the girl was too taken by rage to hear. The side of the building, unable to support her almost one hundred tons, started to crumble. But that didn't concern the giant. She pulled herself halfway onto the roof. The man with the assault rifle wildly fired at her but quickly ran out of ammo.

She raised her arm high in the air to slam her vengeful fist down upon them. Their terrified screams reached Ryo.

Then came the sound of an explosion. Blood streamed from the girl's side.

Sakura shrieked. Princess looked up at the sky, her face blank, her raised arm frozen in place. Then, slowly, she slipped from the building. She fell backward, her hair trailing up in the air. When her back struck the ground, the terrific sound of it rumbled through the streets, and the asphalt cratered beneath her. Fully half of the shopping center was taken down with her. A brown cloud of dust and detritus rose up over the roadway.

A shocked Ryo turned to look at Sergeant Kashihara. In the pale-faced soldier's arms was a still-smoking Carl Gustav.

The sergeant spoke in a hollow whisper. "If I didn't do anything . . . those three would have been killed."

"I know," Ryo said. Kashihara was correct. He'd done his duty as a member of the Self-Defense Force—to protect the lives of the people of Japan.

Ryo cupped his hands over his mouth and ran into the cloud. "Sakura!"

He found her kneeling in the middle of the street, coughing and crying. "She—she's been shot . . ."

"I know." Ryo put his arm around her and lifted her to her feet. The dust was finally beginning to settle. The two of them cautiously approached the place Princess had landed. They readied themselves for the terrible sight of the giant girl, bleeding and dead.

But what they saw was not what they'd expected.

The crater had a diameter of fifteen meters. Water gushed from broken pipes. In the pooling water at the base of the pit lay the helpless, naked, and normal-sized girl.

For a moment, Ryo was dumbstruck, but quickly he found himself and scrambled down into the crater. Stumbling over debris and becoming drenched in the spraying water, he made it to the girl, picked her up in his arms, and checked for a pulse.

"She's alive!" Ryo looked up to see Sergeant Kashihara at the edge of the crater. "Call an ambulance!"

Kashihara gave a forceful nod and ran off, shouting "Medic! Medic!"

"Sakura, call Yojiro!"

"Okay, but what do I . . ." She trailed off.

"The collar! We need to put it on her before she expands again."

After receiving emergency first aid, Princess was taken to a JGSDF medical facility in Camp Kasugai, where she underwent surgical treatment. There was a six-millimeter hole in her right side, but luckily, no major damage to her heart. The doctors predicted a recovery, after which she would be taken to the Meteorological Research Institute in Tsukuba Science City.

A large number of tiny metal bits were removed from her body. To the surprise of those involved, they were determined to be miniscule bullets not even a single millimeter wide—the bullets from the assault rifle had shrunk along with her body.

From the other side of the observation window, Ryo and Sakura watched the girl, still under the effects of the anesthetic, sleeping in her hospital bed.

"She's cute when she's asleep," Ryo said. "To think that innocent face so easily broke the very laws of physics."

"She really is a kaiju, isn't she?"

"We won't know until the DNA test comes back, but I think so. Humans can't create solid light in the palm of their hand. That Mikio must have found her as a young child and raised her."

"Do you think she can actively control her size?"

"Probably. It's rare, but kaiju have been known to do that. The CCI must have kept her in that collar to prevent her from turning into a giant. As soon as she tries to grow her size, it starts to choke her. Once it was off her, she became the giant. It must have been so hard on her, to be confined in that small place. I bet she was happy to be free in a wide open space."

"But now she'll have to keep the collar on forever."

"It's better than being dead, isn't it?" Ryo clapped Sakura's shoulder. "It's ironic. She ended up being saved because she was a kaiju. Without her powers, she would have been killed."

"That's true."

The two turned away from the window and started walking down the hallway.

Sakura asked, "But why did those three try to kill her? If they hadn't done anything, the military would have done it for them."

"Beats me. The leader, Umemiya, died when he fell from the roof, and those other two were just following his orders. They don't know a thing about Princess. Cultists just don't know how to think for themselves."

"And you haven't heard anything about where Mikio is? Something about him worries me."

"We just have to leave that to the police. Oh, that reminds me."

"What?"

"You'd better expect a pay cut after that stunt you pulled," Ryo said.

"Yeah . . ."

Sakura lowered her head, but Ryo caught her faint smile—and he knew what it meant. She was proud to have done the right thing. And she'd do it again.

Kagoshima Airport—

Mikio Izuno watched the news report in the airport waiting area.

"*. . . documents found by a Gifu Prefectural Police raid provided clear evidence that the Creative Cosmology Institute, or CCI, raised a kaiju in secret. Kaiju Six, Princess, that roamed Gifu City earlier this week appears in those documents under the code name 'X,' and . . .*"

He chuckled to himself. The loss of the CCI didn't bother him much. It was only one of many dummy organizations providing him funds and hideouts, nearly all of them filled with puppets, blind believers in whichever religion provided the front. He'd already moved the hidden money into different accounts. He could start over.

The same went for Princess. Just because she had fallen into the clutches of the establishment didn't mean he would necessarily be inconvenienced. Neither the police, nor the Intelligence Agency, nor the SDF—and certainly not the MMD—knew of her real purpose, and he couldn't imagine they ever would.

Not as long as they assumed "X" was merely a letter.

PART THREE

MENACE! ATTACK OF THE FLYING KAIJU!

The first kaiju of 2006 came from overseas.

As Ryo waited for the light to turn at a crosswalk near the east entrance to JR Shinjuku Station, a breaking news report came on the giant television screen on the side of the building across the street.

"And now, for the latest breaking news on the flying kaiju sighted in Nigata Prefecture. A kaiju, thought to be the same as the one seen midday today by several witnesses in Joetsu City, has been reported near Nozawa Onsen. According to eyewitness accounts, the kaiju flew in the direction of Mt. Kenashi. At three o'clock this afternoon, the MMD confirmed the as-of-yet unidentified creature as Kaiju One.

"The witnesses stated that Kaiju One resembled a pterosaur, and estimated it at an MM one or two, with an air speed of roughly fifty kilometers per hour. Citing a lack of additional sightings, the MMD believes with a high degree of probability that the kaiju is hiding in the mountains of northern Nigata. The SDF is working in conjunction with local law enforcement to mount a large-scale search; however, caution is advised for tourists and local residents. The kaiju is thought to be somewhere near the municipalities of Nozawa Onsen, Sakae, Kijimadaira . . ."

Ryo felt a finger poke his side.

"Are you worried?" Eiko Hamaguchi said with a teasing smile.

"Oh no, I'm sure it'll be fine. A one or a two is nothing. Besides, pterosaurs usually eat fish and rarely attack humans."

The light changed, and the couple crossed the street among the jostling crowd of pedestrians. It was mid-January, Tokyo. The clouds hung low in the sky and threatened rain.

"Besides," he said, "winged kaiju always look bigger than they really are. This one might only be a zero. Even if the worst case happens and it's violent, the military wouldn't need anything more than their 7.6 millimeter machine guns to stop it. That said, this time of year, there's a lot of tourists for the hot springs and ski resorts, so there could be an impact on the local economies."

"That's not what I meant," Eiko said.

"Huh?"

"I meant, are you worried about how outrageous it is for you to be thinking about work in the middle of a date with such a gorgeous woman?"

"Oh, sorry."

Eiko really was gorgeous. Ryo never understood how she could be a researcher at the National Museum of Nature and Science—it was such a *plain* job. She probably had what it took to become an actress or a suimsuit model. When he told her that once, fully intending it as a compliment, she got mad at him, although she smiled as she said, "You're being disrespectful to women." She seemed proud that she didn't rely on her beauty to get by in life. Ryo had never met any other woman like that. It was one of the things he found so attractive.

Today was Eiko's birthday. Their plans included a movie starring her favorite actress, followed by dinner at a nice restaurant, and after that, a hotel. Ryo had been looking forward to their date and made both reservations at top-class establishments.

He had the whole day off. It would be a shame if he didn't enjoy it.

Takebashi, Chiyoda Ward, Tokyo. MMD Head Office—

Yuri, who hadn't made it into the office until the late afternoon, looked at the black silhouette on the computer screen and scrunched her face.

"This," she asked, "is a kaiju?"

The image was grainy and low detail, likely enlarged several dozen times from its original. All she could make out was a dark form, shaped like the Chinese character 木, flying over the backdrop of a gray sky. The sideways bar was long and thick—probably the wings—and the two shorter diagonal lines might have been legs.

"And we don't have anything clearer?"

"No," Toshio grumbled. "That's all we've got. A skier at Nozawa Onsen took it with his cell phone. And he sent it to the news networks instead of us, so we lost two hours there. Not that it's good enough for us to analyze anyway."

"They said on the news it has a ten-meter wingspan," Yuri said.

"That's what the person who took the picture said. You know how objects look smaller on the phone's screen than to the eye."

"And it doesn't seem to be a bird?"

"I don't think it's likely. On that account, all of the eyewitness reports match up. Nobody saw it for more than a brief moment, so the details, like its size, are all over the place. But there are three things we can know for sure—it's a lot bigger than a man, it's not feathered like a bird, and it has thin, membranous wings. Look at the picture. See how its wings are a little transparent?"

"You're right. They look a little lighter than the rest of it. So it's a pterosaur?"

"I don't think it's that either," Toshio said. With a click of the mouse, a sharpening filter passed over the image and accentuated the kaiju's outline. "The first witnesses said it looked like a pteranodon, and we all went with that assumption, but look at the wings. They clearly don't belong to a pteranodon."

Yuri was no paleontology expert, but she did know that pteranodon wings extended from an extremely long finger to the sides of their bodies in one swoop. But each wing of the animal in this picture extended at three points.

"It's like a bat," Yuri said.

"Yeah. Some of the witnesses claimed to see it flapping its wings furiously—that would be hard to confuse with a pteranodon's glide. But unlike a bat, it has a long neck and feathers. It could be some variant of a bat. Or some type of chimera we haven't encountered yet."

In other words, they had no clue.

Over the next hour, no new information came in, and little happened in the office. The operators took inquiries from the media outlets and kept in contact with the military—that was about the extent of it. Smaller kaiju like this one appeared all the time, and the MMD staff felt little urgency.

Only one person in the department was impatient—Chief Kurihama. He paced in and out of his office. "Still nothing new?" he asked.

Yojiro's Mobile Unit had arrived at the area of the sightings hours earlier but still hadn't sent any useful information.

One exasperated staffer said, "Chief, can't you just relax a little? They're trying to find one lone kaiju in the middle of forests and mountains. It's not that easy."

"I know that. But what'll happen if the thing flies off before they find it?" Kurihama plopped into his chair and began twirling his pen. "Damn. Big kaiju are trouble, but the little, hard-to-find ones are such nuisances."

"But since it's little, it won't cause much damage."

"Don't underestimate it. Even an MM0 could kill a man with one blow."

One of the women called for the chief, and he turned and snapped, "What?"

"I've been passed information from the National Observatory that I think may be important."

"The observatory? Can't you see I've got my hands full with this kaiju?"

"At five this morning, sailors on a squid fishing vessel in the Sea of Japan claim they saw a UFO. Apparently, they called the observatory as soon as they made it back to port."

Kurihama's jaw dropped. "The Sea of Japan?"

"Yes, sir. They were at 39 degrees thirty minutes north and 135 degrees ten minutes east when it flew overhead to the southwest. Its pale blue body was shiny and flickering, they said."

Red dots on the wall-mounted large-screen display marked the locations of the kaiju sightings over a map of Japan. Starting from the south, there were points at Nozawa Onsen, on Highway 95 near Sekita Pass, and Joetsu City. Farther north, a new point was added in the dead center of the Sea of Japan. The points formed a nearly straight forty-five degree line.

The chief asked, "Are these all the same kaiju?"

Koichiro, whose abilities made up for his lack of experience, had already done the rough calculations. "The sailors saw it about 350 klicks from Nigata. The earliest witness of the creature in Joetsu was at eleven fifty. That would be a little over fifty kilometers per hour—an almost perfect fit."

"A shining kaiju . . ." It wasn't unheard of. There was a kaiju with radiant horns, and another with a bioluminescent back. Not to mention the many monsters that attacked using beams of light. It was entirely possible that this one could look like a pteranodon or a bat during the day and appear as a bright flying object at night.

Kensuke bolted to his feet and cried out, "Now I remember!"

All eyes were on him.

"Yesterday, there was a UFO sighting in Russia."

"Russia?" Kurihama asked.

"Yeah, although when I first heard it, I never thought it would have anything to do with this." Not bothering to sit back down on his chair, Kensuke bent over his workstation and hurriedly searched through his Internet news feed. "Here. A UFO was sighted last night, around seven o'clock in the town of Posyet, a Russian port near the North Korean border. The witness said a pale blue light flew out to sea to the southeast. The Russian Air Force scrambled jets to investigate but didn't find anything. Another sighting last night in a town called Harbin in the province of Heilongjiang in China is thought to be of the same object."

"Bring up a map of China."

Koichiro was already inputting the data.

The map on the wall screen zoomed out to include East Asia. New points at Posyet and Harbin made a nearly straight line with the sightings in Japan.

Toshio said, "It looks like our guy came from China."

"Contact their Meteorological Agency at once," Kurihama said. "See if they know anything about this kaiju. And start searching through their news reports. See if you can find anything about a UFO."

"Yes, sir!"

Activity filled the room as the staffers shouted over each other.

"Does anyone here speak Chinese?"

"Where would UFO news be reported?"

"I need everything we have on Chinese kaiju!"

Kurihama peered between the slits of his office blinds. "It's almost night." From the window, he could look out over the Imperial Palace's East Garden. The time was four forty. If it hadn't been overcast, he could have seen the sun setting behind the Imperial Residence.

He turned back to the room.

"Contact Yojiro. The kaiju glows in the dark. Tell him to keep on the lookout for its light."

Ryo and Eiko were sitting in a nearby coffee shop to kill time before the movie.

"Really," Eiko said, "you're all work."

"I thought I was all play myself."

"That's just what you think. When you talk about kaiju, you get so animated."

"Is that right?"

She nodded happily. "Yeah. Even on your day off, it's still on your mind. That's how you can go on talking about kaiju so effortlessly. It's like your work has become ingrained within you."

"I don't know about that." He frowned. "I'm not that proud of my job."

"Then why did you choose it?"

"It just happened, I guess. It wasn't my childhood dream or anything like that. I joined the Meteorological Agency because I liked science, and I figured that government employees got good salaries. I was placed with the MMD, that's all."

"Even so, it seems like you take your job seriously."

"Of course I do. People's lives depend on it. If there's a disaster because of my negligence, I'd get fired."

"That's the only reason?"

"That's the only reason."

"Hmm . . ." Eiko looked up at the white ceiling. She seemed to look at something Ryo couldn't see.

"It's different for me," she said. "When I was growing up, I always wanted to work at a museum, ever since I was a kid."

"You liked history?"

"I liked yokai—spirits, monsters, the supernatural."

Ryo was taken aback by her unexpected answer. *"Yokai?"*

"Yes!" She leaned forward in her chair. "Ever since I was a little girl, I lost myself reading yokai encyclopedias—the ones aimed at children—and I still do. Sunekosuri, the dog that brushes between people's legs at night; Nekomata, the fork-tailed cat; Kijimuna, the Okinawan wood spirits. They're all so cute!"

"I'm starting to think you're a little weird."

"A *little*? I'm a lot weird." Eiko grinned unabashedly. "All through middle and high school, I never had another female classmate interested in the same things I was. Sure, every girl likes ghost stories and fortune-telling, but if I even said the word *yokai,* their eyes would glaze over. I get it. Ghosts are cool, yokai are lame. But why is that?"

"Who knows," Ryo said.

"Well, anyway, that's why I wanted to work at a museum. I thought that if I wanted to get close to yokai-related materials, I needed to get into natural history. But becoming some scholar sounded like it would be a lot of work, so in the meantime I decided to just work at a museum."

"So you'd say you've found your calling."

"I would. Our main exhibit now, 'The Origins of Human Culture,' was a lot of fun to put on display. Dogon ceremonial masks, Melinke drums, Mandinka magic paraphernalia—all the things museum visitors can only see from the other side of acrylic cases, I get to touch with my own hands." Her eyes glimmered with childlike excitement. "It's the greatest!"

Ryo gazed at her as she talked, adoring her expression.

A waitress came and dropped off an espresso con panna and a royal milk tea.

Stirring his espresso, Ryo said, "I'm jealous of you. Of how passionate you are about your work."

"Really? If I had to, I'd say I was envious of your job."

"Why?"

"You get to see kaiju close up," Eiko said. "Kaiju and yokai are basically the same."

"I guess." Ryo made a wry smile. Western academia didn't differentiate between kaiju and yokai and simply referred to both as monsters. Both were anomalous life-forms. In Japan, supernatural creatures not qualifying for MM0 (i.e., less than one ton of water displacement) were classified as yokai. Some giant monsters written about throughout history were classified as yokai based on their size—including Ushigozen, the bull that killed seven Buddhist monks in Sensou-ji Temple in Asakusa in 1251; Jinjahime, the single-horned mermaid spotted off the coast of the province of Hizen in 1819; the salamander that rampaged through the mountains near what is now the town of Yubara in Okayama Prefecture at the end of the sixteenth century; Oomukade, the giant centipede said to have been defeated by Touta Tawara at Mt. Mikami; and Jinbei-sama, the sea serpent that sunk a great number of ships in the sea off Mt. Kinka (a different mountain, the one in Miyagi Prefecture).

In the past, many yokai lived in Japan—nue, kappa, itsumade, shunoban, arasaraus, jorogumo, hakutaku, raiju, fuuri, kenmun, nobusuma, domeki, shojo, and countless others—but humans drove them from their dwelling places, and the mythical creatures' numbers decreased. Even now, in the deep mountains, there were still the occasional reports of a mizuchi, a tsuchinoko, or a hibagon, but the frequency of such sightings were nothing like in the past.

Since yokai didn't cause significant property damage, they—like other wildlife—fell under the jurisdiction of the Forestry Agency and the Ministry of the Environment. In truth, the distinction between wildlife and yokai was not always clear. If a creature blew fire, changed its shape, flew with wings much too small for its body, grew in ways contrary to the law of preservation of mass, or displayed any other abilities not shared with common animals, it was classified a yokai, but many yokai didn't have special powers. The Ministry of the Environment defined anomalous life-forms as "species lacking the numbers to maintain their continued existence yet which continue to survive." Species of yokai and kaiju were represented by small populations or even a solitary member exhibiting a long life—immortality was one special characteristic of yokai. Cases of reproduction were incredibly rare.

As with other forms of wildlife, yokai were left alone as long as they didn't present a danger to humans. Some more famous ones, like the tsuchinoko and hibagon, became tourist attractions as well as the subject of preservation campaigns. But unlike the Japanese crested ibis, yokai couldn't be bred in captivity, and a sympathetic public held strong opposition to any attempt to keep the creatures confined in cages. The best that could be done was to let them live in peace in the mountains and to watch over them lest they be accidentally killed.

Even overseas, monsters below MM0 were known to appear— the chupacabra in Central America, sasquatch in the U.S., the black dogs of Britain, tatzelwurm in the Alps, yeti of the Himalayas— but such reports only seemed to decrease as cultures advanced. It made perfect sense. A hunter only had to kill a single yokai for its entire species to slip into extinction.

Ryo said, "I get it. You mean the appeal of things that get lost with the passage of time."

"I wonder." Eiko sipped her cup of milk tea then tilted her head to one side. "I have trouble believing that yokai are dying out. Especially the ones with human intelligence. I think they've found a way to keep on living, right among us."

"Huh." Ryo nodded diplomatically.

There were plenty of stories of yokai living in cities. They were typical headlines in occult magazines—I SAW A TEKETEKE IN THE GRADE SCHOOL AT NIGHT! or WOMAN SEEN RUNNING 100 KPH DOWN THE HIGHWAY! or DOG WITH HUMAN FACE SPEAKS!— amounting to nothing more than urban legends. Some thought yokai took on human forms and mixed among people. Experts on the creatures viewed such theories with skepticism, and Ryo didn't much believe in it himself. He wasn't particularly interested in it either way. Even if the rumors were true, it wouldn't fall under the purview of the Meteorological Agency.

"At the museum," Eiko said, "when we do exhibits about ancient cultures or creatures, we get a lot of suspicious-looking people coming in. Like with the one we have now—the very first attendees on opening day were those types."

"Those *types*?"

"A pair of old men, unusually tall and with dark skin. Gaunt, with shifty eyes. They planted themselves in front of one of the display pieces for at least ten minutes, mumbling some gibberish to each other. I'm sure they were yokai in human form."

Ryo thought but didn't say, *That's probably nothing more than two Africans, a long way from home, reminded of their motherland.*

"But if they were yokai," she said, "why should they need to hide? Couldn't they just take their true form? Things aren't like how they used to be. They don't need to fear being attacked just because they're yokai. Heck, they might even make famous TV stars, if you think about it."

Ryo put his thumb and pointer fingers between his lips and stretched his mouth wide, mimicking a yokai right out of the horror movies. "Good evening, ladies and gentlemen, I'm the split-mouth woman."

Eiko laughed. "Well, maybe not. I guess they could just end up being a sideshow spectacle. If I were a yokai, maybe I'd have too much pride for that."

"I could see that."

"And think about it. Say I confessed to you that I was a kappa in human form. Would you still want me?"

Ryo, taken by surprise at the sudden question, chose his words carefully. "Well, I'd hate to be discriminatory, but . . . I guess I'd have some trouble with that. There's definitely a physiological repugnance to it—it'd be a form of bestiality, wouldn't it?"

"Right? That's why I think yokai must be so lonesome." She closed her eyes and tilted her head up. "Living in silent anguish on the fringes of society, unable to reveal themselves to the ones they love."

"You *are* a romantic!"

"Nah, just a yokai geek." She laughed nervously. "I shouldn't talk about that stuff on a date. Let's just forget about kaiju and yokai for tonight."

"Agreed."

"We'll watch our movie, eat our dinner, and then after . . ."

Ryo returned her seductive smile with a genuine one. "I can't wait," he said—though that news report still clung to the back of his mind.

6:00 PM—

With night falling over northern Nagano, Yojiro and the Mobile Unit finally came across something useful. A driver on a road just south of the 1,662-meter-tall Mt. Daijiro had seen a pale blue light on the mountainside. Yojiro and Asaya took a ride toward the scene of the sighting in an OH-6D with the 12th Helicopter Unit of the JGSDF 12th Brigade.

The helicopter held a steady altitude of five hundred meters as it flew east through the evening sky. Points of light dotted the land below them along the Maguse River. They passed over Maguse Onsen and followed one of the small tributaries. Snow covered the mountaintops. One more ridge, and they'd be there. The thunder of the helicopter might spook the kaiju into flight, but they didn't have another option. Nailing down the monster's location was their top priority.

Asaya, seated next to the pilot, peered at the monitor with a live feed on his low-light video camera. A microphone carried his voice back to Yojiro. "Look at that perfect snow over Nozawa."

"Damn, I haven't been skiing in a while."

There was no sense of anxiety in their voices. Why should there have been? The MMD dealt with MM ones and twos all the time. Even Asaya had already encountered dozens of them.

Not that any of the team had ever handled a gun. They observed kaiju to determine their natures and capabilities, then decided on the appropriate measures—leave it, capture it, or kill it. The rest was up to the SDF. They assumed this time would be the same.

Yojiro said, "I hope it hasn't flown away yet."

Even if he didn't feel worried, Yojiro did have a sense of urgency. More than twenty minutes had passed since they received the tip. The main office said the kaiju had flown through the night across the Sea of Japan to the shore. That suggested a high probability the creature was nocturnal. With the sun down, it might resume movement.

"If it escapes by air," Asaya asked, "that means it'll have to be shot down, right?"

"If it appears dangerous, yes."

"With an anti-air missile?"

"Heavens no. We don't go for that kind of extravagance."

The pilot added, "Missiles are expensive. We don't use them for MM twos. An Apache's thirty-millimeter chain gun rips 'em to shreds."

"Oh."

"Around here," Yojiro said, "stray fire from an aerial battle wouldn't cause much damage." He turned an analytical gaze over the twilight-cloaked mountainscape. "But we'd still have to pick the right place."

In the past, there had been instances of civilians caught in the crossfire between kaiju and military. A mistake would result in claims for compensation. Battlegrounds had to be chosen with care.

The pilot nervously said, "Isn't that it over there?"

The bubble-shaped canopy provided a wide field of view, and it took some time for Yojiro to spot what the pilot had seen.

Then he found it. "There, Asaya! Eleven o'clock."

"Oh!"

Within the dark woods on the gentle slopes was a single faint point of pale blue light. At first glance, they knew it didn't come from electricity or flame. This light was more muted, and it swayed, like the glow of charcoal seen through a blue filter.

"Please lower the helicopter," Yojiro said.

The OH-6D drifted toward the glow. Asaya aimed the giant lens of his low-light camera.

He zoomed in. The image of green on the display shook with the vibrations of the helicopter, but in the middle, there it was. Among the mixed forest some large *thing* glimmered. At first, Asaya thought it looked like a tent. Then he saw the minute movements that meant it was alive. He tried to get a full, clear picture of the creature, but trees kept blocking his view.

Yojiro spoke into his mike. "Headquarters, we've discovered a light source that seems to be Kaiju One. The report was right—it's on the southern slope of Mt. Daijiro. Can you see it?"

The video feed was being transmitted in real time to the main office.

Chief Kurihama responded, "Not very well. Get at it from a different angle."

Yojiro instructed the pilot to swing around to the right. The helicopter circled the glowing light, keeping roughly two hundred meters away. Then, finally, they saw the whole thing. It was squatted down with the spiky ridge of its spine to them.

"Its entire body is glowing," said Asaya, still manning the camera controls. "But why? Is it signaling for a mate, like a lightning bug?"

"Then it came all the way here from China to find a mate?" Yojiro chuckled. "I don't think so."

"Yeah, but I don't think it's drawing in prey like an angler either."

No animal would fall for such a ruse—the light was too large for some creature to confuse it for its own prey.

Tentatively, Yojiro offered, "Maybe it's aposematism—a warning signal." Many poisonous animals, including hornets and poison dart frogs, had bright, eye-catching colorations to warn would-be predators away.

Asaya said, "But there are no predators for something that huge."

"Sure there are—and ones fierce enough to kill even the biggest kaiju."

"Huh?"

"People," Yojiro said.

"Oh. Good point."

Suddenly, the kaiju stirred, perhaps annoyed by the helicopter's noise. Even with giant wings, it moved as nimbly as a monkey as it scrambled up the trunk of a nearby tree. About halfway from the top, it flashed open its wings.

Asaya gasped. The creature's batlike wings were covered with a glowing, tightly packed mesh that could only have been the veins beneath its skin. Clinging to the tree with its back legs, the kaiju swiveled its long neck to look up at the helicopter and raised a menacing cry. It looked mammalian, with a face like that of a monkey, but with the triangular, tortoiselike beak of the humanoid yokai known as the kappa. Not only did its face glow pale blue, but the inside of its mouth did as well.

With a single flex and flap of its powerful wings, the kaiju shot up into the night sky. Asaya's breath caught when it seemed like the creature was coming toward the helicopter, but the monster quickly turned and fled, its long tail fluttering behind.

"Headquarters!" Yojiro shouted. "Kaiju One has flown!"

"Follow him!" the chief ordered, but the pilot had already begun to give chase.

The kaiju flew to the southeast toward Mt. Torikabuto. As it drew farther from them, it became harder to make out against the sky. Soon it was nothing more than a faint hazy light. The glowing outline shifted with the flapping of its wings—at such a distance, something a bystander could easily mistake for a pulsating light.

"That could be an MM1.5," Yojiro said. He was no amateur—after decades of live observations, he was good at making a fair estimate of a kaiju's size in mere moments.

An MM1.5 would displace four tons of water—not to be confused with a weight of four tons. Kaiju capable of flight, with hollow bones and lighter bodies, were less dense than earthbound monsters. An MM1.5 might not even weigh a single ton. Still, it was a wonder that something that massive could soar through the air. The amount of raw strength required to move those massive wings was beyond conventional understanding of biology.

"Why is it glowing?" Yojiro asked himself. "And why is it flying in a straight line?"

The AH-64D Apache Longbow attack helicopter of the fourth antitank helicopter squadron took off from Camp Kisarazu in Chiba Prefecture and flew at full speed, 360 kph, on an interception course. But the order to attack had not yet been given. The kaiju was still not classified as dangerous. If it posed no danger, killing it would bring objections from animal preservation groups.

Kensuke enlarged a still frame of the kaiju's glowing mouth opened wide. "Well, these teeth look like they could be dangerous."

In the limited-resolution image, the teeth were only a row of points of light, but they appeared sharp. Sharp teeth indicated a high likelihood the creature was carnivorous.

"Maybe," the chief reluctantly said, "but it might just eat fish. We can't attack until we have concrete proof it poses a threat to humans."

That said, if damages resulted because they were too slow to act, they'd be awash with accusations that they should have killed the ka-iju more quickly. For the chief, that dilemma was a constant source of stomach pain.

"Headquarters," Yojiro said over the communication line, "we will be able to meet up with the Apache in twenty minutes."

Chief Kurihama asked, "Is there a good place to attack?"

"There won't be time before we reach Nakanojo. Beyond there, our only possibility is near the northeast slope of Mt. Haruna."

"Koichiro," the chief said, "show me the map."

Koichiro pulled open the map on his terminal and zoomed in on the area around Mt. Haruna. A red line slashed a forty-five-degree angle just northeast of the summit.

"I see it," Kurihama said. "There are about ten klicks between the towns here, from Higashi-agatsu to Ikaho."

Toshio added, "Luckily the thing is doing us the favor of flying in a straight line so we can predict where it's going."

The chief grumbled, "That's not much of a window for us to act."

"Yeah," Toshio said. "Based on the kaiju's current speed, we'll only have ten minutes to attack. Then it'll reach Maebashi, and it's all city from there to Tokyo."

Kurihama clicked his tongue. "Then there's no choice. Does the SDF have this information?"

"I already passed it on."

"Good." He turned to the microphone. "Yojiro. At its current speed, the kaiju will pass over Nakanojo at seven thirty. You have until then to decide if we should attack."

"Understood. Have Sakura and Kiichi arrived at its resting site?"

The two had stayed behind in Nagano to investigate the forest around Mt. Daijiro for anything left behind by the monster.

"We just heard from them. They entered the forest not long ago, but they still haven't found anything."

"Do they have all the standard mobile lab equipment?"

"Yes."

"Then tell them this. If they find any traces of the kaiju, they should start with the Geiger counter."

Kurihama gaped. "You don't think it's radioactive?"

"That blue light troubles me."

It wouldn't be the first radioactive kaiju. They had become increasingly rare, but back when atmospheric atomic bomb tests were common, there were quite a few instances of giant growth induced in animals as well as ancient creatures awoken by the blasts. The most well known was Ray, the MM5 reptilian kaiju in 1953 brought out by atomic testing in the Arctic Circle. Large quantities of radioactive material were detected in its bloodstream, and even the American military struggled to defeat it.

The chief asked, "Do you think it came from a Chinese atomic test site?"

"I don't know. The light could very well be natural. I'm just asking for safety's sake."

"Okay."

As soon as the transmission shut off, Kurihama gave the order. "Tell Kiichi and Sakura! If they find where Glowbat was resting, inspect the ground with a Geiger counter."

Yuri's face was pale. "If that light is due to Cherenkov radiation, that's an incredible amount."

"I know," Kurihama said, his voice trembling. "I think Yojiro is overthinking it, but if he's not . . ."

After the movie, Ryo and Eiko went to the top-floor restaurant of a luxury hotel in Nishi-Shinjuku.

While Eiko stepped into the restroom before their appetizer cocktails, Ryo opened his cell phone and searched for the latest weather report. The forecast of the kaiju's route came up on the LCD. Since this was a smaller kaiju, no warning had been issued.

At some point, Kaiju One had been named Glowbat. It wasn't a particularly original name, but the chief must have decided the small kaiju wasn't worth fussing over an elaborate moniker. Glowbat was flying southeast, having just passed over the 2,140-meter-tall Mt. Shirasuna and into Gunma Prefecture. Presently, the kaiju was above Shima River approaching the town of Nakanojo at fifty-five kilometers per hour.

The creature was presumed to be a mutation of a bat, but details of its nature remained unknown. There were some reports of it coming from China. As Ryo read the news reports, he shared Yojiro's question.

Why is it flying so straight?

The flight path on the LCD was nearly a straight line to the southeast. Glowbat hadn't altered its course to avoid the tall mountains. Even those flying kaiju that typically ignored topography always had *some* variation in their paths.

The fan-shaped projected path on the Meteorological Agency's website was incredibly narrow. The radius at three hours out was completely contained within Tokyo.

Out of the corner of his eye, Ryo saw Eiko emerge from the restroom. Quickly, he closed his phone and gave her an innocent smile.

7:20 PM—

Toshio stood over the piles of assembled reports—sightings of UFOs and flying kaiju all across Asia—and tilted his head to the side. "That's an awfully long way to fly."

Three days before, a flying kaiju was seen over the Greater Khingan Range. Before that, disturbances over nighttime UFO sightings were reported in Russia near Stretensk, Lake Baikal, and Krasnoyarsk. Going further back, Toshio found sightings in the cities of Petropavlovsk and Oral in Kazakhstan, Kamyshin in Russia, and Donetsk in Ukraine. At first, the UFO sightings seemed to be completely unrelated. Even though the events occurred in the middle of the night, and the light was dim, and it flew over mostly unpopulated regions, many of the reports had been dismissed out of hand as false sightings attributed to aircraft taillights due to the descriptions of a flashing light. Not surprisingly, these seemingly unrelated reports drew no attention.

But placed on a map, the connection was obvious. All those locations formed one continuous large arc. The times of the incidents indicated all were of the same object—the farther west the sighting, the more time had passed.

"How the heck did it slip by the Russian and Chinese air defenses? I'm impressed," Koichiro said.

Kensuke, the most knowledgeable of the group when it came to military technology, explained, "It probably flew too low for most radar systems to catch. Also, unlike metal aircraft, kaiju's bodies don't react as strongly to the electromagnetic waves."

"But it intruded upon thousands of kilometers of Russian airspace," said the chief. "Could they really not have noticed?"

"It's not like it's never happened before," Kensuke explained. "In 1987, before the dissolution of the Soviet Union, a young West German man still in his late teens flew a Cessna hundreds of kilometers into Russia and landed in Moscow's Red Square. The unobstructed intrusion by a Western craft really shook up the Ministry of Defense at the time."

"It's hard to believe their defenses were so inadequate," Kurihama said.

"Well, air defense nets are designed to stop missiles and bombers. I'm sure it's possible a low-speed small aircraft—or a kaiju—could slip through."

Toshio sighed. "Russia doesn't take kaiju defense seriously. They've never had to face a significant disaster."

One of the reasons Japan kaiju were so damaging was the nation's high population density. Wherever a kaiju might appear, city was nearby. Spacious nations like China and Russia faced little probability of a kaiju coming near a major population center, and accordingly, less chance of catastrophe. Even larger kaiju that would have been promptly killed in Japan were kept alive as long as they remained in unpopulated areas, as part of Russian and Chinese environmental protection policy.

Koichiro was deep in thought. "But what is this guy about? It seems to have cut across Asia with no goal."

The room filled with suggestions from the various staff.

"Maybe it's migratory."

"Then it would have to make this journey every year. That sounds strange."

"Besides, migratory birds go north and south, right?"

"To find a warmer place in winter."

"Why would it go in a curve?"

Toshio's eyes were fixed upon the map on the wall display. Then his mouth dropped. "No, it's not doing that at all!"

He put his hand on the mouse and started bringing up one of the programs.

From over his shoulder, the chief asked, "What is it?"

"This map is a Mercator projection," Toshio said, typing in the coordinates. "I'm switching to an azimuthal equidistant projection."

"A what?"

"Typical maps project the globe onto a flat surface. Distances and directions aren't correct. In an azimuthal equidistant projection, all distances and directions from a central point—in our case, Japan—are accurately depicted."

One of the female staffers cut in. "I've heard about that! Like how it's faster for a plane flying from Tokyo to New York to pass over Alaska."

"Precisely," Toshio said. "On a flat projection, Alaska looks like it would be out of the way. But on a sphere, like the earth, it's the shortest route."

He finished typing in the data and clicked his mouse.

A circular map centered on Japan appeared on the main display. Much like on a typical map, the Arctic was depicted above Japan, Australia below it, and Eurasia to its left, but North America was turned on its side and was above and to the right of Japan. Eurasia grew larger and more distorted the farther west it went, and Europe was above and to the left. South America and Africa were so distorted as to not even resemble their shapes and stretched along the edge of the map like curved bows.

Toshio plotted the UFO sightings on the map.

The room buzzed. The red dots stretched from Tokyo at a nearly straight forty-five-degree angle line.

Glowbat hadn't flown in a curve—it came straight to Japan from Ukraine.

"*Japan* is its destination?" Kurihama said.

There didn't seem to be any other explanation. Beyond Japan

lay nothing but the open expanse of the Pacific. Japan—specifically, somewhere in Tokyo—had to be the monster's end goal.

What did it mean? As everyone in the room struggled to come up with an answer, a transmission came in from Sakura in Nagano. There was no picture, but her trembling voice came over the speakers.

"Um, this, this is Sakura."

"Did you find something?" Kurihama asked.

"Y-yes. Um, well, we found where the kaiju seems to have been. The bushes have been trampled down, and it . . . it really reeks."

"'Reeks' doesn't really tell us anything, Sakura," Kurihama lectured. "Be specific and precise."

"Ah, yes. Well, it smells like animals, I guess? Like a zoo." Her voice was nasal. "And we've found glowing spots on the ground. Um, I think, I think it's animal droppings. And, um, Kiichi is using the Geiger counter now, but, well, it . . ."

"'Well' doesn't tell me anything. Just spit it out!"

"It's reacting like crazy!" she said tearfully. "K-K-Kiichi says it's th-th-thirty thousand times higher than the background!"

"What?"

The office was in a commotion.

Kiichi's quiet, steady voice came over the line. "This is Kiichi. The Geiger counter is reading emissions of alpha particles from the glowing spots. At a distance of roughly one meter, I'm measuring eight thousand microsieverts per hour."

Kurihama's mind started putting the pieces together. *Ukraine . . . Chernobyl. If that creature came from Chernobyl . . .*

Sakura cut in, her voice high-pitched and fearful. "C-can I get away from here now?"

"Get ahold of yourself!" Kurihama shrieked, the reprimand half aimed at her and half at himself.

But beneath the creeping terror, he understood that thirty thousand times the normal background radiation didn't pose an immediate danger. Over the course of a year, the average resident of

Japan was exposed to 2.4 millisieverts of radiation from natural and cosmic sources. A stomach X-ray was thought to expose patients to roughly 4 millisieverts each scan. At 8 millisieverts per hour, a half hour next to the glowing spot would amount to nothing more than a single X-ray.

"Leave there at once," the chief said. "Make the area off-limits. There's to be absolutely no rubberneckers allowed near."

"Y-yes, sir!"

"And don't remove anything from the site. Be sure to wipe all the dirt from your shoes!"

"Yes, sir!"

She broke the transmission.

Kurihama wasted no time laying out a succession of orders to the team members. "Contact the SDF. Request the Chemical Defense Unit. Send out warning to all locales in Glowbat's path—if the kaiju lands anywhere, they need to stay far away. And not to touch anything it leaves behind. And get me an expert on radiation."

The staff still had questions.

"Are we going to kill it?"

"Should we shoot it from the sky?"

"Are we going to warn the public about the radiation?"

The chief was flustered. If the SDF fired upon it with a chain gun, radioactive blood could spill over a large area. Besides the obvious hazard to onlookers, there would be a risk of contaminating farmland and causing serious ecological damage.

Even more frightening than anything the kaiju could do itself was the panic of the common man. Not one person in a hundred would understand the amount of danger posed by eight millisieverts per hour at a distance of one meter. If the media announced that a radioactive kaiju was nearing metropolitan Tokyo, the turmoil of fleeing masses could be as dangerous as a riot. But still, the MMD could not *not* tell the truth.

"Wait!" the chief cried out. "Wait! Let me think."

Calm, rational decisions were needed most in times of emergency.

But there wasn't much time to think. In a matter of minutes, Glowbat would pass over Nakanojo.

Kurihama anguished over the decision. The kaiju had flown over ten thousand kilometers straight to Tokyo, and the chief didn't know from where or why. If they screwed up the attack, large areas could be irradiated, but he had a feeling the situation would only become worse if the monster made it to Tokyo.

Yojiro's voice came over the speakers. "This is the helicopter. The Apache has joined up with us. Do we have permission to attack?"

Kurihama clutched at the microphone and yelled, "Wait! We've found radiation in what we think is Glowbat's excrement."

Silence. Then, "How much?"

"Eight millisieverts per hour at a distance of one meter."

"Then if we drop it in the forest, I think we'll get by."

"But the contamination—"

"Will happen wherever it goes down. It would be worse to let it keep flying over Japan. What if it urinates or defecates mid-flight?" Yojiro said.

"But we don't have time to measure—"

"We have to take it out now! If we kill it over farmland or a city, the damages will be in an entirely different league."

Yojiro's words dispelled the last of Kurihama's doubts. "Understood. Take course for offensive maneuvers. But take him down over the forest! And tell the SDF about the radiation. You got that? Be sure to take him down over the forest."

Without delay, the staff began to make contact with the Ministry of Defense. Word was also passed through Yojiro's pilot to the superintendent-general of the Eastern Army. Not two minutes after the decision had been made, the order to fire came back.

Yojiro said, "We've just received the attack order. The Apache is moving into position."

"How long until you're over the target area?" Kurihama asked.

"We are just entering Nakanojo airspace. There's only one problem."

"What's that?"

"It's starting to rain."

After Glowbat passed over Nakanojo Athletic Park and crossed the Agatsuma River, the attack commenced.

To be fair, the pilot and gunner of the Apache did the best job humanly possible. They operated under the harshest of limitations—only fire from above, since shots at the horizon could fall a great distance away and damage residential areas; fire to kill, not to injure, since a wounded but still airborne Glowbat could spread radioactive blood over a wide area; only fire after confirming no civilian homes are directly below. The low visibility due to the rainfall only added to the difficulties. The bad weather reduced the capabilities of the low-light camera by half.

The pilot's ability to follow Glowbat's dim light through the rain was commendable, and on several occasions, the gunner fired at the kaiju. But the monster zigzagged through the air as if it could sense their attacks. The gunner was no match for it. The thirty-millimeter shots fell in vain, cutting holes into forest groves and golf course greens.

At last, the Apache's sights centered upon the fleeing beast. But below twinkled the streetlights of Ikaho City. With a curse, the gunner loosened his finger from the trigger.

The kaiju flew south along Highway 15. Ahead lay an endless patch of houses all the way to Tokyo. They had failed.

8:00 PM—

Glowbat passed over Maebashi City, Gunma Prefecture. With reports of a glowing flying kaiju all over the news, the people of the city, undeterred by the rain, stepped outside their homes and watched the pale blue light cross the sky.

From every street corner came the cries, "I see it, I see it!" "Incredible!" "It's glowing!"

The people, unaware of Glowbat's true nature, gazed up at the creature with naive enthusiasm. Some tried to take pictures with their cell phones, but to their disappointment, its light was too dim to register on the tiny cameras.

The kaiju, unperturbed by the attention, beat its powerful wings and continued its steady course to the southeast. Behind it, two helicopters followed.

Straight toward Tokyo.

Chief Kurihama gave a brief summary of the evening's events to the man on the other end of the line, radiation specialist Dr. Yoshio Iwamura.

The elderly scholar spoke with an affected drawl. "Well, at that amount, from an external source, it is not that severe. Alpha particles have low penetration depth and will not pass deeply into skin. Even with direct bodily contact, following a change of clothes and a thorough shower, there will likely be no serious exposure."

"With quick measures taken, there won't be loss of life?"

"There will not. However, if the material is taken inside the body, the results are different. Even low amounts of exposure to internal organs may cause serious injury. Back when radium was used to make glowing numbers on watches and clocks, the dial painters would use their lips to shape their brushes, and—"

"I'm sorry, Doctor," Kurihama cut in, "but we'll have to leave the history lessons for another time. What about the environmental effects?"

"Would you be more specific?"

"If we were to kill it, how long would the surrounding area be contaminated?"

"It depends on the isotope. Radon-222 and radon-224, for

example, have relatively short half-lives and would not be a problem after a few months. But radon-226 and thorium-230 continue to be radioactive for tens of thousands of years. The fact that you have found alpha particles does not really tell us much. We would have to run more tests before we could know more."

"Do you think we should warn the public? Or would it cause too much panic?"

"Crowd psychology is not my specialty. But I think it would be unwise to expect the general public to comprehend the dangers of short-term exposure to radiation. There are too many who don't understand the different classes of radiation. Some still believe microwave ranges emit radiation. One of my students once told me—"

Kurihama laid the receiver down on his desk. He grabbed the microphone to seek Yojiro's opinion. "Should we tell them?"

"What if instead of telling people to evacuate," Yojiro calmly said, "we instructed them to remain inside their homes? Even if the kaiju were to rain blood, people would at least be safe inside."

"And not say anything about the radiation?"

"I think that would be prudent."

The room erupted in debate.

"The media will skin us alive! They'll accuse us of covering up the truth."

"And if the public doesn't know about the radiation, people might try to get a closer look at its corpse."

"But if we tell the truth, there'll be panic!"

"Is there a way we can break it gently?"

"Are you kidding?"

"The word radiation alone is enough to scare the pants off someone."

"Japanese are sensitive to nuclear issues."

Yojiro offered, "What if we say Glowbat is poisonous? We could say that the poison in its blood is dangerous."

The suggestion sparked a new round of comments. "That could work! Poison won't ignite a panic like radiation would."

"And we wouldn't be lying, exactly."

"Right. Radiation is a form of poison, really."

"Not scientifically speaking, it's not."

"We'll explain to the media afterward."

Kurihama barked, "All right!" The staff quieted to listen. "We'll go with that plan. But we will tell the media the truth beforehand and ask for their cooperation to prevent a panic."

That way, the press wouldn't be able to later accuse them of covering up the truth.

"Let's get the word out," the chief said. "The kaiju is fiercely poisonous. All civilians should keep their distance from its remains and bodily fluids."

At 8:20 PM, Glowbat crossed the Tone River and entered Saitama Prefecture. And still it flew, over Fukaya, ever to the southeast.

As for Ryo and Eiko, they were enjoying their after-dinner wine, absorbed in light conversation.

Neither was aware—nor for that matter, were the vast number of Tokyo residents—of the approaching threat. Television viewers felt only annoyance at the scrolling warnings intruding upon their dramas and variety shows. Few took them to heart. *Don't bother us with every tiny scrap of news about some MM1. Poison? Who cares, as long as I don't get close to it.*

While the MMD and the SDF scrambled under pressures of time and danger, the citizens of Tokyo enjoyed the night as if it were any other.

8:50 PM—

Glowbat passed over Osato District, Saitama.

Chief Kurihama downed his stomach medicine with a pained expression, his eyes on the live display of the kaiju's location. "So it really is headed for Tokyo."

Simply killing the monster wouldn't have been difficult. If it were kind enough to land, army rifles would have been enough to dispatch it. A kaiju of that size wouldn't be able to destroy buildings. There'd be little damage visible to the naked eye. But wherever the battle occurred, that place would be faced with unavoidable radioactive contamination. Unlike the mountainside forests, if land in the heart of Japan's capital with a population of millions were to be contaminated, the economic damages would be in the nine-digit range at best. Of course the chief's stomach hurt.

"Flying *and* radioactive—that's the worst combination."

That was only one complaint of many grumbled by the chief in the past hour. Merely wounding the flying creature would spread its blood—and the contamination—over a wide area. They had to take it out in one shot, when it landed. But with no way of determining where it would land, the SDF remained unable to deploy its waiting forces.

Yuri said, "When the American army chased Ray into an old amusement park, they were able to torch it with napalm."

"Burning it would be pointless." Kurihama sighed. "Radiation doesn't just burn away. Irradiated smoke and ash spreads even farther."

Unlike the Japanese, who had experienced nuclear terror, Americans were soft on the dangers of radiation. In the 1950s, they used to send soldiers unprotected into test site mushroom clouds.

One of the operators said, "What if we kill it with gas? The best way to minimize contamination would be not to spill any blood."

Kurihama dismissed the idea. "How would we force a flying kaiju to inhale the gas? We'd need massive amounts of it, and that would only cause even worse problems to the nearby civilians."

"Besides," Kensuke added, "the SDF doesn't keep chemical weapons on hand. It would be a violation of international treaties."

Now another debate erupted.

"What about anesthetic gas?"

"Same thing. It could beat its wings and spread the gas."

"And it's not that easy putting something that size to sleep."

"Is there anything else we could use besides poison gas?"

"If we got it to inhale large amounts of a not-so-poisonous gas . . ."

"Like natural gas?"

"It would take an awful lot to kill it."

"And what if it ignited?"

"What about car exhaust?"

"That would take too long!"

"No matter what, if we don't have an enclosed space, it won't work."

"So we chase it into an enclosed space. That'd also help keep environmental damages low."

"Like a tunnel or a basement?"

"Or sewers!"

"Yeah, but how?"

"You're all just blueskying—we need something practical."

"Maybe, but if we did find a way to trap it in a small space, the rest would be easy."

"We could even just feed it poisoned food."

"What does it eat?"

They didn't come up with many good ideas.

"And where did it come from?"

Kurihama scratched his head. Just minutes earlier, two new data had been added to the world map—three-week-old sightings of a flying kaiju in the Strandzha massif in western Turkey and a UFO in the Balkans. Glowbat had not been born in Ukraine, but came from somewhere beyond the Mediterranean—in Africa.

The chief asked Koichiro, who was searching through the database, "Is there anything on African flying kaiju?"

"Quite a bit. Kongamato, olitiau, ngoima . . . but the most similar is this one: Guiafairo, a kaiju living in the jungles of southern Senegal."

He pulled up an artist's pencil sketch of witnesses' reports of the creature. Just like Glowbat, Guiafairo had the body of a bat, a hideous countenance, three-taloned feet, and a long tail.

"Senegal?" the chief asked. "Isn't that all the way on the west coast of Africa?"

"That's far, I know," Koichiro said, "but Guiafairo is an MM one or two, and there's something else the drawing doesn't show. Supposedly, it glows pale blue."

"How dangerous is it?"

"It's never attacked humans. But according to local legend, the creature is feared because, quote, 'Just meeting it will make you fall sick and die.'"

"Has it been sighted recently?"

Koichiro read from the English report, translating it on the fly. "In 1995, a man encountered the beast. The guy walked right up to it, and the kaiju exhaled some foul-smelling air at him and the man passed out. He made it safely back to his home, but later, he suffered from headaches, vomiting, and diarrhea. He was admitted to a local hospital, where he was . . ."

He paused.

"What's wrong?" Kurihama asked.

". . . where he was diagnosed with radiation sickness."

"What?"

9:15 PM—

When they entered the hotel room, Eiko went straight to the bathroom to take a shower. Ryo sat on the bed and turned on the TV.

NHK news was on.

"*. . . as we previously reported, Kaiju One, Glowbat, is currently flying over Yoshimi, Saitama Prefecture. The kaiju is continuing its flight to the southeast and is projected to reach Tokyo airspace at nine forty this evening. The Monsterological Measures Department issued a statement earlier today warning that Glowbat's body secretes a strong poison. A battle with the SDF is expected to cause spilled blood. Civilians are advised* *to refrain from going outdoors and to remain inside until Glowbat has been contained. If you see the kaiju, do not approach it. If you find any of the kaiju's blood, do not touch it because it is extremely poisonous . . ."*

"Poison?"

Something about that bothered Ryo. Some kaiju in the past had used poison as a weapon, and the SDF even had guidelines to safeguard against environmental contamination from the rotting carcasses of giant monsters. But something about this seemed different. Even though he knew he was being irrational, he had a bad premonition.

Why didn't it ever deviate course?

Ryo opened his phone. He knew the head office's lines would be choked with calls from all over. A better course would be to call one of the team members' cell phones. Yojiro would be near the kaiju and probably had his hands full. Ryo went with Yuri's number. He figured she'd be the least busy of anyone inside the office.

"Hey, Yuri, it's me, Ryo. Sorry to bother you . . . No, I'm off duty tonight. I just saw the news and was worried . . . Where am I now? Shinjuku . . . Yeah, I saw the warning. Is it serious?"

His face went pale.

"*Radioactive?* Really? How much?"

He grabbed the bedside memo set and started writing everything down.

"Yeah, with those numbers, close contact isn't too much of a worry. The cleanup afterward, on the other hand . . . They said on the news that it came from China."

His eyes widened.

"*Africa?*"

Ryo glanced at the bathroom door. The shower had stopped, but Eiko was still inside. He lowered his voice.

"Three weeks ago? And you say he's flown straight to Tokyo the whole way? Do you know what he's after? Oh . . . No, I don't know either, but I have a hunch . . . I'll call back later."

Just as he hung up the phone, Eiko stepped into the room with nothing but a bath towel over her flushed pink skin. With a wiggle of her hips, she said, "I've kept you waiting."

But every last trace of desire had left Ryo. He put a hand on her shoulder and asked, with his voice tight and intense, "You said there was an African exhibit at the museum?"

She blinked at him. "What? Well, yeah, The Origins of Human Culture."

"Since when?"

"Last month. The thirteenth."

Four weeks ago—the same time Guiafairo was thought to have taken flight.

"Is there anything in the exhibit from Senegal?"

"Why, yes, an item of magic paraphernalia."

"Specifically?"

She spread her arms. "It's about this big. Looks like a wooden oar. It's carved with intricate designs, and there's a blue orb at the tip."

"That must be it."

Ryo pushed her aside, walked to the closet, and retrieved his coat.

"I'm sorry," he said, "but I have to cancel our date."

"What? Why?"

"The kaiju headed toward Tokyo came all the way from Senegal. And it's radioactive."

"No way. *Guiafairo?*"

Ryo froze, his arm halfway through the coat sleeve. "You've heard of it?"

Eiko put her hand to her hip and laughed sharply. "Never underestimate the knowledge of a yokai geek!"

"I wish we had you at the MMD."

"Why thank you. So Guiafairo's on its way to Tokyo?"

"It flew straight the whole way. I have to believe it's being drawn here by something. That exhibit is likely the cause, so I'm going to the museum."

"It'll be closed by now."

"I know. Call one of the night guards. Have them unlock a door for me."

Ryo took a step to leave.

"Wait!" Eiko moved around him and blocked the door with her body. "I'm coming too."

"Listen—"

"The night watchman is strict. He's not just going to open the doors for someone not with the museum. Too many valuable artifacts. You need to go with someone who works there. Do you even know where to find the exhibit if you got inside?"

"Weren't you listening? It's radioactive!"

"Then I really am going," Eiko said. "I'm not going to let it contaminate our precious exhibits and effects. As an employee, it's my duty."

Her eyes were serious.

Ryo sighed. "All right, we'll go together."

She grinned. "Three minutes. I'll get some clothes on."

They dashed out of the hotel and rapped on the window of a taxi parked out front. The driver lowered the passenger-side window a crack.

"To Ueno!" Ryo said.

The driver frowned. "A warning just came over the radio. There's a poisonous kaiju coming, and we're to refrain from going out."

There was no time to argue. Ryo pulled out a ten thousand yen note from his wallet, pushed it in through the cracked window, and said, "Here."

After an initial moment of surprise, the driver unlocked the rear doors. The two climbed in and the taxi took off, rain hitting the windshield.

As soon as they were on their way, Ryo and Eiko took out

their phones—him to call the MMD, and her to call the museum security.

"Yes," Ryo was saying. "There's a strong possibility that the kaiju is headed for the Museum of Nature and Science in Ueno. Please cordon off the area around Ueno Park, and tell the SDF to send forces there. If anyone with the Mobile Unit is free, I'd like some backup."

"Yes," Eiko was saying, "I've seen the news. We're on our way now, so please unlock the employee entrance for me. Thanks."

They hung up at almost exactly the same time. Ryo sighed. "It doesn't look we'll be getting any help from the main office."

"What? Takebashi is closer to Ueno than we are."

"The rest of the Mobile Unit is already out. Our leader and one of the others is in a helicopter, and the other two are still in Nagano. The only people still in the office are all desk workers."

"Can't any of them come?"

"If they haven't had training for field ops, no. People who don't know what they're doing could just end up getting in our way." He gave her a wry smile. "I'm sorry to get you wrapped up in this."

"Wrapped up? I was the one who stuck myself into it."

"I guess."

"But I just can't believe it," Eiko said. "Do you really think the kaiju is being drawn to the museum? All the way here from Africa?"

"It's not like it's never happened before. Eugene went to London from offshore of Ireland to retrieve its child from an exhibition there. And in Japan, in 1969, Niuhi came here from Easter Island. It's generally thought that it came after a statue brought for display at the next year's World's Fair. That's a trip of over twelve kilometers across the Pacific."

The former of the two followed the scent of its child, and the latter could be explained by low frequency sounds emitted by the statue. Still, kaiju behavior often remained unexplainable by scientific rationalism. Many of the giant monsters acted as if they had some form of ESP, and not a few were thought to have been created via occult practices like curses and black magic. These theories were not that incredible under the construct of the parallel anthropic principle, which explained the phenomena as a result of kaiju being creatures not of the Big Bang universe but rather existences of the mythic universe, where our rules of physics didn't apply.

Eiko said, "But when the item was on display in the museum in Senegal, nothing happened."

"I can't explain that. Maybe some curse was triggered with all the attention of the exhibit here." Then it came to him. "What if it was done by those two old men you said looked like yokai? Maybe they were sorcerers or something, and they cast a spell to summon Guiafairo here."

"That could be it!" She made an exaggerated nod. "Ancient African magic brought back to life in twenty-first century Japan! It's kind of fanciful, don't you think? Stirring!"

"Are you high?" Ryo asked.

"Well, I could be—this is so exhilarating! I might be able to see a real live kaiju with my own eyes."

Ryo leaned in to keep the driver from hearing. "You're not scared of the radiation?"

"Maybe a little." If she was frightened, not a trace of it showed in her voice. "But as long as we don't get too close, it won't be dangerous, right?"

"Yeah, I guess. The victim in Senegal said it had terrible foul breath. He probably got too close to Guiafairo and inhaled it, along with a spray of radioactive particles."

"So we won't breathe in its breath. It's just a little MM1 anyway. If we're careful about the radiation, we'll be fine."

"It's not that simple."

Ryo was already beginning to regret bringing her along. She underestimated kaiju. An MM1.5 was small for a kaiju, but it wasn't so small you could let your guard down.

A water displacement of four tons was four times the size of an Indian elephant.

Yojiro announced the location of the kaiju once every minute. "Glowbat is flying along the Tohoku bullet train rail line. It just passed over the Tokyo-Gaikan Expressway. In a few minutes, it'll be inside the city."

On the map display, Glowbat's destination was finally starting to become clear. Its projected location in twenty minutes had tightened to a five-kilometer radius centered on Ueno.

Toshio said, "It looks like Ryo's hunch was right."

"If only I'd realized what it was sooner," Koichiro said, frustrated. The rookie had run across Senegal in his research, but he chose to focus on contacting the Senegalese embassy in Meguro Ward and failed to notice the news of the museum exhibit.

"It won't do any good to say that now," Toshio said soothingly. "Nobody ever anticipated that a kaiju would fly all the way from West Africa to Japan."

Chief Kurihama grumbled, "Why on earth would an African kaiju be radioactive? I'm fairly sure there's never been any atomic tests in West Africa."

Yuri said, "It might be because of biological transmutation inside its body."

"What, like the Kervran effect?"

"Yes. Even enriched natural radioactive elements don't emit that high an amount of radiation. According to the rules of physics in the Big Bang universe, biological transmutation is impossible. But atomic structure in the *mythic universe* doesn't behave in the same way. It's entirely possible that atoms don't even exist there. Like with Princess. It would explain how kaiju can ignore the law of conservation of energy or create radioactive isotopes."

"But if there aren't any atoms, how is Glowbat causing radiation damage?"

"It's possible that the local legends—'Guiafairo glows' and 'Those who meet Guiafairo become ill'—are expressed within the Big Bang universe as radiation. This theory—that the space inside the monster's body is governed by the rules of the mythic universe—would also explain why it isn't harmed by its own radiation. Radiation doesn't exist in the mythic universe. As soon as its blood or urine leaves its body, the fluids are absorbed into the Big Bang universe, and transform into radioactive isotopes."

"And if it dies?"

"The same. When a kaiju dies, its body transmutes into matter consisting of our common atoms. Its appearance won't change, but it will become an existence conforming to our Big Bang universe."

"And the radiation?"

Gravely, Yuri said, "I think will remain."

"That's going to be trouble." The chief sighed.

Yojiro's voice came over the speakers with an update. "The bastard's slowly started losing altitude. It's currently above Toda Station. I can see Ara River now—we'll be within Tokyo shortly."

At that rate, the kaiju would reach Ueno in fifteen minutes.

Ueno Park was already being sealed off. The area around the park was in turmoil, with crowds following the police's advice to flee colliding with small clusters of people coming to see the kaiju despite the warnings. Ryo and Eiko's taxi pushed its way through the jammed streets around Ueno Station, where the two got out of the car and ran the last half-kilometer in the rain.

At the edge of the police cordon, Ryo showed his credentials, said, "I'm with the MMD!" and was let through. Briefly, he considered asking for a few officers to come along for protection, but rejected the thought. Their small caliber firearms couldn't be relied upon. Minor wounds might only incense the beast—or spread radioactive contamination.

Umbrellas in hand, the two sprinted through the empty park.

Ryo's cell phone rang. He answered it without stopping. "This is Ryo."

It was the chief. "Where are you?"

Between deep breaths, Ryo answered, "We're running . . . to the museum . . . almost there."

"Hurry! Glowbat is already in Tokyo."

"And the SDF?"

"They'll arrive at Ueno in minutes. Don't hang up. I'll patch you through to them."

"Understood."

As he ran, Ryo considered the situation. *I can't turn the museum into a battlefield. Like Eiko said, the place is filled with irreplaceable treasures. Besides the usual risk of damage from missed shots, the artifacts could be contaminated with radiation. We have to stop it without guns and without spilled blood—but how?*

They made it to the museum, out of breath, and a watchman in his late fifties opened the door.

"Follow me!" Eiko said. Flashlight in hand, she led the two men through the museum's dark halls. The National Museum of Nature and Science was divided into two halls—the Japan Gallery and the Global Gallery. The Origins of Human Culture exhibit was located in the Special Exhibition Room on the first floor basement of the Global Gallery. They ran down the stopped escalator and into the exhibit room.

Inside, the few scattered emergency lights didn't provide enough illumination for them to see the other end of the large room. As they walked, the beams from Eiko's and the guard's flashlights flickered across the walls and the items inside the display cases. The various objects—African tribal masks and spears, stone tablets and papyrus manuscripts, primitive dolls covered with fur, wooden totem poles—might have been slightly eerie when well lit, but with the lights out, they looked like the decorations of an amusement park haunted house. Even Ryo, who thought himself courageous, was a little rattled. Eiko, who worked around the artifacts on a near daily basis, seemed not to be having any trouble.

"Here it is." Eiko dashed over to one of the acrylic display cases. Inside rested a black wooden tool the same size and shape as a ship's oar. Tightly packed designs were carved all along it, just as she'd described. The patterns resembled the cuneiform script of the Hittites. The end of the oar had a round depression inset with a blue tennis ball–sized orb, possibly lapis lazuli. The display card read "Magic tool used to summon evil spirits."

"Give me the key!" Eiko said to the watchman, who ran back to his desk to retrieve it.

Ryo squinted at the rows of carvings. "Is this writing?"

"It seems like it."

"Seems?"

"The linguists can't decipher it. The consensus is it's probably writing in a lost ancient language."

A great number of languages were extinct, and there were many modern-day scholars still couldn't read—such as Indus, Rongorongo of Easter Island, Khitan of China, Linear A of Crete—and the writing on the oar could have been another.

"Those two men," Ryo asked, "were they in front of this display?"

"Yeah."

"Could they have been reading this?"

"You mean the old script nobody can read?"

"Maybe those two possess incredibly ancient knowledge. They could be one of those yokai you like so much."

"You think that's really possible?"

"Weren't you the one who said they seemed like yokai?" Ryo said. "And yokai and kaiju live longer than natural creatures. It's no wonder they know things humans have long since forgotten." Ryo leaned over the case to look at the backside of the artifact. "Was this crack always here?"

Her eyes widened. She leaned over, put her face beside his, and peered down. A spot on the side of the orb not visible to the visitors had turned gray, and thin white cracks radiated out from it.

"No, it wasn't." Eiko looked at him. "It's not an egg, is it?"

"Could be. There was once an opal smuggled from New Guinea that turned out to be a kaiju egg."

"But we put it through spectroscopic analysis before we took it in the museum. It came back as lazulite and sodalite, that's it."

"We're dealing with a kaiju that produces radioactive elements inside its body. Surely a creature like that could transform an egg shell into stone. Maybe not even just the shell. Maybe it turns its young into stone to protect it for hundreds of years."

"What for?"

"I don't know. Kaiju are like that. They can sleep within the earth for hundreds, sometimes thousands and tens of thousands of years—until something triggers their sudden revival."

"So a magic spell awoke the young from its hibernation? And its mother sensed it and came to get it?" Eiko asked.

The watchman came back with the key. Eiko took it from him and hurriedly opened the case. When she picked up the magic artifact, the three recoiled from the orb's stench.

Eiko held her nose and said, "This is—"

"Hydrogen sulfide!" Ryo said.

"Is the stone reacting with hydrochloric acid?"

The sodalite group of rocks—the common constituents of lapis lazuli—react with hydrochloric acid, softening and producing hydrogen sulfide. The unhatched offspring was likely using its stomach acid to weaken the egg's shell from the inside.

Ryo took the artifact in his right hand. In his left, he held the still-connected phone, which he lifted to his face and said, "This is Ryo. I've recovered the exhibit. It's a kaiju egg."

Chief Kurihama screamed from the other end, "Get out of there—Glowbat has reached the park!"

Ryo turned to Eiko. "It's coming!"

"Let's just get outside," she said.

He put the phone into his pocket and ran. The watchman led the way. If Glowbat pushed its way inside the museum, it could damage the exhibits. They had to get outside before it got in.

Then, just as they were within sight of the exit, a giant figure swooped down on the other side of the glass.

Caught by surprise, the watchman in the lead slipped and landed on his backside. The next instant, the glass door shattered with a tremendous noise, raining a cascade of shards onto the guard.

Ryo and Eiko stood frozen in terror. Glowbat inched its giant, wet, and eerily glowing body into the museum. The kaiju folded its wings and twisted its slender frame to squeeze through the small doorway. The creature's glow brightened the darkness of the entrance hall, its light pale and blue, wavering like sunlight on the seabed.

When the beast was finally fully within the museum, it opened its wings. Fragments of broken glass sprinkled to the floor. The ten-meter-long wings unfurled like a curtain across Ryo's entire field of vision. He could clearly see the bright web of arteries beneath the thin layer of skin. It stood on two legs with backward-bending leg joints, and even stooped over, the kaiju was twice a man's height.

But what really terrified the couple was its face. From the profile, it looked reptilian, but head on, it was simian, disturbingly reminiscent of a human. The effect was far more horrifying than if the kaiju had the face of any other animal.

Glowbat opened its mouth wide and let out a ravenlike cry. Its breath was feral and foul, and Ryo and Eiko hurriedly covered their mouths. The kaiju casually stepped over the watchman, who was prone on the floor, hands over his head, and closed in on the two.

Ryo pulled Eiko with him down a side hallway. "Come on, this way!"

Glowbat gave chase. But the ceiling of the hallway was lower than the entrance, and the walls were narrow. To fit, the creature had to fold in its wings and drop to the floor. It propped itself up with a single finger on each wing and pursued the couple, running on four limbs like a gorilla. Ryo and Eiko had gained valuable distance.

Ryo looked over his shoulder at the kaiju's tortured movements and was struck by a thought.

"Is there an elevator near here?"

"At the back! There's an employee elevator."

Soon they were upon it. Eiko ran up and slid her ID card through the reader. The doors opened, and the two leapt inside. Ryo pushed the button for the bottom floor. Glowbat continued its rage-fueled pursuit.

"Let's just give it over!" Eiko said, plucking the artifact from his hand. She drew back her arm to throw it.

"No!" Ryo snatched it back. While they were fighting, the doors began to shut.

With the passage closed, a thunderous noise rumbled through the elevator. Glowbat had run straight into the doors. For a moment, the couple feared the elevator had been broken, but the car began its descent unperturbed.

As they rode down, a *thud, thud, thud* noise echoed from above.

"Why did you do that?" Eiko asked. "If we gave it back its egg, it might have just gone home!"

"And it might not have. If it tried to raise its offspring here, it would be a mess. We have to kill it, somewhere."

"But . . ."

They arrived at the lowest floor. The doors opened onto a pitch black void. Eiko stepped out of the elevator and fumbled along the wall until her hand found the light switch.

But Ryo didn't move from the elevator car. He pressed the emergency stop button to hold the doors open, and with the artifact in hand, he stood looking up at the ceiling, listening to the monster battering the elevator doors from the shaft above.

Eiko asked, "What are you doing?"

"Luring it to us."

"What?"

"That kaiju comes at this thing in a straight line. It's not smart enough to find a way around. It's throwing itself at the doors right now, but if it would only think to pry them open . . ."

"Then what?"

"It'd come straight down the shaft. But with that body, I'm sure it would get stuck on the way."

Ryo took the cell phone from his pocket to contact the MMD. But the display read SEARCHING FOR SERVICE. *Of course there's no signal this far down.*

"Is there a landline down here?"

"Over there."

At the end of the short hallway was a door with a security keypad mounted on the wall beside it. Eiko swiped her ID and input the passcode. The door opened. Ryo left the artifact on the floor of the elevator and followed her inside.

When he saw the room, he couldn't help but whistle. The spacious room contained rows upon rows of steel shelves tightly packed with binders and cardboard boxes. At the rear of the room was a large steel door that could have secured a bank vault.

As they walked through the room, Ryo looked in all directions. "So this is what the basement of a museum is like."

"We don't let visitors down here. There are too many valuables."

"And that vault? There must be some big-ticket items in there."

"I don't really know," Eiko said.

"You don't know?"

"I haven't been told. It's for safety. Only a few people besides the curator know what's inside. Here's the phone."

Ryo opened his cell phone, pulled up the number for the direct line to the MMD, and called it through the landline. It connected after the first ring.

"This is Ryo. We're in the basement of the museum . . . Yes, the kaiju chased us . . . Yes, we're all right. One of the night watchmen was knocked out by the entrance. I don't think he's badly hurt, but I'm worried about the radiation. He should be brought to a hospital immediately . . . Yes, I have the exhibit. He's following after us, and right now he's trying to get into the elevator shaft . . . You're right. It's the perfect chance." He turned to Eiko. "This is the fourth sub-basement, right?"

"That's just what it's called. Really, we're about eight floors deep."

"Huh?"

"Not only does each floor have high ceilings, there's a lot of space between this storage room and the floor above."

Now that she mentioned it, Ryo realized the elevator had taken an unusually long time to go down from the ground floor.

Ryo spoke into the receiver. "We're about twenty-four meters below ground. It should work well for burying it alive."

Eiko's eyes widened in surprise. "Burying it alive?"

But Ryo kept on talking. "And when it can't move, flood down gas or something to kill it. Then fill the shaft with concrete . . . You've got it. I think it could be our best option . . . Yes, go ahead and make the arrangements . . . I'll wait here until I can confirm it's coming down . . . Of course, if it gets dangerous, I'll get out."

As soon as he'd hung up, Eiko snapped, "Tell me you're joking."

"I swear I'm not. Even if we managed to kill it inside the elevator shaft, by the time we could get its body out, there could already be too much contamination. Burying it would be safer—there are other elevators, or a staircase, right?"

"Yeah."

"Then there's no problem."

"You're saying we'll have to work next to the kaiju's *corpse*?"

"Alpha particles have a low penetration depth. Ten centimeters of concrete would be enough to shield the staff from them completely."

"That's not what I'm talking about. It'd just feel wrong." She pressed her lips tight. "It'd be creepy."

"An employee of a science museum shouldn't say something so unscientific."

"Is killing kaiju all you think about? And to hell with how it interferes with other people?"

"Yes. Of course!" Ryo retorted. "I'm in the MMD. My job is to stop kaiju with the minimum possible destruction. Everything else comes second, or third."

He turned his back to her and walked back to the hallway. Fuming, Eiko followed after him. Ryo stepped through the still open doors of the elevator and looked up. The thudding sound continued from above.

"Look!" Eiko said. She pointed at his feet. He looked down and gasped. The crack on the blue orb had widened to reveal a tiny beak within.

"Turn off the lights," Ryo said.

Eiko flipped the switch. By the time their eyes adjusted to the darkness, the hatchling's tiny head had poked out from the egg. Unlike its parent, it more closely resembled a bird than an ape—and unlike its parent, it emitted no blue light.

"It's not glowing," Eiko said.

"They might not be radioactive when they're young. We might be able to keep it."

The hatchling, eyes still closed, parted its beak and let out a small cry.

Miiiii.

From above came a booming reply.

Kwaaaaa!

Over the next few minutes, the parent and child repeated the call and response.

"Listen," Eiko said, tearfully. "Can't we just give it its child back?"

"Impossible. And even if we did, the end would be the same."

"Huh?"

"With its child back, Glowbat might try to go back home to Africa. Along the same route it came by."

"Wouldn't that be a good thing?"

"On the way, the Chinese or Russian air forces would shoot them down."

"Oh."

"Letting a radioactive kaiju slip through their airspace was an enormous failure. If they learned it was coming back from Japan, they'd be bent on making up for that error . . . No, before that, before the kaiju left the Sea of Japan, the SDF might attack. If we knowingly allowed a radioactive kaiju to escape into another country, there'd be an international incident."

"Is there nothing we can do?"

"It's hopeless. As soon as that creature left the jungles of Senegal, its fate was set. It's only a miracle that the thing made it this far."

"But why? What purpose would anyone have to set it on a course with such a small chance of success?"

"I'd have to guess indiscriminate terrorism."

"What?"

"I can't think of anything else that would fit. Kaiju are uncontrollable, so they can't be used as weapons. But they *can* be used for indiscriminate terrorism. The Zeta Incident proved it, and now there's kaiju terrorism all over the world. This time, Japan didn't even have to be the target. Maybe they wanted to harass somewhere around Russia."

"But . . . that . . ." Eiko's voice trembled. "For people to use kaiju as weapons . . ."

"There are a lot of people in the world who would—plenty of evil bastards who think nothing of stamping out the lives of others if it furthers their goals." Ryo looked down at the hatchling kaiju with sad eyes. It had squeezed its upper body out from the shell and was trying to pull its wrinkled wings free of the egg.

It was trying to live.

"We can't save its parent," Ryo said, "but we can save this little guy. We may even be able to negotiate with the Senegalese government to get it back to the jungle."

"I'm sorry."

"Hm?"

"For saying you only thought about killing kaiju. You *are* a nice guy."

"Oh, stop." Ryo smirked. "A 'nice guy'? That's not in my character."

"But you want to save this infant, don't you?"

"I'm just saying it's all right not to kill it when there's no need to, that's all."

The sound from the shaft above changed. By the time they'd registered the noise of creaking metal, it had been replaced by the unmistakable rustling of flesh scraping against concrete.

"All right!" Ryo said. "It's entered the shaft."

"What do we do?"

"We'll lure him here just a little bit longer. You go to the staircase—oh, but first, bring me a cardboard box or something. To put this guy in."

"I'm on it." Eiko gave him a peck on the cheek before running back into the storeroom.

The rustling noise drew closer, until suddenly, it stopped. Glowbat cried out as it struggled, clearly in pain. Intermittent jolts shook the elevator car. As Ryo had predicted, the kaiju had gotten itself twisted among the cables in the narrow shaft and was now stuck. Howls of despair rang through the shaft.

Ryo gently stroked the crying hatchling's head. "A nice guy, huh," he said softly, his voice tinged with regret. "It must be someone's bad influence."

Three hours later, when all the elevator doors from the first floor down to the fourth basement were completely sealed, a total of 2,400 liters of liquid nitrogen was poured down the shaft. Despite the late hour, they'd managed to gather it from dealers and research organizations. Thanks to the combination of the temperature—negative 200 degrees Celsius—and the vaporized nitrogen pushing the oxygen from the chamber, Glowbat ceased movement. Members of the SDF Chemical Defense Unit equipped with protective suits and oxygen masks entered the shaft and confirmed that the kaiju's heart had stopped. Death by gas carried a risk of the creature's bowels loosening and evacuating excrement, but the cold had prevented that outcome. That had been Yojiro's idea.

The kaiju had become tangled within the shaft and would likely be difficult to remove without opening wounds. In the end, the SDF went with a plan to pour in three hundred tons of concrete to seal the monster's corpse halfway until eternity. That would hinder the museum workers for a while, but as long as the process prevented the building from becoming contaminated, they'd have to put up with it.

Ryo, Eiko, and the injured watchman were taken to the hospital for examination. Luckily, none of them were found to have suffered extensive exposure to the radiation.

When Yojiro came to visit him in the hospital, Ryo cheerfully reported, "They say the chances I'll die from cancer have gone up 0.1 percent." Since three in ten Japanese die from cancer, an extra tenth of a percent wasn't anything to worry about.

"Looks like you'll have a nice long life. I'm relieved to hear it."

"Yes, but this has been awful. They took my best coat away. It was expensive, too. Do you think I'll get it back?" Ryo said.

Due to the risk of contamination, all of their clothes had been confiscated. Even though Ryo wasn't sick, he was wearing a white patient's gown.

"They might return it to you once they've gotten all the dust off."

"And I was off duty too. Am I getting overtime pay?"

"That might be hard, the way our system is set up."

"What?"

"Off-duty employees are just average citizens," Yojiro said. "I guess I can put in a request with Accounting, but I wouldn't count on it."

With a forlorn expression, Ryo said, "You've got to be kidding! I worked that hard and I won't get anything?"

Yojiro clapped him on the shoulder. "What are you thinking about money for? You're the hero who saved Tokyo yesterday. You should be proud. Now, I've got to tidy up the loose ends. See you back at the office."

Yojiro walked out of the room. Behind his back, Ryo muttered, "But I'm not doing this because I wanted to be a hero!"

PART FOUR

SCOOP! TWENTY-FOUR HOURS
WITH THE MMD!

TEASER

> SERIES OF SHOTS—News footage of past kaiju disas-
> ters in Japan:
>
> A two-legged reptilian kaiju smashes through an
> elevated highway;
>
> A rampaging giant fish flips over fishing vessels in
> port;
>
> A four-legged reptilian kaiju bursts forth from a
> mountainside;
>
> A giant bird flies over an elementary school track
> meet, the gust of its wind trail sending children
> and parents into a panic;
>
> A colossal caterpillar leans atop a house, top-
> pling the building;
>
> A giant bull charges down from the distant moun-
> tains and through the fields, a fleeing news crew in
> the foreground.

An ENERGETIC, FAST-TALKING MALE NARRATOR speaks
over a HOLLYWOOD ACTION MOVIE THEME SONG.

>MALE NARRATOR
>Japan, the kaiju nation. Of the nearly two
>hundred kaiju attacks across the globe each
>year, five percent center on our country's
>lands, stealing lives and damaging our econ-
>omy. They could attack us at any moment. We
>live under constant threat of grave disaster.

A collapsed building on its side; a city in
flames; efforts to rescue people trapped beneath
the rubble; the fearful expression of an evacuee.

THEN—

Tanks shooting at a kaiju; battle helicopters
firing missiles; tracer rounds cutting through
the night sky, a kaiju their target.

>MALE NARRATOR (CONT'D)
>But there are those who stand against the
>destruction. They are constantly vigilant
>for indicators of a kaiju emergence, to give
>us precious time to prepare. They observe
>and analyze the creatures to devise counter-
>measures and prevent the worst. This group
>of professional kaiju exterminators is
>tasked with the crucial duty of safeguarding
>the lives of the public. They are the Japan
>Meteorological Agency's Monsterological
>Measures Department.
>(beat)
>They are the MMD.

QUICK CUTS of program highlights:

A little girl flings herself at SAKURA FUJISAWA, knocking the woman over.

> SAKURA
> (*laughing*)
> You're too heavy!

An operator speaks into his desk phone.

> OPERATOR B
> For your own safety, do not approach it.

CLOSE-UP on YOJIRO MUROMACHI seeing the kaiju for the first time.

> YOJIRO
> (*muttering*)
> Of all the places you could've shown up, it had to be here.

The mobile unit flees down a hill, hands over their ears.

A giant object is lying in the darkness of a damaged underground parking garage. Sakura gasps.

SHOICHI KURIHAMA stands with his back to a row of wall-mounted flatscreen displays (FX: the screens are PIXELIZED to prevent spoilers).

> KURIHAMA
> Kaiju Five will be known as Megadrake!

> MALE NARRATOR
> In order to combat a kaiju's threat, we first
> need to learn its nature. Over the next hour,
> we'll report on the front lines of kaiju
> research and reveal the latest shocking
> developments in monsterology.

YURI ANNO is seated with an array of bookshelves
and computers in the background.

> YURI
> (*with a wise expression*)
> Kaiju are, so to speak, beings from another
> dimension.

> MALE NARRATOR
> Our crew was on hand as the MMD rushed to
> the scene of a kaiju attack. An unexpected
> development threw our investigative team into
> danger—this kaiju possessed an astonishing
> power far beyond the MMD's expectations.

The glass windows on a multistory building all
burst simultaneously.

Shaky handheld footage looking down at the kaiju
rampaging through a park—its shape obscured with
PIXELIZATION.

A voice cries, "Run! Run!" The camera shakes
violently and points at the sky—the cameraman
has fallen over.

> RYO
> (*shouting*)
> You fool! Do you want to die?

Then a shrill, dreadful noise followed by a chorus of screams.

SDF soldiers, heavy machine guns in hand, dash down a stairwell.

> SAKURA
> How many floors are there in this place?

An explosion. The camera shudders.

> RYO
> (*pained*)
> Stop! Friendly fire!

A succession of sounds: breaking glass, screams, gunfire, explosions. The picture shakes so wildly as to be incomprehensible.

> MALE NARRATOR
> On tonight's "Tuesday Night Exclusive Report" our embedded team gets an unprecedented close look at the people who battle against kaiju disasters. As we follow their efforts and their daily lives, we sound the alarm against the kaiju menace facing our nation.

LOUD, HIGH-ENERGY MUSIC accompanies the TITLE:

> MALE NARRATOR (CONT'D)
> 24 Hours with the MMD: Protect Japan from the Kaiju Menace!

END OF TEASER

ACT ONE

EXT. JAPAN METEOROLOGICAL AGENCY HEADQUARTERS—DAY

Sakura arrives at the office by motorcycle. VOICE
OVER: a SLIGHTLY JOKEY FEMALE NARRATOR.

> FEMALE NARRATOR (O.C.)
> At 3 PM March 15th, a woman arrives at
> the Meteorological Agency Headquarters
> in Takebashi, Chiyoda Ward, Tokyo. Sakura
> Fujisawa, twenty-one. Three years ago, she
> took the third-class public service exam and
> entered the agency straight after graduating
> from high school. Each year, as few as five
> recruits are hired from all the candidates.
> But Sakura cleared the hurdle and was placed
> in the Monsterological Measures Department.

Sakura walks inside and greets her coworkers.

> FEMALE NARRATOR (CONT'D)
> She works in the Mobile Unit, the group on
> the front lines of the battle against the
> kaiju menace. When a kaiju appears, the
> Mobile Unit goes straight to the scene. They
> must always be prepared for an emergency—day
> and night, at least one team member is on
> standby inside the headquarters.

INT. MONSTEROLOGICAL MEASURES DEPARTMENT—LATE NIGHT

Nearly alone in the office, Sakura, sitting at her
desk, stares at her computer monitor.

FEMALE NARRATOR (CONT'D)
Today, Sakura is on the B-shift—night duty.
She arrives at 3:30 in the afternoon and
remains on watch until the next morning.
It's tough work—the shift lasts for eighteen
hours straight.

Sakura gazes intently at a graph on the monitor.

FEMALE NARRATOR (CONT'D)
Working at kaiju disaster sites enables
Sakura to develop expertise. But even when
there are no active kaiju, she doesn't rest.
To be prepared for the next incident, she
must spend long hours at study. Right now,
she is reviewing data of past kaiju appearances. To catch up with her more experienced
colleagues, she tirelessly continues her
research through the night. Her steady progress will prove useful in a time of need.

"I don't actually spend all night at that sort of thing," Sakura said, shaking her head. Nakakoshi, the pudgy, middle-aged director, had asked her to sit at her computer and let them film her studying.

"Okay," the director said. "What do you do?"

"Anything to pass the time. Late-night TV. I go through quite a lot of manga. And talk with anyone else on the night shift. Surf the net."

"That's no good," Nakakoshi said, clearly distraught. He spelled it out to the woman twenty years his junior. "If we show that on TV, the MMD's image will be even worse than it already is. People will think you're playing around on their tax money. This program's purpose is to turn your bad image around. Didn't somebody explain that to you?"

"The MMD really does have a bad image?"

"To be frank, yes." Nakakoshi put his hands on his hips and

looked down at her. "You make inaccurate predictions. Your responses are often in error and cause damages. A good number of people think you're useless."

"So it's true . . ."

"But I don't agree with them. I want our viewers to understand that you're heroes protecting the people. I want to show them the real MMD."

"Then shouldn't you show the real MMD as it is?"

"Are you saying you never sit at your computer late at night and study?"

"No, I do. It's just—"

"Then what's wrong with us airing it? Now, if we depicted you doing something you never did, that would be fake, but there's no lie in showing something you really do."

Between his look of total confidence and her own lack of experience with the television industry, she had no choice but to take him at his word. Besides, she didn't want her actions to reflect poorly on the entire department. Chief Kurihama had driven it into them in no uncertain terms: they were not to do anything embarrassing in front of the cameras.

She pulled up some relevant data on her screen and pretended to read it. A camera filmed her profile.

"Okay, we're going to get a close-up on your eyes," the director said. "I want your expression stern and serious."

Sakura tried her best to get her face to look stern and serious. The result, however, was something more akin to an awkward grimace, like she was looking at a spot-the-difference puzzle in a magazine and she just couldn't find the last one.

EXT. JOBAN EXPRESSWAY—DAY

Sakura rides her motorcycle down the highway.

FEMALE NARRATOR
Whoever works the late shift gets the next

day off. Sakura is headed for a meteorological research center in Tsukuba City, Ibaraki
Prefecture, to meet someone.

EXT. METEOROLOGICAL RESEARCH INSTITUTE—DAY

A tall steel pylon stands, painted in alternating
stripes of red and white.

> FEMALE NARRATOR (CONT'D)
> The Meteorological Agency's R&D department
> is located here. The spacious grounds
> of the facility house the latest in re-
> search equipment for studying not only
> weather prediction, but the mechanisms of
> earthquakes, tsunami, typhoons, volcanic
> eruptions, and kaiju. One crucial area of
> current research is the ecology of kaiju.

INT. KAIJU CARETAKING FACILITY ROOM—DAY

DR. NAKAYA, a researcher at the kaiju caretaking
facility, and a twelve-year-old girl are playing
with wooden building blocks. The girl is wearing
pajamas and has a leather belt around her neck. The
researcher builds a structure from the blocks, and
the girl knocks it down and raises a gleeful cry.

> FEMALE NARRATOR (CONT'D)
> Some of our viewers may recognize this girl.
> She's Kaiju Six, Princess, from Gifu last
> September. Despite her adorable appearance,
> she is a kaiju. Without that collar, she
> transforms into a giant. Although it's a

little sad that she's forced to constantly
wear such a thing, there's no other choice.

Sakura opens the door and enters the room.

> SAKURA
> Princess! How are you?

Princess makes a cheerful noise and throws herself
at Sakura—who is knocked over by the girl.

> SAKURA (CONT'D)
> (*Laughing*)
> You're too heavy!

"No, really! She's really too heavy!"

Sakura was smiling through the pain. Princess straddled her stomach and let out a merry "*Gyau, gyau.*" The girl bounced up and down like she was riding a rodeo horse.

"Stop laughing and help me already!"

Dr. Nakaya, still laughing, took hold of Princess's arm and pulled the girl off. One of the film crew helped Sakura to her feet.

"I thought I'd die," Sakura said, wheezing. "Has she gained some weight?"

"Seven kilos in the past six months," the researcher said. "She was 140 centimeters tall when she first came here, and now she's at 150."

The crewmember said, "Isn't that really fast?"

Nakaya said, "Four times faster than a typical child. She looks like she's around twelve years old, but we think she was only born three years ago."

Princess noticed the camera with interest and jumped at the cameraman, trying to pry it from his hands. She probably thought it was a new toy. The camera operator ran in frantic circles to keep away from the girl.

The researcher, observing this with a grin, said, "She's managed to learn how to wear clothes and use the toilet, but language seems to be impossible. I believe her intelligence to be on par with a chimpanzee's."

With conflicted emotions, Sakura watched the cheerful child. Softly, she said, "So she isn't human after all."

When it had looked as though Princess was about to be killed, Sakura had risked her own life to protect the girl. At the time, she believed her actions correct. But now that she knew the child was another species and only appeared human, she wasn't so sure.

Did I only want to save the creature because she happened to resemble a human? How's that for being selfish? What about kaiju that don't look human? Saving the ones that look human and turning my back on the grotesque ones—isn't that just some kind of discrimination?

What if, by some chance, she turns giant again? She's grown since then, so she'll already be over MM5. And since she's been designated a kaiju, she'll probably be killed before she has a chance to cause destruction.

Ryo had once declared that nature was the enemy. To the employees of the Meteorological Agency, natural calamities were sworn adversaries in a battle that left no room for personal feelings.

But to Sakura, it wasn't that cut and dried.

Princess clung to the director's pant leg, blissfully unaware of the young woman's internal conflict.

Princess capers around the research room.

    MALE NARRATOR
    Researchers are stumped by Princess's ability
    to change her size at will.

1950s AMERICAN NEWS REEL FOOTAGE of giant monsters:

U.S. Army soldiers armed with flamethrowers face
off against an ant living in the sewers;

A tarantula swaggers across the desert;

An octopus wraps its tentacles around the suspension cables of the Golden Gate Bridge;

A praying mantis clings to the side of a New York City skyscraper.

> MALE NARRATOR (CONT'D)
> Organisms can transform into giants and become kaiju. Until the middle of the twentieth century, this phenomenon was thought to be the result of extraordinarily rapid cellular division. But growth requires a supply of nutrients, and in a great number of cases, the transformation occurs without an increased intake of food. And some kaiju, like Princess, can change size at will—an event which, under the modern study of physics, is a violation of the law of conservation of mass.

CAPTION: The Law of Conservation of Mass

> MALE NARRATOR (CONT'D)
> The law states an object's mass remains constant over time.

ILLUSTRATION: A drawing of a lizard. We zoom in to reveal it's a pointillist construction of many tiny dots.

> MALE NARRATOR (CONT'D)
> All matter is composed of atoms. If this lizard were to suddenly grow into a giant, what would happen?

As the drawing expands, the white space between
the dots increases.

>MALE NARRATOR (CONT'D)
>The space between the atoms grows larger, and
>the lizard becomes less dense. Because the
>number of atoms doesn't increase, its mass
>should remain the same. Kaiju, however, do
>not have reduced density. To the contrary,
>their mass increases in proportion with their
>volume. Where, then, does the extra mass come
>from?

INT. MMD HEADQUARTERS STUDY ROOM—DAY

YURI ANNO is reading from a THICK ACADEMIC BOOK.

>MALE NARRATOR (CONT'D)
>Ms. Yuri Anno is a physicist with the MMD. Her
>job is to uncover the nature of kaiju from an
>astrophysical standpoint. Yuri believes their
>existence can be explained by the parallel
>anthropic principle. Let's hear her explain.

Yuri was nervous.

During her time as an associate professor at the Meteorological College, she often talked in front of classrooms filled with students, and she presented theses at academic conferences. But this would be her first time in front of a camera.

She tried to tell herself, *You don't need to worry. This isn't much different from talking to your students. Just be yourself.*

But how could she not worry—she'd be watched by millions of viewers all across the country. That morning, she put on her makeup with far greater care than normal, and she wore the nice outfit she usually reserved for parent observation days at her son's school. She'd run through the questions and answers in her head. Yuri went into the interview as well prepared as she possibly could be.

But when the director came, crew in tow, he took one glance at Yuri, gave her a dissatisfied look, and said something she hadn't anticipated. "Don't you wear a lab coat?"

She didn't know how to respond. "Ah, not at work, no."

"That may be the case, but typical viewers have certain expectations, don't they? Like 'scientists wear lab coats.' If you're not wearing one, you don't look like a scientist. It'll seem unnatural. It's a symbol of authority."

"What?"

"It's even more necessary for you, Ms. Anno. You don't seem at all like a scientist. You're much better looking."

The flattery did a little to sway her. Yuri found herself thinking, *Maybe it wouldn't hurt to be nice and try to match the typical viewer's image of a scientist.* But then she considered the inevitable jests from her peers if she showed up on TV in a lab coat. She hesitated.

The young cameraman said, "I think you'd look good in white." Then, with a vulgar laugh, "You know, there's a lot of guys out there who have a thing for women in lab coats. The same kind of men who are into nurses. You'll have fans, I can tell."

That settled it. She wasn't about to indulge any strange fetishes.

"I'm sorry, but this is what I'm wearing."

Nakakoshi looked disappointed. "Oh. Well, there's more to the typical image of a scientist than clothing. We could film you doing work instead—flipping through some complex-looking book, typing at a computer."

Yuri thought she could at least do that much for the program. She agreed.

They chose the MMD study room for the location, since it would lend things like computers and books to the background. Inside, the lighting technician unfolded something that looked like an umbrella with its interior painted silver. He put a light in the center of it, affixed it to the top of a stand, and aimed the lamp at Yuri. Then he put a meter to her face to measure the brightness. The process only made Yuri more nervous.

At Nakakoshi's cue, the camera started recording.

Hesitantly, Yuri began to speak. "The anthropic principle was first proposed in 1961 by an American physicist named Robert Dicke. He had his sights on the large numbers hypothesis raised by Eddington. Large numbers, in this context, refers to a dimensionless number—that is to say, a number without units—reached by combining various fundamental constants of physics. Those large numbers would typically be close to ten to the fortieth power, or ten to the eightieth power."

Now that she was speaking about her field of expertise, Yuri began to relax. She spoke easily and fluidly, explaining the history of the anthropic principle, from Dicke's weak anthropic principle and Carter's strong anthropic principle to Collins's and Hawking's theories regarding the flatness problem, and including the mathematical universe hypothesis. She even touched upon the issue of observation with regard to quantum mechanics.

While Yuri had grown relaxed, Nakakoshi watched with an ever-worsening scowl. Finally, he stopped her mid-sentence.

"I'm sorry, Ms. Anno. That's just too complex for our viewers."

"Oh, I'm sorry." She felt ashamed she let herself get carried away.

"Could you leave out the parts about weak and strong and explain it in simple terms? Tell us what the anthropic principle is in one sentence. Short and snappy."

"Snappy? In one sentence?"

"Yes. Snappy."

Yuri's self-doubt returned. How could she explain in a single, short sentence the most advanced theories of modern physics to an uneducated audience? As she sat there confronting the problem, Nakakoshi threw her a lifeline.

"How about something like, the anthropic principle is the theory that our universe exists because people exist in it."

"Well, that's not quite accurate."

"You don't need to be overly concerned about the accuracy. The most important thing is for our viewers to understand the basic picture."

After a little more internal debate, she decided to compromise. After all, this wasn't a scientific conference—there were bound to be areas where the accuracy would be lacking.

The camera resumed recording, and Yuri took another try.

"The anthropic principle, put simply, is the concept that our universe only exists because people perceive it. Why is space three-dimensional? Why does light travel at three hundred thousand kilometers per second? Why are there electrons, protons, and neutrons? If the laws of physics were different, our universe would take an entirely different form, and there would be no Earth. And without an Earth, of course, there'd be no people. Without us here to observe our universe, it wouldn't exist. To put it another way, the simple fact that humans do exist here and now determines the laws of physics and the state of our universe throughout the history of the cosmos. A universe that doesn't allow for the existence of humans isn't itself allowed to exist."

The director told her it was still too complicated and asked her to try rephrasing it. Only after several more tries did she get the okay. Next, she attempted to explain the parallel anthropic principle.

"In 1983, an English physicist named Asprin proposed a theory further developing the anthropic principle. According to him, there was not just one universe capable of supporting human existence. He believed it possible for there to be another universe with different laws of physics from those as discovered by physicists in our Big Bang universe. Kaiju don't obey our laws of physics because they are following the laws of a universe different from our own—one which Asprin called the mythic universe. That's mythic universe, not Miss Universe."

"We can put up a caption there," the director said. "Can you explain the mythic universe with an example? Something easy to understand."

Yuri took a moment to think, then said, "Think of two numbers that result in twenty when multiplied. Say, four times five. But you could also come up with two times ten. Meaning, there's more than one way to multiply numbers together and result in a twenty. The universe is the same way. If you take human existence as the result, the history of our cosmos is the multiplication process. One set of factors leading to our existence is the Big Bang universe. But the mythic universe would also allow for people to live in it. The result is the same, so you can't say that one set of factors is correct and the other wrong. Either works. Therefore, the universe would have two histories."

"That's good." Nakakoshi nodded. "That's the perfect level for our audience. Please continue."

But even after that, whenever Yuri explained something, he either asked her to rephrase it, suggested a possible summary, or advised her on what to say. As they played catch with her words, she gradually lost the feeling she was expressing her own thoughts. She felt like she was just following a script as the director had decided it.

Yet still she endeavored on, believing it her duty to explain the parallel anthropic principle to the common man:

Asprin had been inspired by the theories of Julian Jaynes, a psychology lecturer at Princeton University. Through his studies of ancient texts like Homer's epics, he proposed that up until three thousand years ago, humans did not possess consciousness. Although the peoples of that time had civilization, they lacked the concept of the self. Like present-day schizophrenics, they interpreted their thoughts not as their own, but as the voice of an unseeable third party—namely, a daemon—and, like marionettes, acted by the voices' commands.

One might also say that without the human consciousness to understand the universe, the universe didn't yet truly exist. Looking back from today, the world of that time wasn't real but rather a form of fiction. The Big Bang and mythic universes could coexist without contradicting each other. The world of three thousand years ago was rougher, less exact, and the laws of physics of the mythic universe likely held a powerful sway. The result was a reality that would have tolerated the existence of magic and legendary beings—as evidenced in ancient texts.

But as the human consciousness awakened, the two universes became unstable. Eventually, the mythic universe became less prominent, and reality began to converge on the Big Bang universe in a phenomenon known as the paradigm shift. As the human race stopped hearing the voices of the gods, the old gods, those fairies and yokai, became unrecognized. They were forgotten, and then vanished.

In their stead, people shifted their beliefs to the transcendent beings, dwelling high up in the heavens, of faiths like Christianity and Islam. Unlike the gods of old, these deities no longer took on flesh forms and descended to Earth. They posed no inconsistencies with the Big Bang universe, while the bygone gods, with their corporeal vessels, were unable to survive the trends of history.

The once thriving supernatural beings had nearly become extinct—but kaiju were the exception. They weren't small and powerless like the yokai. By bringing about extensive destruction, the monsters fueled the fears of humanity—and caused humanity to acknowledge the existence of the monsters. And so they didn't die off like the yokai. Kaiju remained governed by the laws of the mythic universe. As long as people recognized the existence of kaiju, the mythic universe would continue to be. The paradigm shift wasn't yet complete.

Through one rejection after another, Yuri was somehow able to convey that much. More than ninety minutes had passed since the start of the filming, and mental exhaustion had set in. But all that was left was the closing summary. She had to try.

"Twenty-five hundred years ago, Democritus proposed that all matter was made of atoms. Three thousand years ago, the concept of atoms didn't exist. Because atoms only exist within the framework of the Big Bang universe, it's plausible that in the mythic universe, there were no atoms. If that's true, then of course kaiju don't behave according to the law of preservation of mass—it's likely their bodies aren't made of atoms at all."

"Could you simplify that?"

Another of Nakakoshi's impossible requests. After considerable effort, she came up with this:

"Newspaper articles sometimes include photographs, right? They're printed on the page in a cluster of small dots. Even the places that look gray are really an array of black dots. When you magnify the picture, the space between the dots grows. Compare that with gray paint applied to a canvas. If you were to magnify the paint, the gray would still be gray. Both grays appear to be the same, but they really have two different compositions. That's why kaiju, not made of atoms, don't lose density when they turn giant."

"We could pop in a graphic there to help explain," the director said. "But why has nobody realized any of this until now? I'm sure there've been plenty of analyses performed on kaiju remains."

"As soon as we attempt to analyze their tissues, they convert into matter typically found in the Big Bang universe. Because atoms aren't visible to the naked eye, we can't tell the difference between Big Bang matter and mythic matter. But with electron microscopes and X-rays and the like, we can observe the atoms. To put it a better way, those machines *cannot* observe matter *not* constituted of atoms. The act of observation itself converts the mythic matter into Big Bang matter. That's why analyzing kaiju tissue doesn't tell us anything."

"That's an astonishing notion."

"Yes, it is. At first, the physicist community didn't support it. But as long as kaiju can't be explained within the laws of the Big Bang universe, we have to acknowledge the existence of another set of physical laws. Because of this, in recent years, the parallel anthropic principle has gained currency within academic circles and is trending toward acceptance."

Finally at the end of her impromptu lecture, Yuri was relieved. But Nakakoshi wanted more.

"Could you sum up that conclusion in one short, snappy sentence?"

Left without enough energy to think of something *snappy*, Yuri feebly asked, "What should I say?"

"How about: kaiju are beings from another dimension."

That wasn't true at all, and Yuri didn't like the idea of something so unscientific coming out of her mouth. But neither did she want to prolong her punishment. Giving up, she repeated the words with a minor adjustment.

"Kaiju are, so to speak, beings from another dimension."

With the lack of enthusiasm, she ended up intoning it more than speaking it, her voice flat and stiff. *How would the viewers see it?*

"Okay," Nakakoshi said, "That'll do."

Yuri released a tired sigh.

Days later, she would watch the program and be astonished at how her extensive talk was edited down to under a minute of air time.

Yojiro ran across Kurihama in the men's restroom, where the chief was straightening his necktie in the mirror.

"This is stifling," the chief said.

As he did his business, Yojiro laughed and said, "Why don't you just take it off?"

The head of the Mobile Unit, at heart an outdoorsman, usually got by without having to wear a tie.

"It's a matter of protocol. Anyway, that's not what I was talking about."

"I know. You mean the TV crew."

"Yeah."

Kurihama had started to regret allowing them to come film. The show's title said twenty-four hours, but the shoot was already on its fourth day. The crew was split into two units. The first unit, a full crew under the director, followed individual members of the MMD through their daily routine. The second unit, consisting only of its own director and a camera operator, reported the activities inside the office.

Not that calling them activities should imply they'd be interesting on TV: monitoring for signs of subterranean kaiju through the EPOS (Earthquake Phenomena Observation System), analyzing data from recent kaiju events, studying kaiju in ancient texts, exchanging information with countermeasure agencies in other countries, and so on. The operators also fielded calls including a well-meaning (but really just bothersome) report from a concerned citizen who'd seen a cloud that looked like a kaiju over Tokyo Bay, which surely heralded the appearance of a great kaiju in Eastern Japan; and an inquiry from a man who'd found a strange organism in his backyard and wondered if it was a kaiju's offspring—usually those were some type of slime mold or a hammerhead worm. Nothing out of the ordinary.

Still, under the constant observation of the two outsiders and their TV camera, the team felt uneasy. They had to keep up a tidy appearance and take care not to make any of their usual crass kaiju jokes. A collected, relaxed man like Yojiro could handle it, but for the nervous chief, it was a punishment beyond reckoning.

"Their crew's getting restless too," Yojiro said. "I overheard some of them grumbling about wanting a kaiju to go ahead and show up already."

"I'd rather one didn't."

With each kaiju, the specter of human casualties gave Kurihama enough worry. But this time, the chief couldn't help but speculate what would happen if their failure was broadcast to the entire nation. It was enough to make his stomach hurt.

As he washed his hands, Yojiro said, "There's been four this year so far, and it's not even March yet. They've been more frequent than last year. I wouldn't be surprised if we had the fifth any day now."

"Don't be so unscientific. Each kaiju appearance is unrelated to the last. There's bound to be a few in a row sometimes—it's just statistics," Kurihama said.

"I know that. But then Murphy's Law has its way of often being correct. Whatever can go wrong, will."

"I hate that law."

The two men exited the restroom together. As they neared the door to the main office, they heard a commotion from inside.

"What is it?" Kurihama asked with a look of concern.

"You know what they say." Yojiro broke into a fearless grin. "Speak of the devil."

```
INT. MMD HEADQUARTERS OFFICE—DAY


The office suddenly bursts into action.
(SUSPENSEFUL MUSIC)


          MALE NARRATOR (O.C.)
          Then, suddenly, in the middle of our report,
          calls begin pouring in with word of a kaiju!


Amidst the activity, we see OPERATORS receive
calls from civilians and police.


          OPERATOR A
          You're calling from your cell phone? And
          that's what you took the picture with? All
          right, could you email the picture to the
          Meteorological Agency's address? I'll read
          you the address . . .


          OPERATOR B
          Please don't approach it.
          (beat)
          Yes, even if it's not moving, it still may
```

be dangerous. For your own safety, do not
approach it. And whatever you do, don't do
anything that might startle it.

OPERATOR C
Yes, cordon off the area and evacuate all
civilians in a five-hundred-meter radius, at
least until we know more.
(beat)
Right, just as a precaution. We still don't
know how dangerous it is.

INSERT: FOOTAGE of a plane taking off from a runway.

MALE NARRATOR
The kaiju appeared in Suita, Osaka
Prefecture—right in the center of the urban
sprawl. The MMD doesn't yet know the size or
nature of the creature. They only know that
if they are slow to respond, there could be
dire consequences. The Mobile Unit is sent
to the scene at once.

INT. ITAMI AIRPORT ARRIVAL GATE—DAY

The members of the Mobile Unit exit the arrival gate.

MALE NARRATOR (CONT'D)
15:05. An hour and forty minutes after the
initial report, ANA Flight 27 touches down
at Itami Airport with the four members of
the Mobile Unit on board. Outside the terminal, a car from the Osaka branch is on hand
to rush them to the scene.

EXT. ITAMI AIRPORT—DAY

SAKURA carries a heavy-looking trunk through the
sliding side door of a waiting minibus. We hear
the director ask if she's all right, and she
smiles and says she's used to it.

EXT. MINIBUS—DAY

Establishing shot as the car drives south down
Highway 175.

INT. MINIBUS—DAY

The four members of the Mobile Unit crowd around
a map.

> MALE NARRATOR (CONT'D)
> Kaiju Five is in a park near Esaka Station
> on the Midosuji subway line. Reports say it's
> a five-meter-tall plant-form kaiju. Because
> botanical kaiju move very slowly—or not at
> all—they are easier to counteract. But that
> doesn't permit recklessness. Plant-form kaiju
> are rarer than animal ones, with a compara-
> tively smaller pool of historical data to
> work from. Previous strategies may not work.
> Tension tightens the team's expressions.

EXT. ESAKA PARK—DAY

The minibus pulls up to the park. The four step
out of the vehicle and greet the police officers
keeping the area sealed off.

MALE NARRATOR (CONT'D)
Then, just as the Mobile Unit arrives on
location—

Kiiiiin! A SHRILL NOISE. The four cover their ears
and crouch. The camera shakes.

MALE NARRATOR (CONT'D)
A terrible ear-splitting sound—the kaiju's
cry.

The camera tilts up. We see a TV helicopter in the
sky. Then—another *Kiiiiin!*

MALE NARRATOR (CONT'D)
It might be responding to the sound of the
helicopter.

Cut to TWO SHOT, policemen looking straight at the
camera, interview-style.

POLICEMAN A
It's been doing this for the past hour. That
kiin sound, once every few minutes.

POLICEMAN B
It just rings right through your skull. I'm
getting a headache.

MALE NARRATOR
But how are the locals being affected?

EXT. SHOPPING DISTRICT STREET—DAY

We're now over five hundred meters away from the park, with a MEDIUM SHOT, interview-style, of a florist.

> FLORIST
> Yeah, it's a lot of trouble, all right.
> (takes a flower from the display)
> Too bad that thing isn't just one of these harmless little fellas.

The camera PANS to reveal the empty street lined with shuttered storefronts.

> MALE NARRATOR
> Classes were canceled at a nearby elemen-tary school, and the businesses are closed. Thousands of residents have evacuated their homes. The Midosuji subway line is shut down and the highway blocked off. Even though the kaiju hasn't yet acted, it has already inflicted economic damage throughout the surrounding area.

EXT. ESAKA PARK—DAY

The Mobile Unit makes their preparations at the edge of the park.

> MALE NARRATOR (CONT'D)
> The Mobile Unit is about to approach the kaiju to observe it. To protect themselves against the noise, they put in earplugs.

A gentle, man-made slope, with a row of trees along each side, leads up into the park. The

Mobile team begins to walk up the smooth incline.
The camera follows after them.

> MALE NARRATOR (CONT'D)
> Because plants don't have sight, the kaiju
> is believed to sense danger through the
> vibration of sound waves. Careful not to
> make any sound, the Mobile Unit slowly
> approaches the kaiju's location. But there,
> in a place where merry, bustling crowds come
> together for springtime flower viewing—

We can see something behind the trees—but obscured
with PIXELIZATION.

> MALE NARRATOR (CONT'D)
> There it is!

END OF ACT ONE

COMMERCIAL BREAK

ACT TWO

After the commercial, we RECAP:

> MALE NARRATOR (CONT'D)
> Inside a park in Suita, Osaka, a kaiju has
> appeared. The Monsterological Measures
> Department's Mobile Unit is investigating
> on-site. Careful not to make any sound, they
> slowly approach the kaiju's location. But
> there, in a place where merry, bustling crowds
> come together for springtime flower viewing—

We can see something behind the trees.

> MALE NARRATOR (CONT'D)
> There it is!

There it is, Sakura thought to herself. The four stopped and nervously looked ahead.

The kaiju had burst through the concrete of a winding, tree-lined path. It was an odd-looking plant, a yellow-green rugby ball as tall as three men—just slightly shorter than the surrounding trees—with rigid, jagged-edged leaves wrapped around its center like furled wings.

They were fifty meters from the kaiju. Asaya carefully set his tripod on the ground, mounted the camera, and adjusted the zoom. The camera transmitted a live stream to headquarters.

Asaya had worked quietly, but something spooked the kaiju. It let out another cry. *Kiiiin!*

The four covered their ears with their hands. At this close distance, the earplugs couldn't keep the sound from sending waves of pain through their heads. Abandoning the camera, they ran back down the hill.

> MALE NARRATOR (CONT'D)
> The kaiju's terrible sound left the Mobile
> Unit no choice but to withdraw. Yojiro
> Muromachi, the leader of the team, had this
> to say.

Yojiro is back in relative safety at the edge of the park.

> YOJIRO
> It looks to be a variant of a mandrake. I
> suspected as much.

CAPTION: MANDRAKE.

ILLUSTRATION: A fifteenth century drawing of a man with leaves growing out of his head.

>   MALE NARRATOR (O.C.)
>   Mandrake. A perennial flowering plant
>   belonging to the potato family. Believing
>   its roots to contain mystical medicinal
>   powers, Europeans in the Middle Ages used it
>   in magic rituals.
>
>   In incredibly rare cases, mandrakes have
>   been known to be mobile and to emit powerful
>   screams when faced with danger—two charac-
>   teristics not commonly associated with plant
>   life. Some believe that mandrake were once
>   a species of kaiju, now devolved into their
>   current state. If that were the case, the
>   giant mandrake in the park may have been a
>   case of atavism, an evolutionary throwback.
>   The park's caretakers, however, insist they
>   never planted a mandrake in the park. Someone
>   must have smuggled it onto the grounds and
>   planted it without permission.

EXT. ESAKA PARK—NIGHT

CAPTION: Reenactment

Three high school-aged girls plant something in the park.

MALE NARRATOR (CONT'D)
In the days following the incident, the Suita
police department, pursuing a lead from an
eyewitness testimony, apprehended three local
seventeen-year-old girls. The police investigation found that the girls purchased the
mandrake root illegally, over the Internet,
and performed a black magic ritual inside the
park. The various spell reagents used in the
ritual, when combined together, caused the
mandrake to grow into a kaiju.

Kaiju transformation is often caused by
radiation or chemical compounds, but the results are not consistent—even by recreating
the same set of circumstances, kaiju effects
are often impossible to reproduce. The
girls hadn't intended to create a kaiju—
they were attempting to put a death curse
on someone they didn't like. But when they
learned from the police the unanticipated
outcome of their dark ritual, it must have
been a terrible fright. Since they had no
way of knowing their act would cause the
creation of a kaiju, their lawful punishment
will not be severe.

Yojiro stood at the park entrance, facing in the direction of the
kaiju. He clucked his tongue and said, "Of all the places you could've
shown up, it had to be here."

Nakakoshi asked, "What's the trouble with here?"

"Usually, we torch giant plants with a flamethrower, but with
that noise, we can't get close enough. That means we need to shoot
it from a distance, but—" He gestured to the row of trees obscuring

the kaiju from view. "—the trees are blocking line of sight, which limits where we can fire from. And all around us are homes and offices. We can't shoot willy-nilly. There's too much risk a stray shot may do serious harm."

Ryo pointed to a glass-paneled office building, home to a life insurance company, across the street from the western edge of the park. "How about the top of that building. It has a clear line-of-fire, and any missed shots would only hit the ground. I think it could work."

"You may be right." Yojiro nodded. "It's a little far, and we'd need the owner's permission, but keeping safety in mind, it could be our only option."

With disappointment in his voice, Nakakoshi said, "This one didn't really turn out that big, did it?"

The TV crew's only footage was long distance, taken from dozens of meters behind the Mobile Unit's line, and the kaiju was only five meters tall—about as high as a second-story window. On a home TV screen, it would read surprisingly small.

"What is it," the director asked, "an MM two or three, at best?"

"We haven't determined that yet," Yojiro said. "We won't know until we've seen the extent of its root system."

Sakura, who had gone looking around the edge of the park, came running up.

"There's an underground parking garage right beneath the kaiju," she said. "Well, it's not quite underground exactly—more like they built a parking lot on top of a parking lot and laid down the dirt for the park on top of that. You can get inside there."

A library sat in the center of the park. Sakura pointed to a garage entrance beside the building.

"We should take a look," Yojiro said. "But I'm not sure we could withstand that sound underground, in close quarters."

The rest of the team agreed. They were also facing another problem—the earplugs they wore made it difficult to communicate with one another.

Yojiro thought for a moment. "Maybe we can ask the SDF for helicopter helmets and bone-conductive microphones."

Bone conduction microphones, used in locations with high background noise, picked up vibrations from inside the cranium and were mostly unaffected by sounds in the air.

Asaya spoke up. "The larger electronics stores have started to carry bone-conductive microphones. For cell phones. I could rig something up with some headphones."

"Go find us some. I'll make sure you're reimbursed."

"Yes, sir."

INT. MMD HEADQUARTERS—DAY

A live video feed streams to a large wall-mounted flatscreen. Other flatpanels along the wall display related data: maps around the park and information on mandrakes.

        MALE NARRATOR (O.C.)
        Reports from the scene reveal Kaiju Five is
        a mutated mandrake. Once the nature of a
        kaiju is determined, it's given an official
        name, which is then reported to the media.
        That authority falls to the head of the
        department, Chief Kurihama.

Kurihama stands at the front of the room.

        KURIHAMA
        Kaiju Five will be known as Megadrake!

"I'm sorry," the second unit director said, "could you say that again for us?"

"What?"

"Your pronunciation was a little muddy. We'll be putting up a caption of the kaiju's name, but this part should be snappy. So if you could, 'Kaiju Five will be known as Megadrake!'"

"You want me to say that?"

"Please."

Kurihama lowered his head and repeated it to himself. *Known as Megadrake known as Megadrake known as Megadrake.*

"Okay Mr. Kurihama, you're on in five, four, three . . ."

The director silently signaled two, one, go.

Obediently, Kurihama raised his voice and announced, "Kaiju Five will be known as Megadrake!"

"Okay, that's good."

EXT. ESAKA PARK

The four members of the Mobile Unit put on their headphones and adjust their microphones.

    MALE NARRATOR (O.C.)
    The Mobile Unit is going underground to determine the extent of Megadrake's root system. They protect themselves from its noise with headphones and specialized microphones. Our crew was not allowed to accompany them, but Sakura agreed to carry in one of our cameras.

Sakura, pro-level video camera on her shoulder, offers an energetic wave.

    SAKURA
    Well, here I go!

What Sakura saw made her gasp.

She quickly drew her hand to her mouth. She'd only let out a small sound—with luck, the kaiju hadn't heard.

The parking garage was almost completely in ruins. Dozens of giant roots thrust themselves down through the concrete ceiling. In color and shape, they resembled sweet potatoes, but these were over a meter thick and many times longer. The roots had scattered the rows of parked cars and cut across the lanes. Some even reached all the way to the library building. The ceiling pipes for the water sprinklers had burst open here and there, and large amounts of water spewed out. One section of the roots had pierced through the floor and extended into the lower lot. Asaya and Sakura, each with their cameras, recorded the scene.

Yojiro decided that with the noise of the spraying water, he could get away with talking quietly. "HQ, do you see this?"

His headphones and bone conduction microphone connected to a pocket transmitter.

Kurihama's nervous voice came over the line. "Yes, I see it."

"This guy's quite a lot bigger underground than above."

"Can you tell how big?"

"This is just a visual estimate, but I'd say the roots are twenty times bigger than what's on the surface. An MM6. I'm sure of it."

Yojiro didn't need to hear the chief's gulp to sense it. It was a natural reaction. They'd thought they were up against an MM3, but this was well over an order of magnitude larger.

Just then, the floor shuddered, as if an earthquake had just begun. The four froze. The cluster of giant roots wriggled as if turning in their sleep. Shards of concrete fell from the cracked ceiling.

Yojiro shouted, "It's still growing!"

Kiiiiin! The kaiju's cacophony rang through the garage. The sound came from above the ground but had made it all the way there. Even through the headphones, the noise sent stabbing pain through their eardrums.

"This is too much!" Yojiro yelled. "We can't take any more of this! We're getting out of here!"

EXT. ESAKA PARK—SUNSET

The SDF arrives on the scene with soldiers carrying recoilless rifles, heavy machine guns, flame
throwers, and assault rifles.

> MALE NARRATOR (O.C.)
> 17:30—over four hours since the kaiju was
> first spotted. As the sun begins to set,
> preparations continue for the SDF's assault.
> Megadrake is still growing, and its height
> reaches more than seven meters above ground.
> Is this transformation a violation of the law
> of preservation of mass—and is the parallel
> anthropic principle right?

We see the top of Megadrake poking out above the
tree line.

At the edge of the park, Yojiro stands in front of
a map, explaining the battle plan to the commanding officer.

> MALE NARRATOR (CONT'D)
> The kaiju must be dealt with as quickly as
> possible. Yojiro, the leader of the Mobile
> Unit, suggests a plan of attack.

> YOJIRO
> The sound is coming from the aboveground
> parts of the plant, so we need to take out
> the upper portion first. In order to mini-
> mize collateral damage, a ranged attack from
> the top of the west building would be best.

We've already obtained permission to use the building.

OFFICER
What about the roots?

YOJIRO
I see only one option—methodically torch them with flamethrowers and dig them out with a bulldozer.

MALE NARRATOR
Muromachi explains the plan in detail. Their biggest fear is the possibility the plant could be mobile. Pain from the attack could trigger Megadrake to pull up its roots and go on the move. It's a perilous gamble. But the kaiju continues to stir—a sign that Megadrake is already about to pull up its roots. A failure to act now could mean disastrous consequences. They have to make a preemptive strike.

GRAPHIC: A map of the park. A red circle in the center of the map represents Megadrake. Three blue arrows surround it.

MALE NARRATOR (CONT'D)
As a precautionary measure, the SDF forces are split into three groups: one on top of the life insurance building to the west and the other two at the northeast and south-east corners of the park. Because surrounding Megadrake on all sides could result in

```
friendly fire, the soldiers are deployed in
three points of a triangle.
```

```
The commanding officer finishes giving orders to his
troops and turns to Yojiro.
```

```
        OFFICER
        We'll be ready within ten minutes. We'll
        commence the attack without delay.
```

```
        YOJIRO
        (bowing his head)
        Thank you.
```

As the soldiers broke to move into position, Nakakoshi clapped Yojiro on the shoulder.

"That was good, Muromachi. Snappy. You delivered it home."

"Yeah?"

He didn't know what exactly it was that he supposedly had delivered. He had only behaved how he always did.

Cheerily, the director said, "All that's left is to exterminate that kaiju. It'll be a great climax for our show."

Yojiro couldn't make himself be that optimistic. "Only as long as everything goes well."

"Is there something worrying you?"

"No, nothing in particular. Just that damned Murphy's Law."

```
        MALE NARRATOR (O.C.)
        The "Tuesday Night Exclusive Report" news
        team obtains special permission to accompany
        the SDF forces onto the rooftop. Ryo Haida
        and Sakura Fujisawa, with the MMD, are on
        hand to observe the operation through until
        the kaiju is destroyed. The head of the
```

MM9

Mobile Unit, Yojiro Muromachi, watches from
the roof of a music college to the east,
ready to respond with a new plan should
anything unexpected occur.

Along with twenty SDF soldiers, Ryo, Sakura, Nakakoshi, and his TV crew crossed the street at the west edge of the park and entered the office building.

"Wow," Sakura said, "this is a swanky place."

A three-story-high atrium wrapped around all four sides of the interior. With glass walls and abundant foliage, the space was more a greenhouse than a lobby. Stairs led up to a second-floor café likely popular with office workers at lunchtime. A large marble-paneled column pierced through the center of the open space—inside would be the elevators. A sky bridge cut across the building, east to west, at the second floor level. To the west was Esaka Station; to the right, the park.

But there wasn't time to stop and admire the surroundings. Chief Kurihama's unsteady voice came over the wireless.

"Ryo, can you hear me?"

"Yes, sir. What is it?"

"The camera you left behind is shaking! Megadrake must be moving. Oh! The camera just fell over."

Ryo shouted to the commanding officer. "It's started to move! We have to hurry!"

They split up to ride the elevators to the top floor and took the stairway to the roof. The sun was setting in the west. Around the edge of the building ran a set of rails for the crane-operated mobile window-washing scaffold. The group hurried across the tracks to stand at the east edge of the roof.

They had a good view of Megadrake. The creature was roughly one hundred twenty meters away. Large cracks in the earth radiated out from the creature. It was pulling its roots up from the ground to crawl along the surface. Even at that distance, they could hear the terrific noise of crumbling concrete.

The officer called out, "Ready!" and the soldiers formed a single line along the edge of the roof. The soldiers were split into two groups: two-man teams with Carl Gustav recoilless rifles and gunners armed with .50 caliber 12.7mm heavy machine guns. The Gustav shooters raised the weapons to their shoulders, and each of the loaders fitted a 84mm caliber shell into the breech and tapped his partner on the helmet to signify the weapon was ready. The machine gunners rested the attached bipods of their guns on the handrail. All of the soldiers wore sound-dampening helmets and received orders via bone conduction microphones.

Ryo turned to the TV crew and shouted, "You're in the way! Don't stand behind them!"

When fired, Carl Gustavs propelled an incredibly dangerous backblast of exhaust. Nakakoshi and his crew were also wearing headphones and bone conduction mics, but theirs were on a different frequency, and they couldn't hear what he was saying. Ryo had to gesture to them to move.

By the time the crew realized what Ryo was trying to communicate, Megadrake had nearly pulled itself completely free of the earth. With a slow twisting of its body, it shook off the clumps of dirt and fragments of concrete. The thing was at least twenty meters long. If the rugby-ball-shaped mass could be seen as its head, it wasn't much more of a stretch to compare the dozen or more trailing roots to people wrapped in rags. The kaiju raised two of the roots like arms high in the air.

Suddenly, the head crackled open. Eight jagged leaves unfurled in eight directions and revealed the thick stalk within. Though covered with rigid scales like a pine cone, the stalk was flexible and bent snakelike—a large pink swelling at the tip was likely the flower bud. The stem had no eyes, but even without them, it looked vaguely reptilian.

Kiiiiin!

Megadrake released a shrill piercing cry at the sunset sky.

"Fire!" the officer ordered.

They fired. One by one the shells flew from the Carl Gustavs in thunderous blasts. The .50 caliber rifles shook like jackhammers, spitting out bullets with a low stomach-churning rumble. Even through the headphones the noise was powerful.

The soldiers had been instructed to aim for the creature's head, but they were at quite a distance, and their target was moving. Most of their shots missed the mark. Some of the 84mm shells tore gouges in the roots. Others missed and exploded in dirt. The machine guns ripped countless holes in leaves and roots, but the skin around Megadrake's neck was unexpectedly resilient, and the shots, at their steep angle, simply bounced off it.

Kiiiiin!

With an angry roar, the kaiju turned its head—its bud—to face the building. It bent its body forward, as if bowing, and pointed straight ahead. For a moment, it seemed as if the creature were about to fall over, but it leveled in a bent-over position. The leaves, which had opened at its necklike stem like a frilled collar, closed partway until they met edge to edge, to resemble an inside-out umbrella.

"What on earth?"

Ryo had a bad feeling.

Yuri watched the live video feed with her own sense of foreboding. She felt like she'd seen that umbrella shape somewhere else before. Somewhere recently.

That's it! That thing the crew used to light me for my interview!

Reflexively, she shouted, "It's a parabola!"

Kurihama spun to her in surprise. "What?"

"It's a parabolic reflector! It's going to focus the sound waves."

Kurihama quickly understood. He grabbed the microphone and yelled, "Run, Ryo! That's a parabola. It's going to focus its sound into a beam!"

Ryo immediately realized the danger. Without a moment of hesitation, he grabbed the commanding officer by the collar and yelled, "We're in danger! It's going to turn its screaming into a beam weapon. It'll focus all the noise into a single point—"

Before he could finish, Megadrake launched its counterattack.

Kiiiiin!

The parabola of rigid leaves reflected the powerful sound into a single focused beam which struck the front of the building. Glass resonated and scores of panels instantaneously disintegrated. Still shrieking, the kaiju slowly raised its body, and, like an invisible monster climbing to the top, the deadly ray worked its way up the facade of the building, tracing a vertical line of shattered panes in its wake. Glass rained down on the street between the park and the office.

"Retreat!" the commander ordered. "Retreat!"

The soldiers ceased fire and pulled back in unison. As Ryo turned to flee, he saw them. Either clueless or fearless, Nakakoshi and the TV crew were affixed at the roof's edge, still taping.

Ryo dove for the cameraman and pulled him away from the ledge and down to the roof.

"You fool! Do you want to die?"

The beam reached the top of the building. Even though Ryo had managed to drag them out of the beam's path, the explosion of noise was tremendous. Waves of pain shot through his head.

Screaming, with hands to their ears, the group ran for the stairs.

Back inside, the sound was dampened, but they didn't have time for respite.

"That thing thinks this building's its enemy," Ryo explained. "It might try to flatten the whole place. We're in danger. We have to get out of here!"

The officer nodded. "Soldiers, withdraw immediately."

The elevators weren't an option because the kaiju's assault could trigger an emergency shutdown at any moment. The SDF unit, Ryo, Sakura, Nakakoshi, and his crew dashed down the stairwell. Even through all of this, the cameraman kept on recording. The display of professionalism impressed Ryo.

Partway down the stairs, Sakura asked, "How many floors are there in this place?"

Ryo barked, "Just think of it as exercise."

Then, finally, when they had made it to the ground floor, Sakura saw it through the greenhouse windows. Hopelessly, she said, "It's here!"

Megadrake had crossed the park and closed in on the east side of the building. From the report of gunfire and explosions, the other two squads seemed to be attacking it from behind.

An off-target 84mm shell blew through the window, smashed into the central column, and burst with a terrible sound. Shards of marble sprayed out into the room.

"Stop!" Ryo shouted. "Friendly fire!"

Megadrake was now climbing across the skybridge connecting the park and the building. Unfortunately for the kaiju, it had no eyes to see its precarious footing. The bridge collapsed under the creature's weight. Megadrake pitched forward. Its head crashed through the greenhouse windows. As the shards of glass cascaded down, Sakura shrieked.

Megadrake struggled weakly. The SDF's relentless assault had torn off half its leaves, and what remained was riddled with holes. The flower bud had sustained serious injury. Syrupy ichor oozed from its shredded roots. It was clearly dying.

But not dead: the bud began to vibrate—an attempt at one last death cry.

"Fire!"

The Carl Gustav fired at close range. The shell smashed into the kaiju right in the tip of its flower bud and pulverized the petals within.

Still the roots persisted, writhing in the street, refusing to stop until many minutes—and hundreds of bullets—later.

EXT. INSURANCE BUILDING—NIGHT

Spotlights illuminate the kaiju's piteous—and
lifeless—body, the creature's neck thrust into the
building.

>   MALE NARRATOR (O.C.)
>   (*somber*)
>   The battle has ended. Only three were in-
>   jured, but the damage to area buildings is
>   severe.

A SERIES OF SHOTS reveals:

A pedestrian bridge crushed beneath the kaiju.

An office building with over half its windows
broken.

Walls pockmarked with bullet holes.

A roadway blanketed with glass shards.

AND—

The four members of the Mobile Unit standing
still, crestfallen.

>   MALE NARRATOR (CONT'D)
>   Their mission can't be considered a complete
>   success.

Asaya looked up at the destruction with a dour expression.
"This is awful," he said. "What do you think the chief is doing
right now?"

"Gulping down his stomach medicine," Yojiro said with a meager laugh. "If he didn't faint outright."

Sakura asked, "Do you think this building is insured?"

"Well, probably," Ryo answered flatly. "It belongs to an insurance company, doesn't it?"

"But who pays out the insurance for an insurance company? Another insurance company?"

Ryo tilted his head. "Beats me."

Sakura glanced to the side and noticed the TV crew filming the kaiju's remains and the state of the building. Nakakoshi saw her looking his way and lowered his head in guilt.

She walked over to the director.

"I'm sorry," he said, scratching his head. "We have to use this in the show. It's just that—"

"I know. I understand. It's television's duty to show the truth."

She turned to look at the kaiju's body. Then, with a rueful grin, she sighed. "I guess it's impossible."

"What is?"

"We're not heroes. We can't settle things snappily and decisively. We have flaws. That's reality. If we were heroes in some fairy tale, we'd succeed every time. We wouldn't come up lacking. We wouldn't let people die." A tear came to her eye, and she quickly wiped it away. "But we have to try. It's all we can do."

As she started to walk away, Nakakoshi called out to her.

"Ms. Fujisawa."

"What?"

"Could you say that again, for the camera? Starting with 'We're not heroes.'"

PART FIVE

ARRIVAL! THE COLOSSAL KAIJU OF THE APOCALYPSE!

"Not again!"

Asaya, who had been staring into the monitor, dropped his head on top of the folding table with a thump. "Ryo," he moaned, "it shut itself off. Again."

Ryo was pushing a machine that resembled a handcart up the reddish clay of the mountain slope. He stopped, turned to Asaya with a scowl, and managed a feeble, "What?"

It was the third time since this morning.

Yojiro glared at the monitor, its actions a personal affront. The complex array of red, black, and yellow stripes had been replaced by the empty darkness of a powered-off screen.

"And we were going smoothly for a while there. Can't we catch a break?"

Even the handcart creaked in protest as Ryo slumped over its handle.

It was the beginning of summer. The sun glared down with a malicious heat, and Kojin Island, a barren, rocky constituent of the Nao Archipelago in the Seto Inland Sea, was as hot as a frying pan. The temperature passed thirty Celsius before noon. Worse still, no trees were around to provide shelter, and the wind was weak. Under those conditions, the long, ceaseless outdoor work was dreary enough, but the intermittent interruptions from mechanical trouble sapped their will to continue.

Eight years ago, a fire destroyed nearly everything on the

uninhabited fifty-five hectare island. Volunteer efforts had begun a few years earlier in order to restore some green to Kojin Island, but the mountain slopes remained mostly dirt and exposed granite—including the area Ryo and the rest of the Mobile Unit were inspecting.

Built into the handcart was a ground-penetrating radar device. By measuring the reflections of its high-frequency electromagnetic pulses, it could find buried objects of differing density to the surrounding material. Despite a modest effective depth of about five meters, the equipment had proven useful in finding kaiju in underground hibernation. But now, every few hours, it stopped working.

And it wasn't just the radar that was having trouble. For several months, local fishermen had reported a variety of electronic malfunctions—from watches and GPS devices shutting off to motorboat engines stalling. Officials in the city hall of the neighboring Nao Island, thinking the phenomenon might be the sign of an imminent kaiju arrival, requested the MMD's Mobile Unit to come investigate.

"Is it just me," Ryo asked, "or is it getting more frequent?"

Yojiro nodded. "You're right. The last one was at eleven forty-five, and . . ."

He looked at his watch. The digits had stopped at five minutes to two. Each time the event happened, all electrical devices, including cell phones and digital watches, stopped working for roughly twenty minutes. When the interference lifted, they all had to reset their clocks. Only old mechanical watches kept on going—and none of the team had one of those.

"Two hours and ten minutes," Yojiro said. "That's shorter than the previous interval. When we're able, we'll have to contact headquarters to get the correct time again. Do we have backups of the data?"

With disappointment, Kiichi said, "Most of it. But the last ten minutes? *Poof.*"

Kiichi was twenty-eight, the same as Ryo and one year older

than Asaya. Although you wouldn't guess it from his heavyset frame and gentle demeanor, he did judo in high school and was physically strong.

The four men—and Sakura, who had the day off—made up the MMD Mobile Unit. At the first hint of a kaiju, they flew to the scene to investigate. When a monster appeared, they observed its actions and provided headquarters with a live report from which countermeasures would be devised. Theirs was an important role in the defense of countless civilians from the kaiju threat. The Mobile Unit required knowledge from diverse disciplines, including geology, zoology, botany, and meteorology; and because their work often encountered danger, physical ability was also a necessity.

Yojiro, himself a veteran of over twenty years with the MMD, led the team of twentysomethings. The youth-centric nature of the team was intentional, as it was believed the next generation of leaders would gain better experience in the field rather than behind desks.

Ideally, Yojiro hoped to foster well-rounded capabilities within his charges, but he also encouraged growth among their respective specialties. Asaya had a passion for science and was experienced with electronics. Kiichi was an earnest learner with a wealth of knowledge and possessed nerves of steel. Ryo had strong decision-making and leadership skills—in him, Yojiro saw the makings of his successor as the leader of the Mobile Unit. Sakura had a youthful recklessness but was skilled behind the wheel, and her determination and drive were second to none. With their individual strengths united, Yojiro found them the ideal team.

"But it's strange," Asaya said. "We haven't detected any electromagnetic abnormalities."

In a low voice, Yojiro said, "Yeah . . ."

Until they came to the island, he had expected the interference to be caused by either magnetic or electrical forces. In extremely rare cases, kaiju had been known to emit pulses of electricity like electric eels or to use high-temperature plasma as a weapon. If a similar creature was about to awaken, it wouldn't be a surprise to find electromagnetic interference mucking up nearby electronics.

But contrary to his conjecture, the team had found no evidence of anything resembling unexpected electromagnetic waves. A field strong enough to kill electronics would have at least been accompanied by some amounts of static noise detectable from nearby ships. Yet there were no such reports. The effect was sudden, absolute, and restricted within a roughly 180-meter radius.

Asaya meekly offered, "So what, we're dealing with a kaiju that can stop electricity?"

Kiichi rebuffed, "Where's the science in that?" But he didn't have the confidence to outright deny it. Orthodox science wouldn't be of use here.

"If it could suppress electrical activity," Yojiro said, "then what would happen to people? Nerve impulses are a type of electrical phenomenon."

Asaya said, "That's right. We'd be killed outright, so that can't be it. Hmmm . . ." He considered the problem but had no further ideas.

"You know," Ryo said, "there's something else that's bothering me."

He pointed to a relic standing on the slopes above. It was a large stone tablet, roughly the size of two double beds and clearly manmade. The monument was thought to be an ancient ritual site, although its age and purpose remained unknown. Without any ash or charcoal to extract from the artifact, carbon-14 dating wasn't possible.

"The name of the island," he said, "Kojin. It means 'violent god.' Maybe that's what the people were worshipping here."

"Like . . . a snake god?" Kiichi offered.

Their radar had picked up an outline of a buried object—a long, three-meter-wide cylindrical body with no arms or legs. So far, the team had found two parallel tube shapes they thought could belong to a giant snake coiled within the earth. Their best guess put it at seventy meters long and around five hundred tons—near the upper bounds of an MM6.

"I wouldn't be surprised," Ryo said. "There have been various forms of snake worship in all parts of Japan. Perhaps some ancient people living on this island stumbled upon a kaiju entering crypto-biosis here and offered prayers to keep it from waking up."

In cryptobiosis, an animal underwent desiccation and sus-pended its biological activity. Some smaller insects, like the African sleeping chironomid, exhibited the ability, but no larger creatures shared the process—except the occasional kaiju. A substance, secreted by the kaiju just before the cryptobiosis, covered its skin and petrified.

The creature would then appear to be made of stone. Buried under the earth, it slept for tens or even hundreds of years, until some catalyst broke through the protective film, allowing moisture back into the kaiju's body and restoring it to life. In the event a kaiju greater than MM5 was discovered before its awakening, the MMD's policy was to destroy the creature with dynamite.

Yojiro said, "Let's leave the analysis to headquarters. Shall we measure the effect's radius?"

Keeping his eyes on his watch, Yojiro walked to the base of the slope. There, eleven small poles with white tape at their tops stood, the stakes placed every 22.5 degrees along a slightly misshapen semi-circle from the shore to the mountain. During the previous electrical disturbance, the team had measured the edge of the effect. About a third of the full circle fell in the waters to the north of the island and was unmarked.

A few steps past the poles, Yojiro's watch sprang back to life. The rest of the team had done the same, walking in different directions with watches and cell phones in hand. As soon as their electronics were working again, they stood in place.

Yojiro raised a megaphone to his mouth and called out to the other three. "How is it where you are?"

"About two meters farther than last time," Ryo said.

"Same here," Asaya said.

"And here!" Kiichi said.

The range was increasing. They all felt themselves get a little more nervous. If the expanding radius of the effect, along with its accelerating frequency, was part of the kaiju's power, the creature's awakening could be near.

"Do we have any more poles?" Yojiro asked.

"Yes!" Kiichi called out.

"All right. Let's mark the new boundary."

They went back to their motorboat and retrieved another set of poles.

Asaya wiped the sweat from his face. "Sakura's lucky to have the day off. This isn't women's work."

"You believe that?" Ryo asked. "She's tougher than any of us."

Yojiro chuckled. "That's not toughness, it's determination. What she lacks in strength, she covers up with enthusiasm."

"Enthusiasm's fine," Ryo muttered. "But she needs to learn to calm down a little. She can't go off on her own again like in Gifu."

As they were hauling the stakes back to the work area, a man, fishing pole in one hand and cooler in the other, approached them and said, "Working hard, gentlemen?"

Ryo held out a hand to stop him from getting any closer to the site. "I'm sorry, but it's dangerous here. Please don't come near. There's a kaiju hibernating."

"Oh, a kaiju," the man said flatly. "And you're with the MMD?"

"Yes."

"Thought so. Me and the other guys've been talking. Something's going on on Kojin."

Ryo perked up. "What do you mean, something? Were you having trouble with electronics?"

"Well, that too." The fisherman shaded his eyes with his hand and squinted up at the rocky slope. "It's felt strange up there."

"Strange?"

"Lately, that area up there's felt a little, well, ominous. Foreboding. Just a feeling." He gave Ryo a dry smile. "I'm sorry, it's not very scientific."

"No, thank you for sharing," Ryo said.

"Isn't there a kind of sixth sense like that? The way animals can predict when a kaiju is going to appear? We haven't been catching as many fish."

"Sure," Ryo said noncommittally.

The belief that animals could foresee kaiju was widespread among the general public and amateur researchers, but specialists in the field didn't buy into it. The supposed indicators—unusually agitated crows, a decline in fishing catches, howling dogs—happened all the time, without a kaiju appearing after.

That said, the notion of a sixth sense couldn't be dismissed as entirely baseless. Although a clear correlation remained unproven, on many occasions animals had indeed seemed to predict a kaiju's coming. But since the observation of unusual animal behavior was by nature highly subjective, such cases were hard to operationalize and were therefore ignored by the experts.

When the last of the ten new posts had been pounded into the earth, the electrical disturbance ceased. The team hurried back to the radar equipment and resumed their search, scanning in five-meter increments the area where they believed the kaiju slumbered.

Kiichi took over the grueling work of pushing the radar cart. As he slowly advanced up the slope, striped patterns appeared on the computer monitor. Kaiju skin was typically denser than their internal organs, and the change of density between the layers altered the speed of electromagnetic waves. The radar measured the time it took for its pulses to return, and built the image from that data.

Not ten minutes after they resumed work, Yojiro cried out in surprise.

"What's wrong?" Ryo asked. When he looked into the monitor, his expression changed. "Is that—"

"Yes, it is."

The two cylinders on the screen had been joined by a third.

Back at the Tokyo headquarters, Chief Kurihama was shocked by the news. When he spoke, his voice was hollow.

"It's a many-headed snake?"

"Either that or a many-headed dragon." Yojiro's face, on-screen, appeared somewhat agitated. "We've been able to confirm at least four heads. There could be more buried farther down than our radar can reach, so there could even be double that number."

Yuri gasped. "Yamata-no-orochi."

Even as an astrophysicist with little knowledge of folklore and mythology, she knew the legend of Yamata-no-orochi—the Eight-Forked Serpent.

"The heads are connected to one large body," Yojiro continued. "We're only just starting measurements of the body itself, so I can't yet say this conclusively, but we should assume we're dealing with something at least ten times bigger than we first thought."

"Five thousand tons? That would mean an MM—"

"Yes. Prepare yourself for it. A nine."

"MM9 . . ."

Kurihama was shaken by the news. Nervous murmurings swept across the room. An MM9—a kaiju larger than four thousand tons—had never been recorded since the advent of monsterology as a scientific discipline. MM9 kaiju were creatures of legend—and the Orochi was the largest monster in Japan's bestiary of mythic creatures.

"We believe it could be about to awaken," Yojiro said. "Give the order to evacuate Tamano City on the mainland coast, along with the nearby islands, including Nao. After that—"

"I know. I'll call in the SDF."

"Yes. Also, we're shorthanded here and could use some more help."

"I'll send people right away. I'm sorry to ask this of you, but I'll need you to keep working through the night. I want a full picture of this beast as soon as possible."

"Of course. We'll keep going until we drop." With a fearless grin, Yojiro cut the transmission.

The chief spun to face the dozen or so dazed workers under his command. "We have work to do, people!"

One by one, he spurred them to action.

"Request an emergency deployment from the Ministry of Defense. Contact the press. Issue an alert to all areas within ten kilometers of the island. Shut down all sea passage in the nearby waters. Get to work on the analysis of the data sent by Yojiro's team and build the CG model. Anyone who doesn't have anything else to do, look up any information you can find on the Orochi. And find me somebody familiar with the local legends. Now get to it!"

Snapped out of their collective stupor, the team started their work. The office sprang to life, its occupants picking up phones, flipping through research, and pounding at keyboards.

Yuri stood amidst the bustle, flustered. "Um, what should I . . ."

Kurihama glanced at her. "Figure out the kaiju's powers. How is it able to suppress electricity?"

One of the operators handed the chief a phone with the Ministry of Defense on the other end. Without waiting for Yuri's response, Kurihama picked up the receiver.

Another man stood up and asked, "What are we calling it? Yamata-no-orochi?"

Kurihama turned from the phone and barked, "We don't even know how many heads it has! Or if it's a snake or a dragon. Until I've confirmed what this thing is, I'm not going to give it a name. For now, stick with Kaiju Seven!"

The chief's temper flared, but his actions remained calculated. This kaiju could cause unprecedented disaster. If he rashly and improperly named the kaiju, the foolish mistake would be preserved in history. The naming of Kaiju Seven required even greater care than Kurihama typically afforded the task.

Of course, he had another reason to hesitate—the hope that the name Yamata-no-orochi *wouldn't* fit.

Meanwhile, in another location in Eastern Japan—

"No, it's too late to go to Kojin Island now," the man said, his voice cool and composed. "The MMD will have already sent for the SDF. I'm not about to get in a firefight with them with what meager weapons we have."

His partner, on the other end of the line, was clearly upset. "But what about One?"

"There's no need to worry."

A computer sat on the table in front of the man. From its speakers came a sound like falling rain. The sound's volume cycled louder and softer, louder and softer. A waveform on the computer screen displayed the rhythmic cycle.

"They may have come sniffing around," the man said, "but they're too late. It'll wake up in a day at the latest."

"What if they destroy it first?"

"That's why I'm going to buy us some time. Get me the necessary people. We'll meet at the place we talked about. Can you do it?"

"Of course, but—"

"Good. I'll lead the first squad. The second team will go to Ibaraki."

"Ibaraki? You mean . . ."

"Yes."

The man—Mikio Izuno—stared coolly at the screen. "Their target is in Tsukuba."

7:00 PM—

In a conference room downstairs from the main office, an emergency meeting convened to explore a possible explanation, offered by Yuri, for the kaiju's electrical dampening field.

Yuri addressed the room, keeping her tone as calm as possible. "As you all know, kaiju follow the rules of the mythic universe, not those of our Big Bang universe. That's how kaiju can ignore gravity and support their incredible mass; how they can ignore the conservation of mass and transform into giants; and how, unlike any other large creature, they can undergo cryptobiosis. Typically, the laws of the mythic universe don't apply past the creatures' skin. But what if there were a kaiju capable of extending its laws of reality beyond its own body?"

Kurihama asked, "You mean the area inside that spherical field becomes part of the mythic universe?"

"Yes. The mythic universe may not have electricity. How could it? It doesn't even have atoms. There would be no electrons or ions."

A team member asked, "What about people? We can't live without the electrical processes inside our bodies."

"Ah, but people do live in the mythic universe. Long ago, *all* people lived inside the mythic universe. It's possible that once someone is taken into the field, his body instantly transforms into one that adheres to the rules of that universe."

"But there was lightning back then, right? We've even seen kaiju use lightning as a weapon," Kurihama said.

"In the mythic universe, lightning isn't electricity. It would look the same to us, but it's a phenomenon with an entirely different basis. This includes any electrical abilities or powers a kaiju may have. We, with our modern understanding of science, only interpret the phenomenon as electricity."

Among the team sat a middle-aged man, with a gentle, handsome face. Stroking his chin, he said, "That's an outlandish theory . . . but a believable one."

The man was Dr. Akihiko Inamoto, a professor of kaiju history at the meteorological college in Kashiwa City, Chiba Prefecture. With doctorates in history and cultural anthropology, Inamoto was an authority in the field of monsterology. Because of the importance of the discovery of an MM9, he had been summoned to the Meteorological Agency headquarters straightaway.

Inamoto continued, "Although we have found organs similar to those of the electric eel inside the remains of electricity-producing kaiju, the actual mechanisms producing the large amounts of energy remain a mystery. The same goes for their beams of destructive light. The creatures' rays of electricity and light are mythical in nature—if those discharges are like what ancient peoples imagined to be the wrath of God, the beams wouldn't necessarily have to follow the laws of physics."

Another member of the team asked, "If that's true, then the kaiju wouldn't need any electrical organs in the first place, right?"

"It could be that our understanding of their internal organs is confined to a rational explanation within the Big Bang universe," Inamoto said. "When a kaiju dies, its body transforms and becomes a part of the Big Bang universe—at which time its flesh manifests in a form most adherent to the logic of our universe."

Kurihama was growing impatient. "Enough talk about electric kaiju. Our concern is Kaiju Seven. Yuri, please continue."

She nodded. "We need to consider the radius of the kaiju's interference field."

At her prompt, Toshio typed on his keyboard and brought up a CG image on the large wall-mounted screen over Yuri's shoulder. In the graphic, a 3-D, half-transparent Kojin Island was overlaid with the monster's silhouette. The parts of the kaiju confirmed by Yojiro's team were displayed in red, and the rest, only a conjecture, were shown in blue.

Kaiju Seven's eight heads (the upper four in red, the lower four in blue) pointed toward the island's shore and appeared to run parallel to the ground, as if the creature were bowing. The heads, each estimated at around thirty meters long, were arranged in a fanlike shape. Its body rested deeper within the earth—beyond the radar's range—and was pure surmise. In order to maintain balance with its heads, the kaiju was likely over a hundred meters long.

A circle over the image represented the area of the monster's antielectrical field.

"At first glance," Yuri said, "the circle appears warped. But once you take topography into account . . ."

A translucent yellow sphere was added to the image. Her audience *ahh*ed. The edge of the sphere intersected with the uneven terrain in a perfect match with the circle.

". . . .as you can see, the circle only appears warped because of the uneven ground. The field itself is an almost perfect sphere. The odd part of it is that if the kaiju is projecting this field from its skin, the area of effect should match the shape of its body. Since that is not the case, and the field is spherical . . ."

She pointed to a spot in the center of the sphere.

". . . a specific organ may be generating the interference."

Kurihama squinted and stared into the screen. "It looks like there's something at that point."

On top of the CG construction's blue, football-shaped body was an indistinct area of red mixed in with the blue.

Directly beneath the rectangular monument.

The chief asked, "Is that another neck?"

"I don't know," Toshio said. "It's outside the radar's range. All I can say for sure is that whatever's there isn't just some rock. We won't know anything more without digging deep."

"Is its shape too different from the others to be a neck?"

"If it were a neck, I don't see how it would connect to the body."

The members of the team traded several possible explanations: the object was a dorsal fin or a wing; the kaiju's tail had curved back over its body; the outline was buried detritus, some decayed tree trunk—but the data were too sparse to give weight to any one theory.

Dr. Inamoto spoke up. "This creature might not even be the Orochi."

All eyes turned to the professor. Kurihama asked, "Even with the radar image we have?"

"Yes. Even though it has several heads, it's still too early to assume it's the Orochi. There are several legends of many-headed snakes and dragons all over the world. The most famous is the Hydra, the nine-headed sea serpent slain by Hercules in Greek mythology. The dragon Ladon of the Garden of the Hesperides, another of Hercules' opponents, is also said to have had many heads. Zeus defeated Typhon, a monster that had a hundred dragon heads growing from its shoulders. In Russian folklore, Zmey Gorynych was a twelve-headed dragon. The warrior god Sisiutl of indigenous Canadian mythology possessed two snake heads, and the Ananta Sheesha of Vedic lore had a thousand. Sumerian cylinder seals often depict the seven-headed dragon Muṣmaḫ, and Egyptian legend tells of a seven-headed snake called Nāu. And here in Japan, we have the Kuzuryu River in Fukui Prefecture, where, according to *The Histories of Echizen,* a nine-headed dragon once lived. Also famous is the red dragon in the Book of Revelation."

With a flurry of keystrokes on his notebook computer, the professor opened a file—Revelation 12.

"Here. 'And there appeared another wonder in heaven; and behold a great red dragon, having seven heads and ten horns, and seven crowns upon his heads.' Let me skip a bit here. 'And the great dragon was cast out, that old serpent, called the Devil, and Satan, which deceiveth the whole world: he was cast out into the earth, and his angels were cast out with him.'"

Chief Kurihama frowned uncomfortably. "Well, yes, I see that, but I'd rather not involve religious matters . . ."

"Please don't misunderstand. I'm not asking you to take it literally. But it's inconceivable that Saint John conjured all of it up from nothing two thousand years ago. It's a rearrangement of prior folklore—of older religions now lost to us."

"So this dragon is Satan?"

"Again, you miss the point. There have been forms of snake and dragon worship all over the world. In ancient Greek worship, Delphyne was a half-woman, half-dragon who guarded the Oracle of Delphi. The sun god Apollo slew the monster and took Delphi as his holy land. This signifies Apollo worship supplanting a dragon deity. Typhon, who was defeated by Zeus, was the offspring of the Earth-goddess Gaia. The snake-woman Echidna begat Hercules' Hydra and Ladon, and the argument for her being an ancient goddess is strong. The same pattern appears in Babylonian mythology with Marduk killing Tiamat, a dragon goddess.

"That pattern can be found among the legends of all peoples. Gods or heroes slay evil snakes or dragons. When a new religion overthrew an old one, the old religion was rewritten, and the once-revered snake or dragon was made into an evil monster. And so, in Christianity, snakes and dragons were seen as representations of the devil."

"So the many-headed snake used to be a god?" Kurihama asked.

"It's possible. The worldwide prevalence of legends with many-headed snakes could mean they were once worshipped on a global scale. The monument on Kojin Island may be from that era. Of course, this is all from a time that predates even Greek mythology— a time so old that not even its legends remain."

"Older than Greek mythology?" Yuri said. "Older than the paradigm shift, then?"

"That would be the case."

The room fell silent as they all considered what that meant.

Three thousand years ago. When the Big Bang universe and the mythic universe coexisted. A world with gods and fairies. The many-headed dragon sleeping beneath a monument built to its tribute that long ago.

No one dared voice the dreadful conclusion.

Kaiju Seven might not be a kaiju, but a god.

9:20 PM—

Geological survey teams from the SDF and Okayama University arrived on Kojin Island, where they met up with the Mobile Unit. Their efforts were divided between two tasks: digging into the ground near the worship site to enable the radar to penetrate deeper beneath the surface, and excavating a section of the slope to unearth a part of the kaiju itself.

The work demanded great care. Because vibrations could awaken the beast, bulldozers and jackhammers weren't an option. All digging had to be done by hand. Adding further hindrance to their operations were the occasional electrical blackouts that forced their work to a halt over twenty minutes at a time.

But with the help of scores of assistants, one of the kaiju's necks was finally exposed to air.

Asaya peered into the hole. "Whoa, look at those scales!"

At the bottom of the four-meter deep hole, the team of geologists skillfully brushed the dirt from the kaiju's exposed scales. Only one fraction of one cylindrical neck had been unearthed, but judging from its curvature, were it an underground tunnel, a car would have been able to fit inside it. A thin layer of fossilized mucus covered the monster, but from its bumps and divots, the scales beneath were clearly discernible—each as big as a roof tile.

Ryo joined Asaya, followed by an SDF soldier, who looked down and said, "So it's a dragon, not a snake, after all."

"I'm not sure," Ryo said. "We haven't found any limbs yet. There's no telling what it is."

"Whatever it is," the soldier grumbled, "we've got our work cut out for us. It's going to take considerable ordnance to get through that armor. And if we have to get all eight heads at the same time . . ."

The evening's investigation had revealed a total of eight necks, not counting the as-of-yet unidentified shape on the kaiju's back. To be assured they had put an end to the kaiju, they would have to destroy all eight. If any remained intact, the wounded monster might only become more violent. Their task required finding the precise location of each head, digging down to it, and setting explosives—all without rousing the monster from its slumber.

In case the demolitions failed, JMSDF destroyers were on their way to the island, and on standby were the JGSDF 5th Antitank Helicopter Battalion from Camp Akeno in Mie Prefecture, the JASDF 303rd Squadron from Komatsu Air Base in Ishikawa Prefecture, the JASDF 304th Squadron from Tsuiki Air Base in Fukuoka Prefecture, and the JMSDF 31st Fleet Air Wing from Iwakuni Air Base in Yamaguchi Prefecture.

One of the geologists called up from the pit. "I'm sorry, could you come down here?"

Ryo climbed down the ladder. "What is it?"

"I want you to listen to this."

The expert placed the cup of a specialized stethoscope on the kaiju, handed the earpiece to Ryo, and asked, "What do you think?"

Ryo listened for a moment. "Flowing blood, right?"

Although he had thought himself prepared for the sound, the unanticipated liveliness of the monster's pulse sent chills down Ryo's back. Its heartbeat was still slow, but the amount of blood already circulating within the kaiju made it clear—the creature's flesh had begun to absorb moisture and it was beginning to emerge from its cryptobiotic state.

Ryo scrambled back up the ladder.

Asaya asked, "Something's wrong?"

"This is bad. It could wake up any minute now. We have to get everyone working faster, or else—"

The work lights went out, their illumination replaced with total darkness. From all across the worksite came moans of frustration.

"You're kidding me!" Ryo grumbled, fumbling inside his pockets for a candle. "It hasn't even been an hour and a half since the last one."

He found the candle, took it out, and lit it. The other workers went around lighting lanterns that had been brought in to cope with the blackouts. Compared to the electric lights, the flames were feeble, but light had returned to the worksite.

Appreciatively, Asaya said, "I guess this means combustion can occur in the mythic universe."

Ryo was unsettled. If the parallel anthropic principle was correct, their bodies no longer consisted of atoms but of pre-Democritean matter. He couldn't imagine what that matter even was and he had no way of finding out. Inside the kaiju's field, X-ray cameras and electron microscopes couldn't operate.

Asaya asked, "Do you think things can explode?"

Surprised by the question, Ryo only tilted his head to the side and said, "Hm?"

"Surely gunpowder couldn't explode in the mythic universe, right? Even though there's volcanic eruptions and the like."

"I wonder. An explosion is just a sudden, violent combustion. I'm not sure, but if there are combustions, I think there could be explosions."

"If not, that'll be trouble," Asaya said. "Our shaped explosive charges will be drastically less effective."

Most modern explosive shells and missiles were designed to use the Munroe effect. The charge was placed behind a hollow cone lined with a thin layer of metal. Upon striking its target, the explosive would ignite and send out a high-temperature, high-pressure jet. The shell would then pass through the enemy's armor not by its own kinetic energy, but with an eight kilometer-per-second jet.

"I'd like to think that won't be the case," Ryo said. "Well, proximity fuses use electricity, so they won't work, but contact fuses rely on basic physical impact and should probably be fine."

"That would be good. But still, if we have to rely on missiles without any guidance systems and only simple kinetic energy . . ."

"You're right. We have to assume the worst. We have to kill it before it wakes up."

"Easier said."

The two men looked across the dark worksite still under a state of confusion after the blackout.

It seemed like they were going to be far too late.

Sakura rode her motorcycle back into Tokyo from her parents' house in neighboring Tochigi Prefecture. By the time she got into the main office, it was already after ten at night. She dashed in through the office doorway and said, "Sorry I'm late—whoa!"

She gaped at the room crowded with five times the usual number of people. Her coworkers bustled about with armfuls of documents and yelled at each other over the constantly ringing phones. This was an emergency, *an MM9*, and the entire department—even those with the day off—had been called in to respond.

It looked like all of them would have to work through the night. Sakura shouted, "Um, should I . . . what should I do?"

But everyone was too busy with their own work to answer. She pushed through the sea of people until, finally, she grabbed Toshio and asked, "Should I fly to the island?"

Absently, Toshio replied, "Huh? What?"

The operator was immersed in his work constructing the 3-D model from the latest underground radar data sent from the island. She tried again, louder.

"Should I fly to the island?"

At that, he turned and said, "No, the SDF and Okayama U sent teams to help. I think they probably have enough people on-site. Besides, on that island, you wouldn't be able to put your driving skills to use. So if you don't have anything to do, we could use your help digging through the archives."

He gestured to a corner of the room and returned to his work. Sakura pushed again through the crowd and headed for the corner, where two desks had been taken over by mountains of books. Around the tables stood seven people with studious expressions, each working through a section of the pile. Sakura was surprised to see Yuri among them.

She approached the group and eagerly asked how she could help.

Yuri looked up from her reading and gestured to the mound of books. There were tomes on history, folklore, and mythology, and more than a few of them looked to be quite old. The books had been dragged out of the Meteorological Agency archives.

"Read these," Yuri said, "and commit anything important to memory."

"What, all of it?"

"As much as you can," Dr. Inamoto said with a kind voice. "We don't know what's going to happen, but if there's some hint in one of these books, we can recall it on the spot, like, 'Now that you mention it, there was something about it in that book.'"

This was Sakura's first time meeting the professor. Having entered the agency as a third-class recruit, she had never attended the Meteorological University. *Wow,* she thought with a little excitement, *I didn't know there were nice older guys like him at the college.*

She asked, "Why can't we just look it up by computer?"

"Not all our books have been entered into the digital archives. There's a lot of data that are still analog. And those are the ones we have here."

"There sure are a lot."

"These are just the ones pertaining to many-headed dragons and snakes."

"Wow."

Sakura grabbed an old softcover from the top of the pile. Since there weren't any chairs left, she leaned her back against the wall. She squinted at the book's yellowed cover. The title read *Yamato Takeru Was a Woman.*

"Um," she said, "what's this kind of nonsense doing with the rest of these?"

"Hm?" Dr. Inamoto looked up from his book. "Oh, Hideyo Tomono wrote that."

"Is he famous?"

"He was a writer in the late 1960s. His writing isn't as fantastical as that title might lead you to believe. He believed that various

ancient cultures had legends of goddesses and heroines, but as so-
cieties became patriarchal, the powerful figures in those tales were
replaced by men."

"So he's literally saying Yamato Takeru was a woman."

"He was dressed in women's clothing when he conquered
Kumaso, wasn't he? And according to some legends, when Hercules
was a slave in Queen Omphale's palace, he dressed as a woman.
Hideyo believed those were remnants of earlier versions of the tales,
when the main characters were women."

Another of the workers added, "There've been others overseas
who shared the notion. Bernard Evslin wrote a novel called *Heraclea:
A Legend of Warrior Women*, with Hercules as a woman."

Sakura asked, "How credible is that theory?"

"That's a tough question," Dr. Inamoto said. "It's difficult to ex-
trapolate from the myths as we know them now. When we think
of Greek mythology, we think of the twelve Olympian gods with
Zeus their ruler. But Zeus wasn't actually a god of the local lands.
Etymology indicates the religion was brought in by Hellenic tribes
around 2000 BC."

"Really? And Athena and Artemis weren't Greek either?"

"No, the goddesses Athena, Aphrodite, Artemis, and Persephone
were indeed worshipped along the coastal regions of the Mediterranean
Sea. The ancient Europe of four thousand years ago was a matriarchy
with nearly no reverence of male gods. But the Zeus worshippers,
the patriarchal Hellenes, came from the east, and transformed and
supplanted the local beliefs. The mighty Athena and Artemis and
Persephone were relegated to become Zeus's daughters. Zeus had so
many children because the invaders absorbed the old religions into
their own."

"So then the tales of Hercules . . ."

"Yes. The many labors of Hercules are clearly a patchwork of
various local legends of other heroes—and possibly heroines. As for
what the stories originally were, no one alive knows."

"So was Hydra really defeated by a woman?"

"That's what Hideyo Tomono proposed."

Sakura folded her arms. "Rewriting the stories like that seems terribly disrespectful. I suppose there weren't copyrights back then."

Her naive remark caused Dr. Inamoto to break into a grin. "Legends were often rewritten on the whim of whoever was ruling at the time. The same is true even within our own classical history, in the *Kojiki* and the *Nihongi*."

"So the Yamata-no-orochi was defeated by . . . what was his name . . . Okuninushi-no-Mikoto?"

The crowd around the table corrected her in unison. "Susano-o-no-Mikoto!"

"Oh, that's right. Was this Susano really a woman?"

"The tale of Yamata-no-orochi is said to have originated in China."

Inamoto reached over to the pile and picked up a book—the *Soshinki*, a collection of myths from the Six Dynasties period. He opened it to a page with a stick-on tab and began to summarize.

"It was in Central Min—that's the modern-day Chinese province of Fujian. A giant snake lived in the mountains there and rampaged through the nearby villages. Each year, the locals, out of fear of the serpent, offered a twelve-year-old girl as a human sacrifice. Nine children over nine years were eaten by the beast."

"Hey, that *is* a lot like the Orochi."

"But here's where it diverges. A girl named Ki, the daughter of Ritan, decided to oppose the monster. Ritan was the father of six girls, and Ki was the youngest. She must have been about the age of the other sacrifices—probably twelve. Doesn't that remind you of Princess Kushinada?"

"Yeah."

"Ki chose herself as the next offering, and she went to the giant snake's lair carrying a concealed sword. The young girl lured the serpent out with a dumpling made of steamed rice, and when the time was right, she struck down the beast."

"If I recall, Orochi was lured out by liquor."

"Correct. And if the Chinese tale was the basis for our story of the Orochi, the giant snake would have originally been killed by Princess Kushinada. When the legend was incorporated into the *Kojiki* and the *Nihongi*, the monster's defeat became one of Susano-o's achievements, and Kushinada went from a hero to just another one of the sacrifices."

As his talk went on, Yuri began to zone out, but suddenly, something he said flashed through the back of her consciousness.

Princess.

"No," she said, "it couldn't be . . ."

At first, the thought was so outrageous she could hardly believe it. But the name wasn't the only point that lined up. In the documents obtained from Izuno's group, Princess was referred to in code as "X."

Just then, Sakura's cell phone rang.

"I'm sorry," she said to the group. "Personal call."

Sakura left the room to take the call, and after a few minutes, she returned with a clearly wary expression.

"What's wrong? Something at home?"

"No, it was one of the researchers at Tsukuba. Her name's Nakaya."

"Why would someone at Tsukuba be calling you?"

Tsukuba, in Ibaraki Prefecture, was home to the Meteorological Agency's research center.

"Well, you know how I visit Princess fairly often? I've gotten to know some of the people there, and we've exchanged phone numbers. Anyway, she called me, crying. I guess Princess has gone out of control."

"Out of control?"

"Yes. Nakaya's looking after Princess tonight. The girl's usually fast asleep by now, but something's agitating her, and she's acting violent. Nakaya wanted to know if I had any tricks to calm her down, since I'm so good with her, and—"

"Sakura!" Yuri sprang to her feet and placed her hands atop Sakura's shoulders, who simply gaped back at her. "Go to Tsukuba."

"What? Now?"

"Yes, now." Yuri's expression was serious. "I want you to check on Princess. If my gut's right, Princess has some connection with what's going on."

"Huh?" Sakura said, but then, finally, it began to dawn on her. As soon as she realized what Yuri was thinking, she couldn't help but laugh. "Yuri, you can't be saying that Princess is . . . Surely you're not suggesting that. Right?"

"I can't believe it myself. But maybe the people who raised her did."

"What do you mean?"

"In their documents, they called her by the letter *X*. At least, that's how *we* read it. What if the 'X' stood for something else—what if it could be read some other way?"

"How else would you read it? Times? Strike?"

"We've been assuming 'X' was the Roman letter. But in Greek, it's the character called 'chi.' Sometimes it's written out as 'ki.' Does that sound familiar? But there's more. *Xi* is one way to represent the Greek letter pronounced 'zai'—it's the letter made of three horizontal lines—which is known in other languages as 'ksi'—or 'kushi.'"

Sakura's smile froze. "I'll be leaving."

"You do that."

Back at the ritual site, SDF soldiers continued to help with the excavation. Without the aid of machinery, the team wouldn't be able to move the giant stone slab. Instead, they dug through the dirt around it and created parallel ditches, each five meters deep, for the underground radar to survey.

Yojiro, who was staring into the monitor, said, "What on earth could that be?"

The protrusion on the kaiju's back had turned out to be larger than anticipated. The mass itself was at least twenty meters tall. With a profile shaped like an old Japanese gold coin, it bent over forward with its tip in the direction of the monster's heads. From its middle, a pair of appendages projected from its right and left. They were thin, with complex folds, and seemed like they could be fins or possibly folded wings. Beneath them rested a narrow stick of flesh.

So far, the team had captured cross-section images at three locations—enough information to make the task of projecting its full shape roughly on par with deciphering a Rorschach inkblot.

Kiichi tilted his head at the image. "What if its whole torso is on its side? Its stomach is facing over that way, and its leg is pointing up . . ."

"And this thin limb is a claw?" Yojiro said. "I think it's too thin—even for that. And where's the other leg then?"

The team's surveys had revealed the beast to be 140 meters long—a definite MM9. But its body was wider than the radar could penetrate, and they still hadn't been able to determine its shape. Assuming the protrusion was in fact a leg, its counterpart, presumably hidden on the creature's underside, was yet to be discovered. The main office had created a simulated image of the kaiju that somewhat resembled a squid, with eight necks extending from the base of a long, slender, triangular torso.

Yojiro continued, "And I can't keep from thinking about how the field of electrical disturbance centers on this organ."

"So what do you think it is?" Kiichi said.

"I don't know," he admitted with a distasteful expression. "It could be a chimera."

Kaiju weren't always merely giant-sized creatures. Some were giant-sized chimeras, mixtures of different animals from entirely unrelated species in one body. Famous chimera included the Gryphon of Greece, part lion, part eagle; the Tarasque of France, part lion, part turtle, and part dragon; and the Kelpie of Scotland, part horse, part fish. There were examples in Japan, as well—a half-mouse, half-dove and a half-mole, half-catfish. Cellular material recovered from the creatures' corpses displayed a mixing of genetic material beyond the capabilities of modern genetic engineering. Some biologists proposed the mixture was a result of horizontal gene transfer through viruses, but no one had been able to explain why the phenomenon only occurred with kaiju.

The parallel anthropic principle offered another explanation: if kaiju's bodies didn't consist of atoms, neither would they consist of DNA. When a giant chimera died, and its matter converged into the Big Bang universe, its genes would manifest as a fusion of its constituent animals precisely because that was what people expected to find.

Kiichi asked, "Are you saying there's something else stuck on top of the Orochi?"

"A many-headed snake in itself is a chimera, of a sort, already beyond the scope of biological science."

One of the soldiers came up behind the two men and said, "Sorry to interrupt, but we found something. Something odd. Could you come look?"

That got their interest.

"Something odd?" Yojiro asked.

The soldier led them to where one of the snake heads was being unearthed. He pointed to an object still mottled with clumps of dirt and said, "This was buried here."

It was a machine, wrapped inside a plastic bag to keep the moisture out. It had an antenna. *A wireless transmitter?* Affixed to its side was an impressively large battery.

The soldier asked, "Your team didn't bury this here, did you?"

"No," Yojiro said.

"I didn't think so. Judging from the condition of the dirt, I'd say it's been in the soil for months."

Yojiro picked up a thin cable that hung from the device. The cable was frayed at the end. "What's this?"

"We accidentally severed it when we dug the object up. This was on the other end." He held up a dirt-encrusted microphone. "It was affixed to the kaiju's skin."

Yojiro and Kiichi looked at each other. Their mobile unit had been sent to the island only days ago, but if the reports sent from the city hall on Nao Island were correct, the kaiju had begun awakening from its cryptobiotic state several months prior.

Had someone been monitoring the monster's heartbeat the whole time?

Astonished, Chief Kurihama said, "You're telling me that Princess is really Princess Kushinada?"

"That's not what *I'm* saying," Yuri replied. "It's what I think the CCI believes."

He looked at Dr. Inamoto. "What do you believe?"

"There's nothing I can say. I can't back up the theory, but neither do I have any basis to deny it."

"I never heard that Princess Kushinada was a giant!"

"But there's evidence that Susano-o was. In the *Kojiki* and the *Nihongi*, Susano-o turned Kushinada into a comb and stuck her in his hair before he set out to slay the Orochi. It's possible the story was created to explain her name, since *kushi* can mean 'comb,' but it also could have signified that compared to Susano-o's size, she was only as big as a comb. And if Susano-o wasn't in the original story, with Kushinada being the one who defeated the Orochi . . ."

"Then Princess Kushinada was a giant."

"It would follow. Now the next part I only noticed when I was reading through the materials anew. Hideyo Tomono thought that the legend of Susano-o slaying the giant serpent was based on Grecian lore. Hercules became Queen Omphale's slave to atone for the murder of a man during a fit of madness and the ransacking of the temple at Delphi. Susano-o was banished from the High Plain of Heaven after similar violent acts. Furthermore, in some versions of his tale, Hercules married the daughter of a bandit during his time in the guise of a woman in Omphale's palace. Her name was Xenodoke."

"Xenodoke? X. Kushinada."

"Yes. Xenodoke's father was a violent bandit known as Syleus, and his daughter may have shared his fiery temperament. It's possible that Hercules' feats were originally Xenodoke's. When he was made into the hero of the tales, she was relegated to the role of his wife, just like the warrior goddesses Athena and Artemis were made into Zeus's daughters. The unusual incident where Hercules dresses as a woman is consistent with incongruities arising from an imposed revision of the legend.

"*Xeno* is Greek for 'stranger,' 'alien,' something foreign. Xenodoke may have been something different from a human. By some route, that name reached Japan and made its way into the basis of stories compiled within the *Kojiki* and the *Nihongi*."

"What about the theory that the legend of Yamata-no-Orochi originated in China?"

"According to Tomono, the *Soshinki* wasn't the direct source of the tale. Rather, stories of a young girl slaying a giant snake or a many-headed dragon are found all across the globe. Although the majority of them have been rewritten to feature a male hero, the *Soshinki* was recorded in a form closer to the original."

Chief Kurihama let out a heavy sigh. "Be straight with me. How much credence should we give that theory?"

"Beats me." Inamoto raised his eyebrows and formed a wry smile. "I don't have the slightest idea. But if that thing isn't just any kaiju, but a creature with the ability to project the mythical outward from itself . . . anything that happens there won't follow the rules of science—it'll follow the rules of legends."

"And what happened in the myths could happen here?"

"It's possible."

Sakura was pulled over for speeding on the Joban Expressway, and thanks to the motorcycle cop's doggedly thorough grilling, she didn't make it to the Tsukuba Research Institute until just after midnight. With the 213-meter-tall meteorological observation tower standing against the night sky to her right, she turned off West Avenue and onto the road toward the main research building.

The campus was home to the Meteorological Agency's research and development efforts. Devoted not only to kaiju research, the R&D department employed 150 and covered fields such as climatology, typhoon research, seismology and volcanology, and oceanography. The institute housed a number of research labs including the meteorological wind tunnel; low temperature lab; radiation measurement, earthquake, and geomagnetic observatory; and kaiju husbandry station where those smaller kaiju (MM0 to MM1) deemed not to pose a danger to humans were raised and studied.

Suddenly, headlights appeared ahead as a cargo van came racing onto the road.

With a start, Sakura thought, *At this time of night?*

Sensing this wasn't just a coincidence, she stopped her bike on the side of the road. The van zoomed by without slowing. In the instant it passed, Sakura caught a glimpse of a struggle through the rear passenger window.

The street was dark, and she hadn't been able to see it clearly, but she thought she knew one of the people inside.

Princess?

After a moment's hesitation, she pulled a U-turn and followed after the vehicle.

She accelerated to close the distance, and soon, her suspicion was confirmed. Through the rear window, she saw several grappling figures. One of them, small, with long, tousled hair, struggled fiercely against the others, who seemed to be trying to hold her down.

What should I do?

Sakura didn't think she could force the van to a stop with her motorcycle. And even if she could, she'd be no match against several men. She'd only end up being captured herself.

She thought of her friend Nakaya inside the institute. *Did they attack her? Is she hurt? Should I call the police?* But to do that, she'd have to stop her bike and pull off her helmet. In the time it took to do that, she could lose sight of the van . . .

"To heck with it! So what if I get my license suspended!"

Keeping her left hand on the handle, she tore off her helmet with her right and tossed it to the side of the road. She took her cell phone out of her pocket, and since she wouldn't be able to dial a full number and drive at the same time, she selected one of her speed dial contacts.

"Hello!" she yelled over the wind. "Main office!"

The chief's face went pale.

"Princess has been kidnapped?"

Sakura's shrieks came from the receiver. "Yes! The van is headed . . . ummm . . . west!"

"Remnants of the CCI?"

"How should I know? Just get me some police backup! And I'm worried about Nakaya back at the institute, so get somebody to check on her."

"Got it. Right away. What's the number on the van's plate?"

"Um, it's a Chiba plate . . ."

She read the number. Chief Kurihama was writing it down when a woman's scream came from across the room. The office was thrown into turmoil.

"What is it?" Kurihama barked. He looked up, and his annoyance melted into shock. Four men in gorilla masks, dressed in all black, stormed into the room. Each carried a submachine gun.

"Don't move!" one of the figures shouted, apparently their leader. The room fell silent. He aimed his gun at one of the female operators. "Hang up."

The other three men faced down the workers in the room.

Kurihama, caught utterly by surprise, simply stared at them. His arm, phone receiver still in hand, hung slack at his side.

"The rest of you too," the leader said. "All of you, hang up your phones."

The operators frantically set down their receivers, and one by one, anyone else on the phone followed suit.

Another of the men pointed at Kurihama with his gun. "That includes you."

Sakura's panicked voice still issued from the line. "Hello? Hello! Chief, can you hear me? Hello?"

With a trembling hand, the chief laid the phone on its cradle. Her voice cut off mid-word.

"Good," the leader said, satisfied. "If you all keep calm and follow orders, you won't be harmed."

As he spoke, Yuri came to a realization. She knew that voice well. "Mikio? You're Mikio, aren't you?"

The leader regarded her. He let out a small sigh, then chuckled. "How did I not see this coming? I should have known you might be here. I guess there's no point in these disguises."

He plucked the mask from his head and bestowed upon Yuri a smile. "Little Yuri, you're all grown up."

Yojiro yelled into the transceiver, "What do you mean, stop setting the explosives? Kaiju Seven could wake any moment."

The chief seemed frazzled. "Um, well, that's because . . . we've, ah, come across some new information. If you kill Kaiju Seven . . . well, there's a strong theory that it would destroy the whole world."

"What?"

"That's what Dr. Inamoto believes. That kaiju could be a god— the god of the mythic universe. And if the god is destroyed, the mythic universe could collapse, the shock of which may prove cataclysmic to the Big Bang universe. We've already informed the SDF, and they are holding off on the explosives."

"I don't understand. Inamoto is saying that? Put him on the line. I want to hear him explain."

"No, he's . . . right now, he's looking through the texts in the other room."

"What does Yuri say?"

"Oh, ah, she agrees with him. At this present moment, attacking Kaiju Seven is too dangerous."

"So what do we do? We just fold our arms and watch as Seven wakes up and goes on a destructive rampage?"

"No, I'm not saying that. We're figuring out how to respond here. We just need to hold off on reckless actions. Since we don't know what may result, we shouldn't carelessly blow it up."

Yojiro clicked his tongue. "Okay. But we'll keep setting the explosives so they'll be ready anytime. All right?"

"Ah, yes, of course. If we discover anything new, I'll contact you. Bye."

Kurihama quickly hung up.

"What the hell is going on?" Yojiro shook his head in bewilderment. "Something isn't right . . ."

Kurihama's face was pale. "Was that good enough?"

"Just fine." Mikio, his submachine gun still pressed against the back of the man's head, snatched the microphone from the chief's hand.

Deliberately, he scanned the room with fierce eyes and said, "You're all going to follow our orders for a while. You'll be spreading false information in order to delay the blasting."

"I-it won't take long before you're found out," Kurihama said, his voice wavering. "S-s-someone will notice something's strange."

"I'm aware of that. I'm not planning to keep this up for days. Just a few short hours, until dawn. That'll be enough."

"Until dawn?"

"For years we've been monitoring what you call Kaiju Seven. We've listened to the sound of its blood flow for half a year, and we've collected a lot more data on the frequency and duration of its mythical field than you have. Within hours, at most, the field will no longer be intermittent, but a continuous projection. At that time, it will awaken."

Dr. Inamoto spoke. "You . . . you know something about the nature of that kaiju?"

"I certainly do," Mikio boasted. "It might not be in your folklore, but it is in ours. The great nine-headed dragon."

"Nine heads? But—"

"Nine heads, Dr. Inamoto. It has nine heads. We call it Kutoryu."

Kurihama yelled, "Wh-who are you people? What do you want? Global domination? Or global destruction?"

"Global destruction?" Mikio laughed. "No, no, don't be ridiculous. We want the opposite. What we want is the world to continue."

"What?"

"What I had you tell your colleague before—that wasn't a complete fabrication. Kutoryu must reawaken, and it must spread terror across the world. Were humanity able to trivially dispatch it, then and only then would the world cease to exist."

Sakura shook her phone up and down in frustration as she chased the van down the midnight highway.

"What's going on? Why won't you connect?"

With one hand, she speed-dialed the MMD's number again and again, but the call wouldn't go through.

She had no way of knowing that, aside from the bare minimum of lines to keep in contact with the media and the Ministry of Defense, the terrorists inside the main office had pulled all the phone lines from their jacks.

The kidnappers' van fled southeast, avoiding high-traffic roads and densely populated areas. Rice fields spread out along each side of the road. At that late hour, there were few people out.

Sakura, unfamiliar with the area, didn't know where they were heading.

"I guess I'll have to call the police."

She started to push the numbers, 1-1-0.

Just then, the rear door of the van lifted open in a flash. Inside, a man all in black was crouched on one knee. Behind him, a girl struggled with two other men.

Sakura's eyes widened. "You're kidding!"

In the beam of her motorcycle's headlight, she saw the gun in the crouching one's hands.

She ducked down and put on the brakes. A moment later, the man fired. Possibly a warning shot, the bullet flew far over her head.

"What is this, some action movie?"

Sakura stared dumbstruck at the van as it sped away. The man, apparently satisfied he'd scared her off, lowered the rear door.

She noticed her hand no longer held her cell phone. She'd dropped it in her panic. The road was dark, and it would be hard to go back and find the phone. And even if she did manage to find it, it probably would have broken in the fall.

The van's taillights shrank into the distance.

Sakura quickly regained her composure.

They're taking Princess.

And I'm the only one who can stop them.

"Your bullets don't scare me!" she shouted after them, and to herself.

She sped up her bike and resumed chase.

"They're nothing more than tiny lumps of metal!"

Mikio, submachine gun still in hand, sat himself on top of Kurihama's desk, gazed across the room, and said, gleefully, "We're a family of what you call yokai."

His men had collected all the workers' cell phones, and only a few landlines were still connected. Whenever a call came in from the media, the operators, from the end of the barrel of a gun, would give their callers nonanswers like, "We don't know anything about it yet," or "We're still investigating and can't comment," or "The person in charge of that is out of the office at the moment." Still, their voices faltered from fear, and some of their callers may very well have thought something was suspicious. But none would imagine that terrorists had seized the office.

"We're not particularly special for yokai, mind you," Mikio continued. "The only power we have to boast about is our ability to transform into the guise of humans."

Yuri was in shock. She'd known the man since she was a young girl. Of course she'd heard stories of yokai living as humans, mixed in with the public. But she never took the idea seriously. She never believed it could be true.

"We can't just take any form we please, but at least our ages, we can fake. I'm older than I look. My parents were able to obtain a family register in the confusion of the Meiji era, and we've lived as humans ever since. Because we age slowly, every few decades we have to make ourselves look young again and find new identities so as not to draw suspicion. It's all a bit of a bother, really, but we manage it.

"We live long, which, don't get me wrong, is nice, but it's difficult for us to bear offspring. A yokai couple having a child is a rarity separated by centuries. Neither can we mix with humans. So our numbers only decrease. The situation is grave enough, honestly, that we should be placed on the endangered species list alongside the Iriomote cat.

"I want to make myself perfectly clear: we don't hold any animus toward mankind. We've never been persecuted by you. Besides, how could we be? Most humans don't ever notice us. It was our own choice to live in hiding. Our slide toward extinction is not anyone's fault; we are caught in the currents of time. We've lived among humans our whole lives. We've even loved them."

He looked at Yuri, and for a moment, he allowed the sadness to slip through and tinge his face.

"And if it were possible, we'd wish to keep on living with you."

Yuri cut in, "Then why—"

"Please, let me finish. I had come to accept our species' fate. But I wanted to know where I came from. I wanted to know why yokai and kaiju exist in this world. My quest led me to astrophysics, and to my studies with your father.

"As I pursued my research of the connections between our people's ancient tales and the parallel anthropic principle, I reached a conclusion. I envisioned it—the birth of a new world."

Mikio sighed, and as if the words tasted foul inside his mouth, he spat, "A world without kaiju."

Inside the cargo van, the struggle continued.

"Can't you get her to calm down?" said the man at the rear window.

"Easy for you to say," said one of the two grappling with the girl, "she—*oof*!"

He howled in pain. Princess had a pretty good knee lift.

There were four kidnappers—the driver, their leader stationed at the rear window, and two men attempting to bind the girl with rope. Unlike in the movies, tying up a conscious and unwilling subject wasn't so easy. And although Princess looked like a twelve-year-old girl, she was undoubtedly a kaiju. She howled like a wild animal, flailed her arms and legs, and bit at the men. Even for two large men, pinning her down proved a difficult task.

The kidnappers' original plans had been to knock her out with an injected sedative, but Princess had resisted them and batted away the syringe, which shattered on the ground. Instead, they had to drag her into the van by sheer force.

The leader, his face pressed against the rear window, watched the motorcycle headlight on their tail. With a curse, he grumbled, "She's stubborn."

The bike had gained speed and was closing in. *Isn't she afraid of getting shot? I shot at her and she's still following us? How dumb can she be?*

If this keeps up, she'll find our hideout. I didn't want to kill anyone, but there's no other choice.

He opened the rear hatch and aimed his gun at Sakura.

Princess saw it. Her senses were sharper than those of a human. She'd recognized the roar of the motorcycle's engine, and she knew it belonged to Sakura. She didn't fully understand what a gun was, but intuitively, she knew *that man meant to harm Sakura.* The girl wanted to leap forward and stop him, but the two men held her back. She had to do something.

She reached her arms toward Sakura and opened her right hand.

A pale blue orb of light appeared from her palm. The orb floated out a few centimeters from her hand, then spun and flattened into a disc. It spun faster and faster, becoming thinner and wider until it was as big as an old LP record. One assailant, sensing danger, tried to pin down her arm. She turned her hand, and his made contact with the disc of light.

In an instant, his hand was severed at the wrist.

The leader, only moments from firing at Sakura, instead spun around. The man who'd lost his hand screamed and clutched at the wound, trying to hold back the spouting blood. The other man let go of her in surprise.

Princess was free.

She looked at the severed hand on the floor of the van. At last she knew how to correctly wield her power. She tilted her head back and drew the light to the leather collar around her neck.

Even though he knew he was in danger, the leader didn't fire upon the girl. Mikio had ordered him to keep her alive. Kutoryu was to be allowed to rampage, but if the dragon were to get out of control, she would be needed.

His hesitation would end his life.

The spinning disc made contact with the collar and sliced cleanly through the thick leather strap. She cut just slightly too deep and left a thin slash down her neck, but the wound was minor. Now nothing remained to restrain her.

She thrust her bare foot at the man's face, and for a brief flash, he heard the tearing of pajamas and saw the bottom of her foot growing at him, like through a camera quickly zooming in. Faster than he could pull the trigger, Princess kicked him out of the van.

"W-what?"

Sakura gasped as she saw the man tumble from the back of the van. She jerked the handlebars to the side to avoid hitting him.

She slammed on the brakes and brought her bike to a quick stop. Protruding from the rear of the van was something that looked like a white tree trunk several meters long. The vehicle's suspension dropped low and the van began to weave. One after the other, all four tires burst. Its frame was no longer able to support the increasingly heavy weight of matter not conforming to the law of conservation of mass. The van bottomed out, kicking up sparks as it screeched to a halt. Its roof bulged upward like a grilled rice cake.

The side doors slid open, and two men rolled out to escape, one gushing blood from his arm. After them, two arms burst out the sides of the car. With a scream, the driver dove out from his door.

The ballooning roof ripped apart, and like a butterfly emerging from its cocoon, the girl's pale back was exposed to the night. When she had been a human's size, a collar was enough to confine her. But now, with the weight of several tons and the strength to match, the van's metal frame was as flimsy as a wadded-up ball of paper.

Sakura watched the spectacle with a shudder. The girl still continued to grow, and as she slowly rose, the scraps of the van's frame fell around her, each fragment striking the pavement with a terrible sound. The three men scrambled away from the scene.

At last the girl stood upright, stark naked under the pitch-black sky. Sakura hadn't seen the child in her true form since the events in Gifu, and the girl had grown. She was now as tall as a seven-story building, with the illumination of the streetlights reaching no higher than her thighs, the rest in darkness. Princess shook her head, and her hair fluttered in a slow-motion silhouette against the night sky.

She looked up into the heavens and let loose a fearsome howl.

"Oogaaauu!"

Mikio continued, "In the universe of the anthropic principle, the law of causality reaches into the past. Causes do not necessarily precede effects. If mankind is the result—or, we could even include beings like us yokai and say that sentient creatures are the result—the past is shaped to provide a matching origin. Humans observe the universe, and therefore the universe's past is established. If mankind's observations change, then the past is also changed with it.

"In the earliest universe, the mythic universe, a many-headed dragon was the creator of all things. Humans were only bit players in the grand scheme of things. They weren't even self-aware. We call this the first age.

"As mankind spread across the earth and came to possess self-awareness, the world changed. Each individual person was weak, but with their great numbers, their observations overwhelmed the many-headed dragon's influence. With the birth of legends of god-desses and giantesses destroying the dragon, the stories reached into the past and became the real history. Those women became the new gods, and the many-headed dragon fell from the creator's throne. We call this the second age.

"But the second period was short-lived. With the advent of patri-archal society, the women's triumphs were rewritten with male gods and heroes in their place. Apollo defeated Delphyne, Hercules de-feated the Hydra, Susano-o defeated Yamata-no-orochi. Again, the past was altered. This was the third age.

"After that, polytheism fell out of favor, and the majority of hu-mans gave their faith to monotheistic religions. The world had not been created by a many-headed dragon, and neither by a pantheon of humanoid deities of flesh and blood, but by a singular, unseeable, and transcendent being. This was the fourth age.

"Now the fifth age is nearly upon us. With the advancement of science, a great number of humans think the idea of a creator God was incorrect. Instead, they have come to believe the universe was born out of a Big Bang 13.7 billion years ago.

"But the transition to the fifth age is not yet complete. We know this because of the kaiju. In the Big Bang universe, kaiju do not exist. Our world hasn't stabilized; influences of the second, third, and fourth ages still reverberate. This is because human observation isn't uniform. There are some who don't believe in the Big Bang and many who have never even heard of the theory. Therefore, we exist within a mixture of different universes.

"One might compare it to Schrödinger's cat. You're a physicist; I'm sure you've heard of it. According to quantum physics, the wave function doesn't collapse until the observation is performed. In the-ory, the cat exists simultaneously alive and dead simply because it is beyond human observation. The universe works the same way."

Yuri said, "But we *are* observing the universe."

Mikio shook his head. "No, no. I was just using Schrödinger's cat as a metaphor. Besides, we are not presently the true observers. The observers are in the future. The laws of cause and effect ripple back into the past. The people of the future grasp the ability to determine what form our universe, our history, and our laws of physics take.

"Right now, people believe in kaiju strictly because kaiju cause destruction, year in and year out. How could anyone deny the creatures' existence? But because of the efforts of the MMD, and those of groups like yours, this past century has seen a decline in the number of victims to kaiju attacks. Along with the ever-increasing destructive power of human weapons, kaiju-inflicted disasters will soon be a thing of the past.

"When that happens, people will no longer fear kaiju. Then their observations of the universe will shift. The Big Bang universe will grow ever more dominant, and kaiju will appear less and less frequently. The change in human observation will reverberate into the past. Kaiju disasters will fade from history.

"The people of the future will believe only in the Big Bang universe. They'll probably think that kaiju were nothing but legends. As soon as the last kaiju disappears from history, at that moment, the fifth age will truly be complete. The age we live in now will change with it. The kaiju disasters will *never* have existed and history will be reconstructed to remove any inconsistency with the new age. The smaller disasters will simply vanish and be forgotten. The larger ones, catastrophes that claimed tens of thousands of lives—those will likely become earthquakes and typhoons."

Chief Kurihama cut in. "W-well, wouldn't that be a good thing? If there weren't kaiju, then—"

"You think that would be good?" Mikio glared at Kurihama. The chief trembled under his gaze. "Weren't you listening? Without kaiju, only the agent of the disaster will change. The victims will of course remain. And the kaiju won't be the only ones to cease existence. We yokai will vanish with them!"

Mikio scowled. To Yuri, he seemed to be fighting back tears.

"Try to imagine it," he said. "Try to imagine how terrifying that would be. I'm not afraid of dying. Everyone dies. I can even accept

the inevitability of our extinction. But the total and complete nega-
tion of our family's tens of thousands of years of history, and each
and every real experience I've been through . . ."

Mikio clenched his fist. "It's the greatest terror—it's the shameful
feeling of utter helplessness."

Dr. Inamoto asked, "That's why you're doing this?"

"It is. Humans need to be afraid. When they think of kaiju, they
need to feel dread and awe. With this great disaster, we will instill
within them a terror they will never be able to forget and they will
never be able to deny—not for thousands of years, not for tens of
thousands of years, until the day the very last human dies. We will
prevent the completion of the fifth age and preserve the current universe, the overlap between the mythic and Big Bang universes, and
space where kaiju and yokai can exist.

"To achieve that goal, Kutoryu is perfect. It was passed down
in our traditions: 'In the house of the violent god, dead Kutoryu
waits dreaming.' The story was passed down from the second
age. Once every thousand years, the many-headed dragon and the
giantess awaken somewhere in the world, and their battle unfolds.
The legend even appears in the Book of Revelation, Chapter 20. The
dragon—the devil, Satan—is defeated by God, cast down into the
earth, and bound for a thousand years. Every thousand years, he is
released for a short time.

"We think it last occurred some time around AD 1000 somewhere in inner South America. Before that, in the Middle East.
Before that, China. Each time the number of heads was different.
Eighty years after the battle in the Middle East, the news reached St.
John on the island of Patmos, where he wrote it into his Revelation.
In the twelfth chapter, a giant woman appeared in heaven and was
faced with a seven-headed red dragon. Of course, John, a worship-
per of Christ, made the woman to be Mary, Mother of God, and the
dragon a being seeking to destroy the unborn Savior.

"Along with the sleeping Kutoryu, we found Princess, who had
already awakened, and we secured her. Her fate is to defeat Kutoryu.

But we're going to change that. We're holding her captive to delay their confrontation. Kutoryu will spread destruction. His victims will number in the millions."

"All for that?" As Kurihama spoke, his voice cracked. "You're going to harm all those people just for your own sake?"

"Not just for us," Mikio said with a smile. "Think about it. You'll all disappear too, won't you?"

"What?"

"Wouldn't you? The MMD exists only because kaiju exist. A world without kaiju won't have the MMD. All of you here in this room will be erased from history."

The room fell silent.

"Try to imagine it. Can you handle it? How about it? All proof of your existence—faded to nothing. All of your struggles, all of your love, all of your pain, everything. All of it will never have happened. Can you accept something so senseless?"

Mikio dropped his voice, barely above a whisper now. "You can understand my pain, can't you? Now that I've told you everything, I hope I can have your help."

He looked across his transfixed audience, then spoke, this time with force. "This world needs kaiju."

Meanwhile, on Kojin Island—

"This is bad!" Yojiro cried out in the darkness. The electricity had cut out, and the earth periodically rumbled beneath their feet.

With a fearful expression, the commander of the SDF unit asked, "Does this mean it's about to wake up?"

"No, I think it already has. I've felt shaking like this before. The kaiju is pushing against the dirt, trying to break through the surface."

The commander turned and shouted to his subordinates, "Evacuate everyone immediately!"

They scattered in all directions, calling out, "Evacuate! Evacuate!"

The teams split among ten inflatable boats waiting on the shore. With the electrical interference, none of the engines worked, and the passengers were forced to row themselves.

Oar in hand, Ryo cursed and said, "What the hell is headquarters doing?"

The soldiers had finished setting the explosives on each of the kaiju's eight heads. The charges were even equipped with remote detonators ready to ignite on command. But within the disturbance field, the remote was incapable of transmitting the signal.

There had been a chance just minutes earlier, before the latest blackout. They could have set off the explosives and dispatched the beast before it awakened. But with the orders from the main office, they had been forced to watch the perfect opportunity slip through their fingers. With the kaiju revived, they had no choice but to assume that the explosives were now useless.

Two clusters of lights on the water ahead belonged to two JMSDF destroyers, the *Hisame* and the *Shigure*. The ships had anchored one kilometer north of Kojin Island. Their 72mm .62 caliber rapid-fire naval guns and 20mm Phalanx systems were trained on the island, ready to attack as soon as the monster revealed itself.

But the permission to engage still hadn't come from the MMD headquarters. The Mobile Unit hadn't heard anything from them at all.

Chief Kurihama paused in thought, then said, "What are you trying to make us do?"

"Nothing." Mikio beamed at him. "Don't do anything. I want you to keep on doing nothing. Don't give any orders to the team on the island. With what you told them about the end of the universe, I highly doubt they'll strike. Before they know it, they'll be too late."

"In order for us to continue existing, the kaiju has to wreak havoc?"

"Precisely."

Mikio turned his back on the chief and presented the room with a wide, yet forced smile. "We don't intend to harm you. Just be patient a little while longer. Then we'll take our leave, and you all can get back to your jobs. Just don't forget: you, us, we all exist only as long as kaiju also exist."

Then, Yuri saw it. Behind Mikio's back, Kurihama slowly began to rise. *No, he can't! Mikio's looking away, but what about the other three? They'll notice!*

Swiftly, Yuri yanked on the cord of a nearby phone. The receiver clattered to the ground. Mikio—and the other three—spun and pointed their guns at the woman. For just that brief second, no one had their eyes on the chief.

Kurihama took his chair into his hands, lifted it up into the air, and swung it back down on Mikio's head. Mikio staggered. His three underlings turned in surprise and snapped their guns to bear on the chief. But he stood too close behind the yokai, and the three couldn't fire without endangering their leader.

As they hesitated, Kurihama swung the chair once more and landed a second blow. Within an instant, the office workers swarmed the terrorists from behind. The three were quickly overwhelmed by the greater numbers and brought to the floor. One submachine gun let out a clipped burst-fire roar, but the bullets only opened holes in the floor. The team had worked in unison as if on signal. Not even twenty seconds had passed from Kurihama's first strike until the four intruders were disarmed.

"Don't underestimate the MMD!" The chief sneered down at Mikio, who had curled up on the floor, hands on head. "As part of the Meteorological Agency, it's our duty to save every single person from disaster we possibly can. To hell with the anthropic principle! What does it know anyway? We defend humanity against kaiju. Just you watch us."

Kurihama looked back and gave out orders in quick succession. "All the men, tie these guys up. There has to be some duct tape around here somewhere. You women, contact the police. And get our phone lines up and running. Tell the SDF they have permission to attack!"

The room filled with activity. The four yokai were bound in a haphazard winding of duct tape and plastic wrapping cords. The phones were reconnected, and emergency communications went out to all quarters.

But the tie job had been too quick and too careless. Mikio shook free from his binds and took off running. He shoved past several of the MMD staff, scrambled atop a desk, and, moving as nimbly as a monkey, leapt to the window, unlocked the latch, and cast open the blinds.

Yuri called out for him to stop, but he only flashed her a remorseful glance before diving out the window and into the dark. The women screamed.

Yuri and a few of the others dashed to the window, expecting to see Mikio on the ground in a pool of blood. But they didn't. What they saw was something black, shrouded in torn scraps of human clothes, skittering down the side of the building on its multiple long legs.

When it reached the ground, it fled into the darkness and out of sight.

A few of the men turned from the window to give chase.

"He got away!" yelled one.

"What the hell was that thing?" said another.

Kurihama shouted over them both. "Let him go! Catching him is the police's job. We have our own work to do. First, what's happening on Kojin Island? What about Yojiro's team?"

Five minutes earlier—

"It's moving!" Ryo shouted. He stood on the deck of the *Hisame*, watching the island through a pair of binoculars. Yojiro, Asaya, and Kiichi hurriedly raised theirs to their eyes.

Under the illumination of the two ships' searchlights, the island shore slowly swelled upward. One neck lifted up and shook off the sand, followed by another. Up close, the kaiju's motions probably created a cacophony, but at the ships' distance, the noise was drowned out by the waves. The result—a silent movie, no background music, no sound effects—was all the more unsettling for it.

Kiichi cursed. "And we *still* can't attack?"

The F-15 Eagles had already scrambled from the Tsuiki Air Force Base and were on their way. All that was left was to wait for the order to engage.

Asaya whispered, "It's red."

In the ships' lights, the dragon's necks were blood red.

After such a long slumber, the beast did not awaken in a good mood.

The last place it had hibernated, a millennium prior, was in a faraway land. The end of the great battle six thousand years ago, the savage clash against the Elder God for the rule of Earth, had left its body destroyed, the essence of its soul sealed away deep underground. In the languages of the humans, the state was called death. But to this creature, death wasn't any more than a temporary dream.

Such rules of life—*The dead don't come back to life,* and *New life is born to a mother*—did not apply. Though its body might be destroyed, its essence was immortal. It had no creator but came forth from nothingness.

For what could create the Creator?

It had once ruled the world but now was bound by chains repugnant and mythical. Its strength had diminished. Only once each thousand years did the Elder God's curse break and grant him a new body so that the First Battle could be reenacted. The defeated would be sealed away for the next thousand years—for the two opponents, it was a custom, a law. Consumed by hatred and burning with a ferocious ambition, the beast had dreamed of nothing but victory over the Elder God and the rightful return of the world into its clutches.

Humans had once lived in terror of the beast. Even after it fell from the throne of the gods, they had feared it. The megalithic cultures of the world, their peoples in touch with the spiritual world, predicted where next the beast would arise. They erected worship sites and attempted to appease the dragon's spirit—although their efforts would always prove futile.

Now it had again awakened. The beast was bathed in a bright light and affronted by it. The beams were being cast by two ships floating in the sea. Such a dazzling, unpleasant light had not existed the last time the dragon had arisen. In these thousand years, humans had again claimed some impertinent scraps of knowledge.

How arrogant.

It scoffed at them, then came to a decision. Before the fight against the Elder God, it would mete out a bit of punishment for these puny, dimwitted, and impudent creatures. It would teach them who the true ruler of this world was.

The time had come to herald the return of the king.

Ryo shouted, "It's coming up!"

With the emergence of the last of the eight necks, the dragon shook its body and began to advance. As the mountainside crumbled around it, the rear half of the kaiju's body came up from the earth, and along with it, the unidentified appendage on its back—

The lights cut out.

Yojiro and the others looked around in confusion. All of the destroyers' lights had gone off. Darkness shrouded the ships.

"What the—" Yojiro said. "It can't be. Not this far!"

Ryo slapped him on the shoulder, pointed off the port side, and said, "Over there!"

To the west of Kojin Island, over two kilometers away from the kaiju, the lights of Tamano City port disappeared in succession, as if covered by a sweeping curtain. The eastern island of Nao-shima had already gone dark.

"Number Seven!" Asaya cried out. "It's glowing!"

The four men of the Mobile Unit looked through their binoculars at the kaiju.

Bright red and yellow lights flickered above the creature. It became quickly apparent the intense flashes emanated from the mysterious appendage on its back.

Yojiro gasped. "Is that . . . humanoid?"

With the scant background illumination, he couldn't discern any details, but the outline formed by the points of light appeared to be the head and arms of a person. At first, Yojiro thought the figure sat astride the kaiju, but he realized the silhouette's lower half seemed to merge *into* the dragon's back. Then, as though issuing a proclamation, the shape slowly and deliberately raised its arms into the sky.

In the next instant, one of the dragon mouths opened and shot out a beam of light. The brilliant glare filled the lenses of the four men's binoculars, and they screamed and covered their eyes with their hands.

The beam was golden white and jagged like lightning, although this lightning cut straight across the sky, nearly parallel to the ocean's surface. The ray connected with one of the *Hisame*'s cannons—a full kilometer away—and cut through the armored hull with a shower of sparks. Seventy-eight-millimeter shells exploded in a chain reaction, and the gunner, enveloped in flames, spilled out onto the deck, screaming and writhing, his hands to his face.

Another mouth let loose a bolt of light. This one hit the *Hisame*'s mast. The mast's center glowed bright red and slowly melted down toward the deck. A third shot grazed the bridge. With a bright flash, the glass windows shattered, and the sharp fragments left serious injuries on the captain and several of his crew. The fourth beam cut into the sky, but the fifth was on target and smashed into the ship's hull just above the waterline.

The kaiju continued its barrage. The *Hisame*, without any power to its systems, was incapable of mounting any counterattack. The large ship, dead in the water, was a perfect target. The *Hisame* was helpless. It sat under the relentless bombardment, increasingly damaged, in flames, and riddled with holes. Sailors screamed, ran in all directions, and dove into the water.

After a few dozen blasts, the kaiju relented, likely tired from the display of force. But the respite didn't last even half a minute. The eight necks slowly swiveled to their next target—the *Shigure*. This time all eight heads fired simultaneously. From the side of the ship came a brilliant explosion, the noise of it rumbling across the night sea.

It was the hammer of God.

Within minutes, flames from the two ships rose tall into the dark sky. The kaiju, satisfied with the scene, ceased its attack. It advanced to the shore and dove into the waters with a giant splash.

There wasn't time to play with these small fry. The true opponent awaited.

"Stop!" Sakura leaned out the police car's rear window and shouted, "Princess, stop!"

Two cops in a patrol car had driven by, and she filled them in and got permission to ride with them.

Princess was running down the road ahead. She moved as if in slow motion—more than four times slower than a human—but her stride was tens of times larger. At full speed, she could top forty kilometers an hour.

Ignorant of traffic rules, the girl strode right down the center of the highway. Each footstep, with the weight of over a hundred tons slamming down from the sky, left deep holes in the asphalt. She tore through power lines and uprooted traffic signals and highway lights. The clamor woke up nearby residents from their sleep. Thankfully, at night, traffic was light. Drivers, startled by the giantess in their rearview mirrors, caused a number of accidents, but the girl hadn't squashed any of the vehicles under her feet—yet. Had it been daytime, a great number of casualties would have been left in the girl's wake.

The chase proved to be incredibly dangerous. Princess left behind a trail of craters, and to maneuver past them at forty kph was to risk their lives. Luckily, the policeman behind the wheel was a skilled driver, and he deftly wove through the debris and destruction like a skier on a slalom course.

The officer in the passenger seat held out his personal cell phone and said, "I got the MMD on the line."

Sakura snatched it from him. "Hello! Headquarters?"

"Sakura, is that you? Is Princess really on the loose?"

She quickly filled him in on what had happened, then said, "We were on the 356 for a little while, along the Tonegawa River. We just passed Inzai, and—" She peered into screen of the GPS navigation system. "We're headed southwest on Highway 59, almost to Shiroi, and still going forty."

Kurihama's gulp was audible. "You'll be in Tokyo within the hour."

"That's true."

"Stop her!"

"What?"

"Do whatever it takes to stop her. Don't let her cause any damage. Please! You're the only one who can."

Sakura considered the gravity of his order. Kurihama made a habit of saying he didn't want any martyrs so long as he was chief. For him to issue such a dangerous command, the situation must have been truly dire.

"I understand," Sakura said. "I'll do what I can."

She looked at the driver. "Can you get in front of her?"

"If we find a side road, I can pull off."

His partner pointed to the GPS display. "If we turn left at the T-intersection one block past the NTT building, I think we can overtake her."

"The problem is after that," the driver said. "Will she keep going southwest, or will she turn west onto the 464?"

"West," Sakura said without hesitation. "She'll go west."

He didn't ask why. There wasn't time to. He yanked the steering wheel and said, "I'm going for it!" The car veered left, maintaining almost all its speed through the turn. The centrifugal force pressed Sakura against the right-side door.

The shocking news came in from Kojin Island.

"Kaiju Seven," Kurihama said. "It got away?"

Yojiro's face on the screen looked haggard. He had just come out of the water and still wore the orange life vest. "Yes. It was a total defeat. As soon as it came up from the ground, its antielectrical field widened drastically. All of Nao Island and even Tamano City on the mainland were under a complete blackout. I'd say the radius was five kilometers—"

"Five kilometers?"

"Yes. The destroyers were helpless. And the ships, unable to move, were struck by the light beams—"

"Light beams?"

"From each of its eight heads. I think it's using a kind of lightning. It appears to be able to send the lightning bolt's path straight across the sky. It can fire them in one concentrated burst or in a sustained rapid fire. The *Hisame* and the *Shigure* were completely destroyed. There were many casualties."

An operator came up to the chief holding the latest printout of data. "Chief, wreckage of the two F-15s we lost contact with have been found off the coast of Nao Island. Their engines shut off when they entered the kaiju's field."

"God help us."

Kurihama felt dizzy. His worst nightmare had come about. Kaiju Seven had already left a staggering number of victims—and if they didn't do something, that number would only spiral higher.

The chief returned his gaze to the main monitor. "Where is Seven now?"

"It entered the water," Yojiro said, "and went around the north shore of Nao Island toward the east. We believe the kaiju should just be passing Te Island and headed for Shodo Island. And Chief, you need to hear this. The thing on its back? It's human."

"Human?"

"It's a chimera. The top half of a human is on the dragon's back. There wasn't much light, and we were at a distance, so I don't have any more details than that. But it definitely appeared human, and it twinkled all over—yellow and red, like a deep-sea fish."

Yuri said to herself, "A human-dragon chimera . . ."

She remembered Mikio's words. *The dragon has nine heads. Was the ninth head a human's?*

Kurihama turned to face his staff. "Contact the SDF. There is to be absolutely dead airspace within a five-kilometer radius of the kaiju. And warn the press! Issue an alert to all areas with shores in the eastern Seto Sea. Call for evacuation."

Kensuke, the military geek, was still attempting to process the situation. "But how do we attack something like this? Missiles and ASROCs won't be of any use inside that field, and it's next to impossible to hit a moving target with artillery fire at five kilometers. And once on land and inside the cities, it'll have too much cover. Besides, without wireless communication, it would be difficult for forward observers to report where the shots land."

"That's why we need to think of something," the chief said. "It's our job to come up with a plan."

The bank of operators had been busy entering all the incoming data into the computer system. On the large wall-mounted monitor, the kaiju's current location and projected path were displayed over a map of Japan. Number seven was following the northern shoreline of the Seto Sea, headed east at twenty kilometers per hour. Its estimated location in twelve hours covered a wide area from Himeji all the way to Osaka.

Yuri and Inamoto stood next to each other, looking up at the map. Princess's path was included on the eastern edge of the display. The girl was headed west.

"They're being pulled toward each other," Yuri said. It couldn't be a coincidence.

"They intend to have their mythical battle," Dr. Inamoto said. "The legend that repeats every thousand years . . . and this time, here, in Japan."

"But if they do, the damage will be . . ."

"Yes. If we can't avoid the battle, we have to lead them somewhere away from population centers."

An operator shouted, "I've got a question from the media! What are we going to call the kaiju?"

Kurihama hesitated. He'd rather not use the name those men had called it. But there wasn't time to think of anything else.

"Kutoryu. Kaiju Seven is hereby known as Kutoryu!"

On Route 464, a four-lane divided highway running alongside the Hokuso Rail Line, the patrol car stopped three hundred meters in front of Princess. Sakura brushed aside the policemen's protests and hopped out of the vehicle.

"Princess!" she yelled from the bottom of her lungs. "Stop!"

She waved her arms and jumped up and down. Princess drew steadily nearer.

Will she see me? she worried. *Maybe I'm just too tiny to draw her attention . . .*

But Princess saw her. She slowed to a stop just a few paces in front of the patrol car, plopped her knees to the pavement, and bent over above Sakura.

Even though this wasn't Sakura's first close encounter with Princess in the kaiju's true form, she felt her face tighten with fear. The two cops stumbled back and drew their weapons with trembling hands.

"Kooo?"

Princess gazed down with giant eyes at the woman, and tilted her head in puzzlement. Sakura spread her arms wide, welcoming, and forced a wide smile.

"P-Princess, do you recognize me? It's me," she said, then, pausing between each syllable, "Sa. Ku. Ra."

Princess understood. Her voice boomed happily, *"Aaaaahh!"*

Like a shriveling balloon, she rapidly shrunk down.

Once again in human size, she threw herself into Sakura's arms.

Kurihama was pleased. "You've recovered Princess? Good. Nice work. There's an SDF base nearby. You know the one? Take her there. I'll fill them in and have them prepare a helicopter for you."

He turned to the bank of operators. "Koichi!"

"Yes, sir!" Koichi hadn't waited to call up an Internet search for the Shimofusa Air Base. "They have an Air Rescue Wing UH-60J. It should be ready 24-7."

"What's its range?"

"Five hundred eighty-four kilometers. Just enough to make it to around Osaka and Kobe. If we're going to need it for combat operations, it might have to refuel along the way."

"Get them on the line immediately!"

"Hold on!" Sakura cut in over the phone. "Do you mean it? Are you going to make Princess fight a kaiju? Isn't that just sending her to her death?"

"We don't have any options," Kurihama said with a pained expression. "As long as there's that antielectrical field, the SDF can't get close to that thing. And right now, it's headed for Kobe. If we allow it to make landfall, we'll have another '95 on our hands."

Sakura fell silent.

Yuri said, "Put me on," and took the receiver from the chief, who went back to giving orders.

"Sakura?" she said. "I know this is tough. But there really isn't any other way. It's fate. Princess was born to fight Kutoryu."

"But—"

"We need to have faith in the legend." Yuri kept her voice gentle, but firm. "I know it's strange for a scientist like me to say, but science isn't going to do us any good against that thing. We must rely on the legend, and it tells us that the girl will defeat the dragon without fail. Of course, we'll do everything we can to help her win."

"But—"

"Think. What's our duty?"

After a brief pause, Sakura answered. "To save people from kaiju."

"Exactly. And we have to give it everything we possibly can."

For a few seconds, they were silent. Then Sakura said, "All right. I'll bring Princess to the air base."

The plan hit an unexpected snag.

The helicopter departed from the Shimofusa Air Base with Sakura and Princess on board and, after an hour flying at full speed, touched down at the Komaki Air Base in Aichi Prefecture for refueling. Princess quickly became impatient at the delay and grew back to full size, intent on heading west. Sakura managed to calm her down, but not before the girl had wrecked the helicopter. The vehicles and crew at Komaki had been sent to JGSDF Camp Yao to help with the evacuation of Kobe, and a precious two and a half hours were spent finding a replacement.

Dawn broke. When their light helicopter finally was in the air, Kutoryu had already passed the Ie Islands. Because the creature was headed directly toward Princess's location, it was expected to make landfall at Kakogawa City. In a last-ditch effort to change Kutoryu's course, Kurihama sent Princess's helicopter south over Ise Bay.

The gambit worked surprisingly well. Kutoryu turned due east and seemed like it would pass through the Akashi Straight.

Kurihama stood in front of the map display, wake-up coffee in hand. He took a sip from the cup and made a face at its bitterness.

"I wonder if we can just lead it into the Pacific," he said. "There's nothing for it to destroy out there."

"I don't think that'll work," Toshio said. "If we try to take Princess in any direction away from Kutoryu, she'll go nuts. Besides, an ocean battle will leave her at too great a disadvantage. The dragon seems like a good swimmer."

The operator was right. A creature over a hundred meters long swimming underwater at twenty kilometers per hour was a small wonder—and a violation of the laws of physics.

"How's the evacuation of Kobe?" the chief asked.

"A long way to go. A lot of people are still sleeping and are unaware of the alert."

Kurihama clicked his tongue. "That's bad. If that thing comes out of the water near the city, who knows how many will die?"

"According to the Mobile Unit's report, Kutoryu's movements are sluggish aboveground. We have to draw it out and bring the fight on land, somewhere where there aren't many people around."

"He's right," Yuri said. "The dragon must be somewhere around sixty times more massive than the girl and four times her size. That means time flows half as quickly for it as it does for her."

Kurihama nodded. "You're talking about the time scale."

Kaiju experience time differently than humans, at a rate inversely proportional to the square root of their size.

"Yes. To put it another way, Princess can move twice as quickly as Kutoryu. Speed may be her only advantage. She might be able to dodge the dragon's light beams and get around behind its back."

"Then we need to find a place on land." Kurihama pointed to the map of the Hanshin region from Kobe to Osaka. "Soon, Kutoryu will pass through the Akashi Straight. That means we're too late to use Awaji Island. After that, it would have to be somewhere in Kobe. If we limit it to nonresidential areas, then . . ."

He pointed to a man-made island jutting out into the sea from Kobe City. Port Island. South of it floated a second, smaller island, home to a newly opened airport.

"How about here?" the chief offered. "The airport will have plenty of open space, and a battle there won't endanger any lives. The runways might get a bit dinged up, but—"

"No!" Kensuke cut in emphatically. "That open a space is absolutely no good."

"Why?"

"Kutoryu uses energy projectiles, right? And from the reports, it has a range of over one kilometer. A location with few obstructions will be disadvantageous for Princess. She'll get shot before she can get close."

"So where do you propose?"

"We need to lure it somewhere with a lot of cover. Somewhere she can hide herself as she advances to close range and brings the battle to it. That's her only chance."

Kurihama's eyes widened. "Cover? You mean . . . buildings?"

"Yes."

"You're saying we should let two kaiju battle it out in the middle of the city? Do you have any idea the kind of damage—"

"What about old buildings nobody cares about anymore?" Kensuke said.

"Oh, and there's going to be some place that convenient for us?"

A female operator said, "There is!"

An online map of Port Island was on her computer screen. In the center of the map, part of the island blinked red.

"But that's . . ." Kurihama said. "An amusement park?"

"Yes," replied the operator. "I'm from Kobe. I went there several times when I was growing up. But the park closed this March, and now it's being torn down."

Kurihama thrust his finger at the operator. "That's our place! Call the owner. And get the word out. Make sure we've evacuated that island. Get Sakura's helicopter headed there."

"Yes, sir!"

A little under an hour had passed since they took off from Komaki. The OH-6D, a light helicopter from the Flying Training Wing, closed in on Port Island.

"Looks they made it on time," Ryo said.

He stood at the Kobe Heliport, located near the island's western edge, and gazed up at the gray sky, watching with relief as the helicopter came in from the east.

The Mobile Unit had made it onto land at Tamano with their lives intact and raced to the island by car. With all the evacuees, traffic had stalled in the oncoming lanes, but the eastbound lanes were clear, and their team had been able to overtake Kutoryu.

Next to Ryo, Yojiro reported to headquarters.

"Yes," he said, "We just now can see the helicopter. It's about to land. Hm? Hello? Hello?"

Ryo turned to him. "What's wrong?"

"The connection dropped."

Ryo took the cell phone from his pocket and flipped it open. The LCD was blank.

Asaya paled. "It couldn't . . . It's not supposed to get here for another twenty minutes."

They had miscalculated. Kutoryu swam too deep for sonar to reach, so the MMD team had been estimating its progress from the antielectrical field. They had failed to notice that the dragon increased speed as it felt Princess draw near.

"This is bad." Ryo turned around and shouted up to the helicopter. "Go back! Sakura! Go back!"

But there wasn't a chance she would hear him. Even if she had, it was already too late. The helicopter's engine stopped.

"H-hey, wait! The engine shut off!"

In the rear of the four-seat helicopter, Sakura was overcome by panic. She had the sensation of her body floating up, and reflexively embraced Princess.

The pilot pulled back on the collective pitch lever and shouted, "Don't worry! Helicopters don't crash that easily."

He spoke truth. Even if a helicopter's engine stopped, and the vehicle began to drop, pressure from wind at the front would keep the blades spinning like a child's bamboo toy propeller and allow the helicopter to maintain a slow, steady descent. Pilots were trained for autorotation emergency landings.

But that only held true if the helicopter's airspeed was fast enough. Since Sakura's helicopter had already begun to slow down for its landing, the autorotation was extremely difficult to control. As hard as the pilot pulled the collective pitch lever to adjust the rotor blades, the aircraft still lost altitude. Resistance from the transmission started to roll the helicopter to the left. The pilot slammed down on the right pedal to counteract the rotation. The cyclic stick, which provided forward and sideways control over the craft, was of no use at all.

Sakura screamed, "We're going to crash!"

Through the half-sphere of the canopy, she had seen the Ferris wheel approaching, only an instant before the impact.

Several seconds after the rotors completely stopped, the copilot hesitantly asked, "Is everybody all right?"

Sakura replied, "Y-yeah. We're okay—" She looked down. "Eek!"

The helicopter's landing skids had caught on the very top of the amusement park's Giant Wheel, a twenty-story-tall Ferris wheel.

The pilot spoke in a near whisper. "Keep very still. If we lose our balance, we'll fall."

"H-how are we going to get down?" Sakura asked.

"This is a search-and-rescue helicopter, so it's equipped with a hoist . . . No, wait, that won't work. The motor's electrical."

"So what are we going to do?"

"All we can do is to just keep calm and wait for someone to rescue us."

"Any rescue helicopter's not going to be able to fly here either. Besides, that kaiju will get to us first."

The two airmen were silent. There was nothing more they could do. Princess, quickly losing her patience, moaned "*Ooohooooh*," and twisted her body in Sakura's arms. Sakura tightened her hold to keep the girl under control.

Below them spread the amusement park grounds, which had yet to be torn down. From atop the Ferris wheel, they could see it all—roller coasters like the Double Loop Coaster, the Munich Autobahn, and the BMR-X, and other rides like the Flying Carpet, the Condor, and the Golden Hinde.

"I know we're in an amusement park," Sakura said, her voice shaking, "but I'm not amused."

"You think this is a good time to make jokes?"

"If I didn't, I don't know how I could make it through this."

Just then, the Ferris wheel creaked under the helicopter's full ton of mass. Sakura shrieked.

"Sakura!" Ryo's voice came from afar. "Sakura!"

She regained her composure and looked down to see Ryo and Kiichi waving at her. Slowly, cautiously, she slid the door open a crack and popped her head out.

"Ryo!"

"Is Princess all right?"

She thought, *What about me?* but said, "She's fine."

"Hang tight. I'll think of a way to get you down."

"I'll look forward to it."

It was nice of him to say, but she well knew there was no way down.

"It's here!" Asaya pointed to the sea.

Yojiro, who was standing at the edge of the man-made island, watching the water through a pair of binoculars, had already seen it. Choppy waves rose above a gigantic, black underwater shape rapidly approaching the quay. The two men ran to shelter under the shade of a nearby warehouse.

As the underwater shape neared the edge of the island, the sea swelled up, then split apart in an explosive burst. The massive spray cascaded down to reveal the monster's writhing body. Its eight necks danced in the air as if suspended by invisible threads, and from its eight mouths came a surprisingly birdlike cry that sounded something like, "*Pi-lu-lu-lu.*"

The creature was bright red. Glistening scales the color of blood covered its body. It hooked its short front legs slowly atop the quay and dragged itself out from the water. Yojiro, seeing its form under broad daylight for the first time, shuddered with fear.

What had terrified the man was the top half of a human growing from the kaiju's back.

It was a woman, maybe twenty meters from her head to her waist. Her skin was a mottled mixture of red and purple, her bosom ample, her long black hair trailing down. Her body was covered with glowing spots of red and yellow, as if her skin had been inlaid with precious gemstones. From her back sprouted two batlike wings folded in like a cloak, though those seemed to serve no apparent function. But evolutionary necessity had no place here—this was a being from the mythic universe.

Her face, kaiju or not, had a beauty to it. Her irises were elongated like a cat's, and her ears too were pointed and feline. Her red lips were opened wide and her fangs on full display. Two large horns, alongside eight smaller ones, sat atop her head like a crown. Across her forehead were rows of shapes that could have been lettering. Yojiro was reminded of the seventeenth chapter of the Book of Revelation.

> And I saw a woman sit upon a scarlet colored beast, full of names of blasphemy, having seven heads and ten horns. And the woman was arrayed in purple and scarlet color, and decked with gold and precious stones and pearls . . . And upon her forehead a name written, MYSTERY, BABYLON THE GREAT, THE MOTHER OF HARLOTS AND ABOMINATIONS OF THE EARTH.

Yojiro felt his head go numb. "This is insane."

Was it true? he wondered. *Two thousand years ago, did this monster appear in Palestine, just like this, only with a different number of heads? John must have witnessed it, or at least heard the account. Delphyne, Hydra, Typhon, Tiamat—all had either been chimera, part serpent and part goddess, or many-headed dragons borne from a goddess.*

The world had once been ruled by a goddess dragon.

Kutoryu's 140-meter long body was now fully onshore. It shook off waves' worth of water and advanced on four short lizardlike legs. Asphalt crumbled beneath each five-thousand-ton step, and its legs sank deep into the landfill. The creature walked with some difficulty, as if traipsing through mud, but following an ancient battle instinct, it pressed on toward its fated enemy. A warehouse stood in its way, but not for long, crumpling like paper beneath the kaiju's mass.

It was an MM9—the largest kaiju in the history of the MMD.

"Can you reach them?" Kurihama asked.

"No," one of the operators said. "We've lost communications with nearly all of central Kobe."

When Kutoryu made landfall faster than they'd predicted, the main office was thrown into confusion.

Yuri looked at the tiny high-angle video feed on the monitor and whispered, "That's Kutoryu . . ."

Through the morning fog, the kaiju looked like a small red lizard, kicking up a cloud of dust as it crawled between wooden building blocks. The video was being broadcast from the Nunobiki Herb Garden atop a mountain six kilometers to the north.

Kurihama howled, "Can't we get this any larger?"

"Impossible," the operator said. "Any closer, and we'll enter the antielectrical field."

"But at this angle, it's going to walk into a blind spot."

On Port Island, a number of tall buildings obstructed the view from the north. None of the amusement-park-turned-battlefield would be visible.

Along the way, Kutoryu slipped behind a high-rise hotel and out of sight.

"Don't we have any other cameras?"

Displayed on the other monitors were additional live feeds, including one from Rokko Island to the east and another atop a large Ferris wheel on Osaka's Mt. Tenpo over ten kilometers away, but each of the cameras was either too far away or obstructed by buildings.

"Damn it, what's going on over there?"

"It's here!" Sakura said with a shudder.

From atop the Ferris wheel, they had a clear view of the approaching monster. It shoved through everything and anything that got in its way. Now, having just passed the sewage treatment plant and knocked over the elevated Port Liner railway, Kutoryu was only moments from the park.

Princess couldn't hold back any longer. She cried out, *"Ugau!"* and wrested herself free from Sakura's grasp. The girl leaped at the door handle and pulled it open. She'd seen Sakura do it before and learned from it.

"Don't!"

Sakura tried to stop her, but it was too late. Princess jumped from the helicopter down onto the roof of the adjacent gondola. There, she started to grow. As she enlarged, the added weight started the wheel slowly turning.

Sakura and the two soldiers screamed in unison.

Just as they had completed a quarter turn around the wheel, Princess's gondola snapped under her weight, and the girl fell thirty meters to the ground. But by the time she landed, she had nearly returned to her true form. A thirty-meter fall to her was nothing worse than a two-meter fall to a human. She struck the ground with an impact that shook the earth and sent fragments of brick and concrete high into the air. Her feet had dug ankle-deep into the dirt. Immediately she turned and gently caught the tumbling helicopter.

The girl was now fully twenty meters tall, and the helicopter rested in her palm like a radio-controlled toy. She softly set it down on the ground. Sakura and the two men stumbled out and onto their feet. Ryo and Kiichi ran over to them.

Sakura waved up at Princess and said, "Thank you!"

The giant girl grinned down at her and returned the gesture with a nod.

Just then, an enormous rumbling sound swept through the park. Princess spun to face the noise. Kutoryu had entered the fairgrounds, snapping through the tracks of the Munich Autobahn as if they were twigs.

Its eight mouths opened and prepared to fire their beams. Princess made no move to evade. She crouched down, held out her hand, and formed a disc of light.

The dragon shot out one dazzling golden ray of lightning after another, each accompanied by the boom of a thunderclap. The beams undulated through the air but traveled straight and true at their target. Princess used her light disc as a shield, blocking the attacks, but she couldn't stop them all. The lightning grazed her side and her knee, shredding through her skin and sending blood spraying out. Princess winced but held her stance.

Sakura stood behind, calling up at the mountain of a girl.

"Come," Ryo said. He took her by the hand and pulled her away. Princess was protecting them. Until they got to safety, the girl couldn't move.

From the corner of her eye, Princess watched them escape. Then she moved. She ducked down and ran behind the eaves of a merry-go-round. Kutoryu tracked her and fired a succession of lightning beams in her direction. Its heads wavered in the air, and its aim was sloppy. Bolts exploded into the mast of the Golden Hinde and a strip of old European storefronts and set them ablaze.

Princess dove behind the storefronts. Kutoryu lost her. The dragon waded into the pond in the center of the park, rested its front legs on the Hinde, and slowly scanned its surroundings with an intense glare. The woman's beautiful face distorted with rage, and from her mouth came a voice that sounded like a slowly winding tape.

"Ph'nnn-gluu-ii-fh-hu-iä-fhta-gn!"

Ryo gasped. "It's talking?"

It was certainly possible. If the dragon were indeed the god of ancient times and had been the creator of the mythic universe, it would of course possess intelligence.

Despite Kutoryu's provocation, Princess remained hidden. The dragon resumed its assault and fired wave after wave at the fairground's buildings. Explosions. Flashes of light. Fire. Debris kicked up like confetti. As the flames spread, smoke filled the air, further restricting visibility.

Even the great Kutoryu couldn't sustain that attack forever. It paused, short of breath. In that instant, Princess jumped out from the smoke. The eight necks swiveled to follow her movements, but she was faster. She leapt at the beast without giving it a chance to ready another shot.

With her left hand, she grabbed one of the necks, then swung her right hand down. As if her disc of light was a spinning saw blade, she severed the neck in one clean blow. Blue blood sprayed from the wound and fell down to the ground like a waterfall. All at once, the remaining seven necks of the dragon and the woman atop it let out screams of pain.

Ryo shouted, "That's it, Princess!"

Sakura joined in. "Princess, you can do it!"

But then, one of the dragon heads clamped its fangs down on Princess's right ankle. It pulled her off balance and yanked her to the ground. She tried to shake free, but another head bit down on her left ankle. Her attempts to resist were futile, and it lifted her up into the air and dangled her upside down.

The other five heads all opened their mouths and aimed at the flailing child, ready to unleash a concentrated, close-range blast to scorch her from existence. The woman folded her arms, formed a triumphant smile, and loudly proclaimed something in an unknown language. Probably something like "This is the end of you."

Sakura shouted, "Princess!"

Princess threw her light disc. Spinning, it flew straight toward the woman's head. At such close range, the chimera couldn't dodge it. The monster could only stare at it, dumbfounded. The disc connected with her forehead. Her flesh tore open, and blood sprayed from the wound.

"*Ugaaaaaaaooooooooohhhh!*"

The woman howled in slow motion. She put her hands to her head in agony. Her grip on Princess slackened, and the girl fell to the ground. One of the necks swung around and struck Princess on the face. Another swooped in to bite the downed child, but she rolled out of the way and dodged out of range. The seven dragon heads, writhing in pain, indiscriminately fired their beams of light. One ray grazed Princess's side, and blood bubbled up from the cut. Her long hair fluttering in the wind, she nimbly maneuvered her giant body into a backflip and dodged the rest of the dragon's attacks. The surface of the man-made island shook violently from the pitched battle.

For a moment, a break came in Kutoryu's barrage. Princess swiftly moved to flank the beast. She dug her fingers into the cracks of the dragon's scales and climbed up its side and onto its back. Several dragon heads turned to bite at her, but the necks could only reach the beast's own side, and their clumsy attempts found no success.

Princess grappled the woman from behind. She put her left hand on the creature's wings, wrapped her legs around her torso, and rode the woman like she was at a rodeo. The monster shouted in protest, but Princess ignored the cries. She recreated the disc of light and struck it against the woman's head, again and again. The woman screamed and flailed her arms but couldn't shake the girl off.

Kutoryu, in a frenzy, fired lightning in every direction. One bolt clipped the top of the ticket booth Sakura and the others were hiding under. Other shots flew beyond the amusement park, disintegrating the roof of a youth science center to the north and blowing a hole through the side of a high-rise hotel to the west.

At last, the woman's head had been so savaged as to be unrecognizable. Kutoryu's massive body heaved, and the monster collapsed on its side, all five thousand tons striking the earth with a thunderclap. Princess was flung to the ground.

The girl sat up and shook her head. Kutoryu writhed in pain. Its ninth head, the one with intelligence, the one in command, was destroyed. The seven remaining ones each tried to assert its own command over the whole. The result was fruitless: its body shook and thrashed; its feet stomped. Every once in a while, another lightning bolt fired, but each shot flew off into the distance.

Princess sprang to her feet and raised her right arm high above her head like a baseball pitcher preparing for a throw. She focused all of her energy into her right hand, and the disc grew larger and larger. After half a minute, the disc was wider than she was tall.

She hurled it.

The shining disc rotated through the air as if rolling above the surface of the earth. It cut a thin, straight groove along the pavement and slammed head-on into the writhing dragon. The disc, imbued with tremendous power, kept on going straight through the beast like a spinning saw blade. Kutoryu's seven heads howled in pain. Sparks and blood and guts sprayed into the sky. The disc cut clear through all 140 meters of the dragon's body, and made it past the Double Loop roller coaster before it lost power and winked out.

The two halves of the kaiju flopped to the ground.

The eight necks, four on the left and four on the right, still weakly floundered about. One turned up to the sky and let loose a final lightning bolt. The blast made it to the clouds but quickly grew thin.

And when it had finally disappeared, Kutoryu ceased to move. Princess slumped to her knees and fell forward.

"What happened?" Kurihama said, frustration in his voice. "How did it end?"

During the battle, all the telephoto lens of the video camera saw were lightning bolts shooting out from the park, clouds of dust, and fire. When calm settled, it was clear the battle was over—but the victor was unknown.

"Chief!" It was a female operator. "Yojiro is on the line."

"What?"

"This is the Mobile Unit." Yojiro's quiet voice came from the speakers. The office fell silent as everyone inside it held their breath in unison.

"Kutoryu has been completely destroyed. Let me repeat. Princess has won. Kutoryu is dead."

Cheers filled the room. Workers tossed papers into the air, shook each other's hands, clapped, hugged, and shared in their delight.

Kurihama's eyes teared up. He hugged one of the women and basked in the victory high.

But as the passion subsided, the chief called out, "Attention, please!"

All eyes were upon him.

"It's still too early to celebrate. We have work to do. We need to contact the SDF, lift the alert, announce to the press, assess the damages. But first," he said, putting his hand to his chest, "a silent prayer for the twenty-seven brave soldiers who lost their lives."

Kurihama closed his eyes, and his subordinates followed suit.

Then, after a time, he opened his eyes again. Quietly, proudly, he said. "We're almost done. Let's finish up."

Sakura held Princess, now human size after expending the last of her strength, lovingly in her arms and said, "That last move had a long warm-up time, so I guess she could only use it to finish that thing off."

The girl's wounds weren't severe, and they'd done what first aid they could. Now they only had to wait for the ambulance to arrive.

"We'll have to give it a name," Sakura said.

"That move of hers?"

"Yeah. If she's going to be using it from now on, it'll need a name, right? Let me think . . . Something, something guillotine. No, wait, it rotates, so—"

"You said 'from now on.' You mean we're going to have her help us from now on?"

Sakura laughed and waved her hands at him. "No, no, no. We'll be doing our part, of course. But when we've done all we can and it isn't enough, I think she'll come save us like she did now. She's a friend of the people. Haven't you heard the saying, 'Do our best and leave the rest to Providence?' The MMD is our best, and this girl is Providence. I'm sure of it."

"You're always the optimist." Ryo chuckled, but then his expression darkened. "But if what Mikio said was right, no matter what we do, it'll all be as if it never happened."

"Who cares? Say kaiju disasters end up in history as natural disasters. Everything we do now to protect people from kaiju will have protected people in the new universe from natural disasters instead, right? I think that would be pretty cool."

Ryo's smile returned. "I never thought of it that way."

He thought to himself, *But now that I do, I want to keep trying. If our work affects not only our universe, but the one in the eventual fifth age—the one with no kaiju—then what we do here is not meaningless or useless at all.*

"Wait a minute," he said. "In the new universe, kaiju are all fictitious, right?"

"Yeah."

"That means, maybe, all our work will become fiction too. Like a weekly TV show."

"That'd be fantastic!" Sakura beamed. "Some really popular show with top ratings. Maybe they could rewrite us to be cooler than we are."

"With our own jet planes and laser guns."

"Yes! Perfect!"

Their laughter echoed through the devastated amusement park.

The sound of an ambulance siren wailed in the distance.

Photo by Tatsuya Jinbo

Hiroshi Yamamoto was born in 1956 in Kyoto. He began his career with game developers Group SNE in 1987 and debuted as a writer and game designer. He gained popularity with juvenile titles such as *February at the Edge of Time* and the Ghost Hunter series. His first hardcover science fiction release, *God Never Keeps Silent,* became a sensation among SF fans and was nominated for the Japan SF Award. Other novels include *Day of Judgment* and *The Unseen Sorrow of Winter.* His novel *The Stories of Ibis* was published in English by Haikasoru in 2010. Aside from his work as a writer, Yamamoto is also active in various literary capacities as editor of classic science fiction anthologies and as president of To-Gakkai, a group of tongue-in-cheek "experts" on the occult.

HAIKASORU
THE FUTURE IS JAPANESE

TEN BILLION DAYS AND ONE HUNDRED BILLION NIGHTS BY RYU MITSUSE

Ten billion days—that is how long it will take the philosopher Plato to determine the true systems of the world. One hundred billion nights—that is how far into the future Jesus of Nazareth, Siddhartha, and the demigod Asura will travel to witness the end of all worlds. Named the greatest Japanese science fiction novel of all time, *Ten Billion Days and One Hundred Billion Nights* is an epic eons in the making. Originally published in 1967, the novel was revised by the author in later years and republished in 1973.

THE NAVIDAD INCIDENT: THE DOWNFALL OF MATÍAS GUILI BY NATSUKI IKEZAWA

In this sweeping magical-realist epic set in the fictional south sea island country the Republic of Navidad, Ikezawa gives his imagination free rein to reinvent the myths of twentieth century Japan. The story takes off as a delegation of Japanese war veterans pays an official visit to the ex-World War II colony, only to see the Japanese flag burst into flames. The following day, the tour bus, and its passengers, simply vanish. The locals exchange absurd rumors—the bus was last seen attending Catholic Mass, the bus must have skipped across the lagoon—but the president suspects a covert guerrilla organization is trying to undermine his connections with Japan. Can the real answers to the mystery be found, or will the president have to be content with the surreal answers?

ALSO BY HIROSHI YAMAMOTO
THE STORIES OF IBIS

In a world where humans are a minority and androids have created their own civilization, a wandering storyteller meets the beautiful android Ibis. She tells him seven stories of human/android interaction in order to reveal the secret behind humanity's fall. The stories that Ibis speaks of are the "seven novels" about the events surrounding the announcements of the development of artificial intelligence (AI) in the 20th and 21st centuries. At a glance, these stories do not appear to have any sort of connection, but what is the true meaning behind them? What are Ibis's real intentions?